ATM

a novel by
Joseph Keough

cover art by **Margaret Keough: Madeira** Island

Copyright © 2012 Joseph Keough
All rights reserved.
ISBN-10:1475230346
ISBN-13:9781475230345

Also by Joseph Keough
Shattered Peace

Praise for *Shattered Peace*

"…… an intellectually stimulating and emotionally thrilling book. Reading the surprising conclusion of the story, one is left craving a sequel or an excellent motion picture version."
Christopher Ackerman for Independent Professional Book Reviewers.

"In Shattered Peace, Joseph Keough reminds us what Aristotle proclaimed so long ago: character and plot go hand in hand. Upbeat, alluring, spry in sound and sense, this is as much a novel as it is a motion picture."
Mark Fitzgerald, poet/author, *By Way of Dust and Rain*, Cinnamon Press.

"The author tells a great story through masterful development of interesting and compelling characters. It is all at once a thriller, a murder mystery, a love story (or two or three), and a study in human nature. I highly recommend this: it is well written, hard to put down, and a joy to read."
Matt Cairone, author, *The Brit*.
Amazon/Kindle

Chapter 1

FIVE MILLION DOLLARS? Lynn O'Brien gasps aloud, alarming a man who is standing at the ATM she just finished using. He turns to ask if she is all right. Staring in shock at the astounding account balance on her receipt, Lynn does not hear him. She can hardly believe her eyes, but there it is in black and white. Five million dollars. And $892.24. Bold and clear as can be, and no mistake about it. Mistake? Of course it's a mistake! Not the $892.24. That is what it should be. To the penny. But $5,000,892.24? Who could have made such a blunder? Some careless bank clerk? An errant computer? A power surge somewhere? That arrogant ATM? She looks up at the machine and would swear she sees it smirk.

The man asks again, "Are you all right, miss?"

"Oh," Lynn mutters, "yes, yes, I'm . . ." Her voice trails off. She watches him extract his cash, retrieve his bank card, examine his receipt. "Excuse me," she says when he steps away from the machine, "your receipt, is it correct?"

"Quite correct," he answers, his condescending frown indicating an attitude of superior electronics sophistication. He strides toward his car, eyes rolling, thinking her just another lost soul of the computer age, unable to operate a simple automatic teller machine. Lynn, whose only problem with ATM's before today was an occasional struggle to see in bright sunlight the dimly displayed messages on some of their peculiarly green screens, does not observe the misplaced disdain of her fellow supplicant at the ATM altar.

She checks her receipt again. It is unchanged. The five

million dollars is still there. Oh, if only it were correct. She indulges herself in what-iffing. Pay off the house, buy Patrick a new car, the best colleges for the kids, new clothes, family travel. If only! But the five million is not hers. It's not real. It's just an error. A cruel error. Still, the receipt bears the correct day and date: Wednesday, October 16th, and the right time: 8:37 a.m. 8:37? She checks her watch. The time is now 8:42. Her aerobics class starts in eighteen minutes. She must get going. There's nothing to be done here at the bank now. It doesn't open until 9 a.m. She will come back to straighten out her account after her group fitness class, and someone will get a piece of her mind for putting her through this aggravation.

Her musings turn to this morning's class. Today's session at Patcong Health Club, where Lynn works part-time as a fitness instructor, is the most grueling of the half-dozen classes she leads. The members of this group are not the overweight beginners vying for invisibility in the back of the room, not the struggling intermediates, not the non-strivers content to look good in cute outfits while mainly exercising their tongues, not the seventy-five percent who drop out on the sweaty road to fitness. These are the animals, the killers, the no pain – no gain athletes who like nothing better than to out-dance, out-kick, out-spin, out-jump, out-climb, out-lift, outlast and generally outperform their instructor. Lynn relishes the challenge, confident the new tape she has put together and choreographed for today's dance aerobics session will keep her a couple of steps ahead of the pack.

Changed into her gym clothes, Lynn pauses to look herself over in the locker room mirror. 5'7" tall, 130 pounds, hazel-eyed with short blond hair and a smooth, problem-free complexion, she is satisfied she looks pretty good. A more objective viewer would describe her as a very pretty young woman but might fail to observe how supremely fit, strong, and full of stamina she is, such an observer perhaps deceived by her slim, feminine shapeliness. Despite being thirty-six years old and the mother of two adolescent children, she has the figure of a lithe twenty-year-old, the result of good genes, healthful eating habits and rigorous physical conditioning.

Lynn greets her class at 9:05 a.m., receiving a few disapproving glances for her brief tardiness. She dons her headset microphone, inserts her new tape, and turns on the stereo, filling the studio with loud, lively, drum and bass-driven music. For the next hour she champions her charges through one intricate maneuver after another in a relentlessly exhausting, fast-paced drill that leaves every one of them gasping for air at its close. Lynn, however, feels better at the end of the class than she did at its beginning, endorphin-invigorated, ready to take on a spinning, stair climbing, strength training or treadmill workout without even a break, and not at all contrite at having unjustly punished her bevy of bowed and breathless beasts for her ATM-inspired annoyance.

At the front desk on her way out of the building, she passes Charlie Jacobs, her boss, the owner of Patcong Health Club. "Hey, Lynn," he calls her over. "I stuck my head in during your class."

"I saw you, Charlie."

"You were really pounding them into the floor."

Lynn shrugs and smiles. "They love it."

"I know. When are you going to be ready to take over this place?" For months he has been offering her the opportunity to manage the club, a prospect Lynn has consistently turned down. It is a full-time commitment she will not make, content to remain a part-time instructor and full-time mother rather than reverse those roles, at least for the next few years. She thinks about her five million dollars and shows Jacobs her ATM slip.

"Whoa!" the owner says. "What the hell is this?"

"ATM slip. My bank balance," Lynn answers.

"Hey, maybe you'd like to *buy* the club."

"And then you would work for me. There's an idea, but of course it's not actually my money. Some kind of bank error."

"Damn. I never heard of something like this. A five million dollar mistake. Sheesh! I'm glad I don't have my account there. Or am I?"

"I'm going to the bank now to show them what they've done."

"Good luck. Maybe they'll let you keep it. Finders-keepers?"

"Right. See you later, Charlie."

At Seashore National the one officer on duty is busy with a customer. Lynn takes a seat outside his cubicle until he waves her in. "What can I do for you?" the young man, whose desk nameplate identifies him as William Meeks, Bank Officer, asks agreeably. He invites her to sit, which he also does.

"Well, uh, my name is Lynn O'Brien, and . . ."

Before she can finish, he jumps to his feet, exclaiming, "Mrs. O'Brien! It's a great pleasure to meet you." Startled by his unanticipated exuberance, Lynn shrinks back in her chair. But his bright smile encourages her to shake his extended hand, despite her confusion. After an awkward moment he settles back down and asks again how he can help her. She produces her ATM receipt and lays it before him on his desk. The broad smile returns to his face, and he nods enthusiastically.

"You see the balance?" Lynn asks.

"Uh-huh!" Meeks responds, his head nodding with the gusto of a contented canine's wagging tail.

"It says five million dollars."

"Yes, I know, and, uh," he reads the slip, "eight hundred ninety-two dollars, twenty-four cents."

"But that's not my balance. It's a mistake. A huge mistake."

"I suppose it's a bit of a surprise, Mrs. O'Brien, but I assure you the receipt is quite correct. It's not every day we get five million dollar deposits here at our little branch. And I might venture to add that I am quite sure we even less frequently make five million dollar errors." Meeks chuckles, appreciating his own wit. "Let me show you," he says. To allay her continuing doubt he enters her account number into his desktop computer. "There you go," he announces, turning his monitor in her direction. Lynn sees that the bank's record of her account balance is exactly the same as it is on the tiny piece of paper she holds.

"Does this prove anything? I mean, wouldn't your computer and the ATM show the same amount whether or not it's accurate?"

Meeks leaps to his feet. "Come with me, please, Mrs. O'Brien. I would like you to meet our branch manager." She follows him, wondering if Meeks might be delusional or if perhaps she has entered some alternate universe. He knocks at the open door of the bank's one actual office. "Excuse me, Mr. Terwilliger, allow me to introduce Mrs. Lynn O'Brien," he says. "Mrs. O'Brien, this is our branch manager, Mr. Terwilliger."

Lynn acknowledges the introduction with a slight smile, but Terwilliger springs from his chair, bounds across the room and shakes her hand heartily. "Mrs. O'Brien," he gushes, "so you got my message. I am so pleased to meet you."

"Message?"

"On your answering machine?"

At a loss to comprehend what he is talking about, Lynn merely shakes her head and shrugs.

"I called you this morning, maybe an hour ago, to invite you to come in and see me," Terwilliger says. "No matter. Here you are. Please, won't you take a seat?" She does, allowing the fawning, sixtyish, mustached, graying, balding, bifocaled branch manager to push a chair under her in gentlemanly fashion.

Eager not to miss any of this unprecedented entertainment in his otherwise mundane workday, young Meeks seats himself on Terwilliger's office couch. He earns a fleeting frown of disapproval from his superior, which Lynn sees but the young assistant does not.

Terwilliger immediately beams his mustachioed smile in her direction. She thinks he has the pretentious demeanor of an overly solicitous maitre d' who expects a hefty tip. Reinforcing her impression, the branch manager continues cloyingly, "My dear lady, let me explain." He tells her that five million dollars has been deposited to her account. Lynn replies that there must be an error. Terwilliger maintains there is no error. Lynn says the money must belong to a different Lynn O'Brien. Meeks's head swivels back and forth from one of them to the other like a birder on a May morning in a warbler-filled grove of budding birches.

"No, I assure you, the money was properly deposited," Terwilliger says, "to the account of Patrick and Lynn O'Brien of 368 Willow Avenue, Somers Point, New Jersey."

"But neither I nor my husband deposited five million dollars," Lynn objects.

She recalls her conversation with Patrick after the kids had left for school this morning. "You remember about the dress and shoes, Patrick?" she had asked when Kerry and Sean slammed the door behind them and ran for their school buses.

"Dress? Shoes?" Patrick had echoed, emerging from behind the sports pages appearing simultaneously quizzical and pained. Quizzical because the dress and shoes had slipped his mind, pained because of the impact such feminine apparel purchases have on their limited family budget. Quizzical and pained was precisely the expression Lynn expected to see on her husband's handsome face. If she were a caricaturist she could have sketched it before he lowered his newspaper. She had tried not to smile.

"For Kerry's Freshman Welcome Dance," she said.

"Oh, that, right, the dance," Patrick murmured. "When is it?"

"Saturday night. I'm picking Kerry up from school today, taking her shopping."

"Today," Patrick acknowledged. No objections, no challenges, no discussion of the merit or lack thereof accruing to the expenditure of hundreds of dollars for a fourteen-year-old daughter's first high school dance. Instead, he sighed, nodded, sipped his coffee and settled back in his chair, having no desire to reignite their heated discussion of the issue some weeks earlier.

Neither had Lynn. Winning battles with her husband is no fun for her. She loves him, after all. And on the one hand she considers the expense for their daughter's dress and shoes as extravagant as does Patrick. On the other, though, is the consideration that all of Kerry's female classmates will be wearing new outfits. How can Lynn let *their* daughter be slighted?

"How much did you say you'll need?" Patrick had asked.

"Three or four hundred," Lynn replied, her tone conciliatory. "Do you think I should charge it or get cash from the ATM?"

"I don't know," Patrick answered. "Aren't the credit cards close to maxed out?" Lynn nodded. "What's our checking account balance?" he asked.

"Close to thirteen hundred dollars," she had answered then.

To be more precise, their account at the time had been worth $1292.24, she reflects now, an amount which, minus her withdrawal of $400 for Kerry's dress and shoes had since magically morphed into $5,000,892.24.

"No, no," Terwilliger is saying now, "we know that you and your husband did not make the deposit. It arrived by wire transfer. I'm sorry we could not notify you immediately upon its receipt. We had to make certain the transfer was authentic and that it was indeed meant for your account. We were not sure of all that until late yesterday. As I've said, I tried to reach you first thing this morning."

Growing mentally numbed by the insistence of these two bank officials who appear genuinely convinced that she and Patrick have inexplicably become five million dollars richer, Lynn nevertheless manages to ask reasonably, "Since you know my husband and I did not deposit the money, I presume you know who did?"

Undaunted, Terwilliger replies, "We do not know who the depositor is." He pauses briefly before adding, "I think you should know, however, that the money was sent specifically in *your* name."

"My name?" Lynn stares blankly at him. Haven't we already established that? she asks herself.

Terwilliger sees her confusion and elucidates. "What I mean to say is the money was electronically transferred to *you*, not to Mr. O'Brien or to Mr. and Mrs. O'Brien, but to *Lynn O'Brien*, using your joint checking account number."

"To my husband's and my joint account but in my name?"

"Exactly."

"And the depositor is unknown?"

"Anonymous."

"Okay, anonymous. Well, if you don't know who he or she is, how do you know the deposit is genuine?"

"I guarantee you it is, Mrs. O'Brien. We were quite able to establish that fact. For whatever reason he may have, the depositor wired the money in a manner designed to ensure his anonymity, by means of a series of electronic transfers through Lisbon and New York to Seashore National's headquarters and finally to our branch. That was what made our verifying the deposit rather more complex and time consuming than usual."

"You said Lisbon. Lisbon, Portugal?"

"Yes, and frankly I don't believe I am betraying the depositor's confidence by telling you that the transfer originated at *Banco Espirito Santo* in Funchal."

"*Espirito Santo*? Holy Spirit? That's appropriate for money out of the blue, wouldn't you say?" she quips. Terwilliger is anything but fanciful, but Meeks giggles appreciatively. "A bank in Funchal. Where is Funchal?" Lynn asks.

"On Madeira Island."

"Madeira?" She starts to feel like a parrot.

"Yes. Funchal is its capital city."

"Uh-huh, and I suppose Madeira must be where they make the wine, but whereabouts is it?"

"In the Atlantic Ocean off the coast of North Africa. Portuguese," Terwilliger adds. "I must confess I had to check an atlas to locate it. Perhaps you know someone in Funchal?"

Lynn shakes her head. Africa? Portugal? Madeira? Why in the world would someone in Madeira send her money? She refrains from asking the bankers, who evidently don't have a clue. Instead, she sighs and says, "This is all so overwhelming. Apparently it's real, so I suppose I should be happy, but I feel as if I'm about to cry."

"Would you like a glass of water? Some coffee?" Terwilliger asks.

"No, thank you," Lynn responds. She falls silent for a moment. Bank Manager Terwilliger waits patiently. "What do I do now?" she asks finally.

Bank Officer Meeks can't resist answering. "I don't know, but, whatever it is, I imagine you can afford it." He laughs, but Lynn is too nonplussed to respond.

Terwilliger, exasperated by his young assistant, waves Meeks from the office. "There are a couple of things I might suggest, Mrs. O'Brien," he says when Meeks is gone. "As a first step you would do well to transfer some of the money to other accounts. You don't want to keep five million dollars in one checking account. Secondly, you should consult a competent financial planner for investment and tax advice as soon as possible. The bank will be happy to recommend someone if you like."

"Thank you," Lynn says absently, struggling to assimilate what is happening into her established ideas of how the world works. Patrick will never believe it, she thinks. "I had better call my husband right away," she blurts. "May I use your phone?"

"Of course. Be my guest, Mrs. O'Brien. Sit here at my desk. I'll step outside while you talk."

Lynn calls Patrick at work. He picks up the shipping dock phone after being paged by the plant manager's secretary and is initially concerned that there must be some emergency. Lynn rarely calls him at work otherwise. He customarily checks in with her once or twice a day rather than take calls out on the plant floor wherever he might be busy. She tells him nothing is wrong, exactly, but she needs him at the bank.

"You mean now?"

"Yes."

"You're at the bank?"

"Yes, Patrick. Didn't I just say that?"

"Uh, well, you said there's no problem, but you sound as if you're on the verge of tears. What is it? Why must I leave work and go to the bank? Isn't there enough money in our account to cover Kerry's dress and shoes?"

"More than enough."

"Well then?"

"Five million dollars more than enough."

Chapter 2

"Five million dollars?" Patrick yells and immediately lowers his voice. Lynn pictures him scanning production lines, hoping no one has heard him. He whispers into the phone, "Lynn, what are you talking about, sweetheart? You sound like you're losing it."

"Patrick, someone deposited five million dollars in our checking account. I can't explain it. I don't know who did it or why they did it. The bank doesn't know either."

"Obviously it must be a mistake," Patrick says.

"It's not."

"Of course it is."

"It is *not* a mistake, Patrick." Her voice takes on a hands-on-hips, foot-stomping timbre.

"No? But I don't . . . I can't . . ."

Lynn interrupts him. "Just come over here, will you please?"

Patrick comes to the bank where he meets Bank Officer Meeks, who escorts him to Terwilliger's office. Lynn is seated across the desk from the branch manager, sipping coffee, having accepted the offer she declined earlier. Meeks announces Patrick and takes advantage of the moment to regain entrée to the office, taking Lynn's seat as she joins her husband on Terwilliger's couch.

Patrick O'Brien is thirty-eight years old, a big man, 6'3", 235 pounds, with a ruddy complexion, curly black hair and deep brown eyes. His arms and legs are still as muscular and powerful as they were when he made the second string all-state football team as a high school senior. In the past few years, though, his loosening abs have allowed his belly to sneak up to nearly the size of his broad chest. Lynn has kept after him about starting some kind of exercise program, which, until recently, Patrick resisted. Always a competitive athlete in his youth, he was accustomed to getting his exercise on the football field and the basketball court gratis of the game. He dislikes workouts that lack the competitive element of team sports. Besides, until just recently he thought he always seemed as fit and firm as ever. Now that his mirror is reflecting what his wife has been telling him, he has joined a senior basketball program, started watching what he eats, and begun to do some weight training.

Patrick is a loving husband, as evidenced by his huge arm embracing his distraught wife. Although he has a big man's easygoing nature, as his smile now demonstrates, he has little tolerance for persons or situations that upset Lynn. "All right," so what's going on here?" he demands without preamble.

An hour later Patrick and Lynn leave the bank. Branch Manager Terwilliger has covered the same ground with him as he did with her. Lynn takes her husband's hand as they walk to their cars, each as mystified as the other by the apparent reality of their impossible fantasy. "It's almost noon," she remarks. "Are you going back to work?"

They decide to have lunch together, taking Patrick's car, leaving Lynn's at the bank. Patrick calls his boss, Atlantic Glass Company's plant manager, and takes the rest of the day off. They eat at their favorite place, The Anchorage, a Somers Point bay front restaurant and bar. Foregoing a table in the busy dining room, they opt for one in the bar area, quieter at this time of day. With deserted pool tables behind them and an exquisite view of Great Egg Harbor Bay before them, they gaze at each other over pre-lunch drinks.

Lynn's pensive expression eases into an impish smile. "So

what's new?" she asks.

Patrick grins. "I can't believe all this, Lynn. Can you?"

"I don't know what to think. A few hours ago we were worried about spending three or four hundred dollars. Now we're millionaires."

"So it seems, unless we're both just having the same dream."

"Want me to pinch you?"

"Not right away. I'm not sure I want to wake up," Patrick says. "To be suddenly so rich, it's like . . . like winning the lottery without buying a ticket."

Lynn nods. "If it is true it will save us ten dollars a week on lottery tickets."

"You spend ten dollars a week on lottery tickets?" A note of reproof enters Patrick's tone but as quickly disappears. Lynn detects its arrival and smiles at its quick departure.

"Not any more," she replies.

Patrick is silent for a moment. Lynn realizes what is coming. Finally it does. "You know what bothers me most about it?" he asks.

"Yes, I do."

"What?"

"The money was sent in my name."

"Bingo! So who do you know in Madeira, Lynn?"

"Nobody."

"Some nobody there simply decided to give you – not us, not me, mind you, but *you* – five million dollars?" She doesn't comment. "For no good reason?" he adds.

Lynn won't be provoked. She shrugs and sips her vodka and club. "Guess so."

"Just happened to pick you out. Kind of like random violence in reverse."

"That's good, Patrick. Okay, you've got me. I guess I'll just have to confess." He sighs, knowing he is in for it, takes a slug of his Coors Light – only about a hundred calories per twelve ounce bottle; he has also switched to non-fat milk – and waits. Her voice dripping wifely sarcasm, Lynn continues, "I have a lover who wants to carry me off. Since I refuse to leave you and go with him, his unrequited passion has driven him to provide me the financial wherewithal to have a happy, secure life with the man I love. That's you, Patrick, by the way. Unable to bear remaining on the same continent as I without possessing me, he has fled into exile on Madeira Island."

Patrick nods. "I can buy that." He takes Lynn's hand. "It's not true, though, is it?"

"No."

"But assuming the money is really ours, there must be some reason for it, right?"

"Has to be."

"So what we do now is . . ."

" . . . find out who sent it."

Patrick points out that the bank people were unable to identify the depositor. Lynn considers for a moment and says, "True, but they really don't care all that much about who sent the money.

They're only interested in making sure the deposit is authentic."

"Uh-huh," Patrick agrees. He purses his lips and rubs his chin. His eyes turn upward in thought. "I don't know, maybe we can somehow trace the money to its source. I mean, whoever your fairy godfather is, he could have done more to hide his identity, don't you think?"

"How do you mean?"

"Apparently only three banks are involved: Seashore National, *Banco Espirito Santo* and someplace in New York City. He could have used a more roundabout route: more banks, say, or dummy charitable trusts, some kind of foundation, phony company names that couldn't be traced, a numbered-only account from some Swiss or offshore island bank. Whoops! Offshore island. Madeira. Maybe the money did come from a numbered account. Dead end if that's the case, I guess."

"We don't know that, though. All we know for sure is what Mr. Terwilliger told us," Lynn says. "If we check Seashore National's home office ourselves and talk to officials at the other banks by phone, maybe we can learn something."

"Or we can just leave the money alone, not spend any of it for a few months until we're sure nobody is going to demand we give it back. We don't have to know who sent it, do we?" Patrick asks.

"Yes, we do. Absolutely. If we don't find out *who* sent it, we'll never learn *why* he did. I know you, Patrick. You'll never believe it's ours until you know exactly why it was given to us. Neither will I."

"I guess you're right, Lynnie. I'm certainly having trouble believing it now." Patrick suggests they not tell anyone about the money right away. Lynn admits she showed her ATM slip to Charlie Jacobs at the health club earlier, before Meeks and Terwilliger told her the deposit was not just a colossal mistake.

Patrick thinks that if Jacobs considered it just a bank error, his knowing probably does not matter, and the bankers are likely to be close-mouthed about it. "But it will be easier on both of us if we don't tell your mother, my sister, the kids or anyone else until we know for certain what's going on." Lynn agrees, with the proviso that her assent is limited to the present. She doesn't want to face a host of questions without having answers, either.

Seashore National's main offices are in Atlantic City, where the institution was founded eighty years ago and from which its third generation of owners rule their family's fifty-four branches up and down the New Jersey coast. Through the years they have steadfastly resisted innumerable attempts by the merger-mad banking trade to acquire their solidly profitable, wholly family-owned enterprise. Because Atlantic City lies a mere twenty-five minute drive across salt marsh, over bridges and up beach through Absecon Island, the O'Briens begin their investigation with a personal visit to Seashore National Bank headquarters.

Lynn and Patrick are greeted royally by each echelon of cordial managers they meet on their way up the line right to the bank president himself, Oliver Higbee III, grandson of Seashore National's founder. Grandfather Oliver's portrait stands watch over proceedings at the helm of his empire from the wall above Oliver III's desk, unafraid to display a slight smile of confidence in his progeny's competence. But, although the helpful bank president questions his own minions in great detail and personally further explores the matter by telephone with the New York clearing house that brokered the money transfer from Lisbon to Atlantic City, Lynn and Patrick learn nothing about their mystery benefactor.

They leave Seashore National with scarcely time enough to drive to Linwood, their own community's neighbor to the north, arriving at Mainland Regional High School as their daughter exits the student entrance. Looking around for her mother's car, Kerry overlooks her father's. Patrick taps his horn to get her attention, and she hurries to them, surprised to see him at this time of day. "You sick, Daddy?" Kerry asks as she climbs in. Patrick never misses work.

"Hi, sweetheart. No, I'm fine." Patrick lets Lynn explain how he comes to be there, which she does while mentally reserving certain rather salient facts, merely telling their daughter that they had conducted some bank business, then hurried directly to school to meet her. Patrick transports them to Lynn's car, gives them each a kiss, and they watch him drive off.

Back home later in the day, after Patrick duly admires Kerry's new party dress and shoes, and the girl and her brother go outside to shoot some hoops, Lynn asks her husband if he had learned anything more while she and Kerry shopped.

"There's a five hour time difference between us and Portugal, so I couldn't call the banks there," Patrick says. "I spent a couple hours on the internet checking out *Banco Espirito Santo* and reading about Lisbon and Madeira. Good bank. Beautiful part of the world, especially the island. I managed to find the bank's phone numbers. Nothing else helpful, though." Exhausted by the day's staggering mental assault, Lynn falls asleep on the couch during the 6:30 p.m. national news, not unusual for Patrick, but something she never does.

Thursday morning when Patrick and the children leave the house Lynn immediately gets on the phone to *Banco Espirito Santo* headquarters in Lisbon. She is transferred to an obliging, English-speaking Portuguese woman, only to learn what she already knows: the money originated from a bank branch in Funchal, and its Lisbon headquarters in turn wired it to New York. The woman says their main office, of course, verified the deposit with the Funchal branch, but, at the depositor's request, were not given his name.

The man with whom Lynn eventually gets to speak at *Banco Espirito Santo* in Funchal is its director. He is every bit as affable as the woman in Lisbon, but, although he says he would like to be cooperative, is not. A full ten minutes into the call Lynn asks, "So the transfer was not from a numbered-only account?"

"No."

"The account is in a person's name?"

"Yes. A gentleman's."

So! A man; not a woman. "But you will not tell me his name?"

"I cannot, *senhora*. The depositor insists we do not reveal his identity."

"Why is that?"

"*Não sei*. I do not know, *senhora*."

"But you know who he is."

"Of course."

"And he lives in Funchal?"

The banker pauses before answering hesitantly, "On Madeira."

So! On Madeira but not in Funchal. Lynn presses on. "He must be very wealthy."

"Yes."

"Are there many millionaires on Madeira?"

The man laughs lightly. "Very many."

"Dozens? Scores?"

"Hundreds easily."

Lynn is discouraged by the banker's estimate, having hoped

she would find a way to narrow down a smaller population of wealthy Madeirans to single out her benefactor. She persists in her questioning anyway, but her phone correspondent, though he seems as if he would like to disclose the information she seeks, tells her nothing more of value. He does willingly furnish his own name, which she notes for possible future reference. Eventually she gives up, thanks him courteously, hangs up the phone and sits considering what more she can do. Soon she decides her course of action. She calls Seashore National President Oliver Higbee III.

"Mr. Higbee," Lynn begins, "I need a card with a substantial line of credit. Can your bank issue one backed by my account?"

"Certainly. Will a million dollar line be sufficient?"

Lynn gulps so as not to choke on the amount. "More than sufficient," she says. "I would like to get it as soon as possible."

"I expect you would like a card in your husband's name as well?"

"Oh? Um, yes, I would, please," she replies, feeling instantly guilty for not even considering a card for Patrick. Not that he ever used one much in the past, but his outlook may well change in their new financial circumstances.

"Of course," the bank president agrees. "Well, Mrs. O'Brien, let me see, it's ten o'clock now. We can have the cards for you by, say, two this afternoon."

"Wonderful. Shall I pick them up from Mr. Terwilliger or at your office?"

"I'll have Terwilliger issue them and someone from the bank deliver them directly to your home if you like."

The cards are in Lynn's wallet when Patrick arrives home from work. He listens attentively while she recites every word of her telephone conversations with bank representatives in Lisbon and Madeira. "I guess that's it then, hon," he ventures when Lynn finishes. "We'll have to sit tight until we're sure no one swoops in to demand we return the money."

Lynn shakes her head. "No," she replies and hands him his new credit card. "Boot up your computer, Patrick, and book me a flight and a hotel room. I'm going to Madeira."

Chapter 3

Patrick searches for his wife's smile. Nope, she's serious. "Come on, Lynnie, you can't go to Madeira without me."

"I'd rather not. Come with me." She knows he can't, or, rather, he won't, because of his job. *Can't* would have been accurate last week, but now that they have five million dollars he could if he would, but she is sure he won't.

"I can't leave work now. My shipping foreman goes on vacation this weekend."

"I know."

"His trip was arranged and paid for months ago."

"I know."

"I only have three vacation days remaining this year, which we agreed I would save for Christmas week."

"I know."

"Our production line people are working overtime because of seasonal demand."

"Especially for the company's two hot new items," she finishes for him. I know you won't go with me, Patrick. That's why I have to go alone."

"It's not that I won't go. I can't."

"Have you thought about quitting your job?"

He is crestfallen. Her question seems to stun him. "Quitting? No." Lynn watches him consider the possibility for the first time. "Funny," he says, "I always laugh when a lottery winner says he's not going to leave some awful job just because he has won a few million dollars. I'm saying the same thing, huh?"

"Except your job is not awful. Anyway, I think you're right to stay with Atlantic, at least through the next two months. I wouldn't expect you to leave now. After the first of the year," Lynn pauses, shrugs, completes her thought, "who knows?"

Patrick sits flipping his new credit card absently in one huge hand, considering his gorgeous wife, self-confident and self-sufficient though she is, traveling to Portugal and Madeira without him. They have never been apart for longer than a weekend in their seventeen years of marriage, since Lynn was nineteen and he twenty-one years old. "I don't like it, Lynn," he mutters.

"I don't either, but I'll be okay," she says and kisses his cheek.

Patrick focuses on the credit card. "Where did you get this?"

"Seashore National sent it over."

"Sent it over? Delivered it here? To the house?"

Lynn beams. "We seem a lot more credit-worthy all of a sudden."

Patrick returns her smile. "How much is it good for?"

"A million dollars. Total for the two of us. I have one just like it," Lynn says, and they enjoy a hearty laugh together.

Three days later, on Saturday afternoon, Patrick drives Lynn to Newark Airport. He is skeptical that she will find their benefactor, and he remains uneasy at the prospect of her traveling so far without him, becoming involved in who knows what. Also he is still reluctant to use any of the money, fearing something will yet go wrong and they will be forced to replace it. Lynn has tried to allay his concerns in the dozens of related discussions they have had these past few days, insisting she will be fine, she won't be gone for long, the kids are old enough and responsible enough to get by without her for the week or so she is away, Patrick's sister Theresa can take them to any scheduled events that he can't attend or transport them to. As to spending some of the windfall, if it should turn out that the money in their account is a mistake, the expenditures for her trip will be the error-maker's cost of his carelessness. "And serves him right," she added each time her husband voiced his apprehension about spending the money.

Patrick booked her flight online, at top dollar since it was so imminent. The cost made him wince. However, they both thought the price of the accommodation he reserved for her at Funchal's Hotel Savoy, reputed to be among the island's finest lodgings, was pretty reasonable. But she did persuade him to splurge an extra hundred dollars for an ocean-view room.

Lynn is confident that Kerry and Sean will get along perfectly well with Patrick and Theresa taking care of them. As she and her husband cruise north on the New Jersey Turnpike, she recalls her phone conversation of Thursday evening with Molly, the couple's fourteen-year-old niece, who had answered the phone when she called for Theresa.

"Hi, Aunt Lynn."

"Hi, Molly."

"I have an easy one for you," the girl had said. Lynn smiled, anticipating what was coming. Molly always greets her with a movie trivia question. She and her brother Danny are movie buffs, avid about it, can name everyone in any recent film, know all the old classics, can tell you what songs are on a film's sound track, are up on the history of film making, stay on top of Hollywood gossip, know the biographies and relationships of everyone in the industry: actors, actresses, directors, producers. Molly, being two years older than her brother, developed the interest first. Danny picked it up from her because of her enthusiasm for the subject and the closeness between the siblings. It has become a competition as well as a shared interest. Lynn used to challenge Molly with questions, but as her niece's knowledge surpassed her own their roles in the game reversed.

"*Casablanca*," Molly announced over the phone.

"*Casablanca*. All right," Lynn replied.

"Play it again, who?"

"Sam. Play it again, Sam. That's an awfully easy one. You're toying with me, Molly, right?"

"The name of Humphrey Bogart's nightclub?"

"Come on," Lynn said. "Rick's."

"The character played by Paul Henreid?"

"Uh . . . Laszlo. Victor Laszlo," Lynn said after a moment.

"Who played *Señor* Ferrari?"

Lynn didn't remember. She took a shot at it. "Peter Lorre?"

"No. Sydney Greenstreet."

"Oh, that's right."

"Who directed the movie?"

Lynn had no idea. "I surrender, Molly. Who was it?"

"Michael Curtiz. Just one more, Aunt Lynn."

"All right, just one."

"You've seen Natalie Forthright's films?"

"Some of them."

"Good. In what movie did she play Attorney Rebecca Belanger?"

"Oh, I don't know, Molly. Was it *Personal Request*?"

"Bzzzz," Lynn's niece buzzed like a game show's annoying disqualifier. "Good try, Aunt Lynn, but no cigar. In *Personal Request* she was a reporter named Tracey Curtis. It was in *Written Consent* that she played the lawyer."

"I remember that now, sweetheart. Let me talk to your mom, okay?"

When Molly told her that her mother was out food-shopping, Lynn drove to the supermarket and waited until her sister-in-law emerged, pushing a cart filled with bags of groceries. They greeted each other warmly. "You here to shop?" Theresa asked.

"No, I came to see you."

"What? Something's wrong?"

"No. everything is fine. Where's your car?" Theresa pointed toward it. "Come on, I'll walk you over. We can talk there."

"In my car? We have to talk in my car? It *is* bad, isn't it? You never behave this way, Lynn."

"Relax. I don't have bad news. It's good news. I just don't want you screaming here in the parking lot when I tell you what's happening."

"You're pregnant!"

"No. Shh. I'll tell you everything."

-28-

Lynn's sister-in-law Theresa O'Brien Conlin is thirty-five years old. Like her brother, she is blessed with naturally curly black hair, but radically unlike Patrick she is tiny and slight at 5'2", 115 pounds. The brother and sister are both grateful for that fortunate dispersal of genetic and hormonal-induced traits.

Theresa's relationship with Patrick has always been familialy warm and loving, but the fondness she and sister-in-law Lynn share is truly remarkable, like that of particularly close sisters who are also great friends. The two women are only months apart in age. Their daughters Kerry and Molly were born just weeks apart, as were their sons Sean and Danny. The girls are classmates at Mainland High; the boys seventh graders at Jordan Road School. Lynn and Theresa regularly alternate on transporting the kids to school affairs, sporting events and social get-togethers, and they turn to each other any time a sitter is needed. This last is the subject Lynn wants to discuss with Theresa, but, of course, it is instantly overshadowed by the announcement of her five million dollar bonanza.

After emitting the scream Lynn expected and had fore-sightedly prevented from echoing through the supermarket parking lot, Theresa unleashed a torrent of omigods and questions. Lynn tried to answer between ecstatic embraces and successive shouts of disbelief and unbridled excitement. Finally, restraining Theresa's wildly gesticulating hands and shushing her to a trembling speechlessness, she related all that had transpired since her ATM visit two days earlier.

Once Lynn had decided to embark on her odyssey, she and Patrick realized that their covenant of concealment could not continue. Patrick would need Theresa's help while Lynn was away. Theresa would have to know what was going on. So would Kerry and Sean. And Lynn's parents.

Patrick told Kerry and Sean, who were thrilled at becoming rich and thought their mom's trek to track down the font of their family's good fortune was cool.

When Lynn completed her in-car conference with Theresa, she drove directly to her parents' Northfield, New Jersey, home, seven miles, twelve minutes from the Somers Point supermarket, calling in advance from her cell phone to announce her visit, knowing there was no real need to do so. Her mother and father would almost surely be at home. Her dad had turned on the porch light and was waiting at the front door when she arrived.

Michael Gallagher, age sixty-nine, is four years retired from a career with Atlantic Glass Company. He looks older than his years, but, despite his white hair and somewhat stiffened gait from a touch of arthritis, he is in generally good health. His TV-viewing evenings are sedentary but are offset by his vigorous lawn, garden and tool-shed active days. Lynn returned his always affectionate hug and kiss as she smelled the aroma of brewing coffee wafting from the kitchen. Decaf, she knew, for her early to bed, early rising folks.

"Pat's not with you?" Michael asked. Most people call Patrick by that typically abbreviated name. Only his mother, father, sister and Lynn customarily use his full first name. Some of his high school friends still call him Knute, a nickname bestowed because of his football prowess, the appellation coined by a teammate who watched old movies and knew that his buddy's namesake, actor Pat O'Brien, played the great Notre Dame University Football Coach Knute Rockne in the 1940 film, *Knute Rockne, All American.*

"Not tonight, Dad," Lynn answered.

"What's up?" her father asked.

"You might want to turn off the television while I get mom. I've got some good news to tell you both."

Lynn kissed her mother's cheek, exchanged hellos with her and carried in the coffee, cream and sugar-free sweetener while her mom fussed with arranging cheese, crackers and cookies prettily on a tray.

Donna Ryan Gallagher is sixty-five years old, 5'4" in height and overweight. Despite her superbly fit and health-conscious daughter Lynn's urging, she paid little attention to diet and none at all to exercise until two years ago. During a routine doctor visit at that time she learned she was hypertensive, and a follow-up blood test revealed she had also developed Type II Diabetes. Donna was quite obese then, weighing as much as 190 pounds. The physician advised her to lose weight in an attempt to reduce her blood sugar and lower her blood pressure without resorting to drug therapy, words of wisdom she heeded from him as she never had from her daughter.

Motivated by these presages of her mortality, Donna adopted a more healthful lifestyle with Lynn's enthused and educated guidance. She began eating more carefully and eased into an exercise program. Initially her regimen was prudently light, but now it includes brisk walks interspersed with a fair amount of jogging, out in the fresh air in decent weather, on her treadmill on inclement days. She engages in weight training to benefit her arms and upper body and a program of daily stretching to ease the strain on muscles, ligaments and tendons and keep her limber. Her weight has fallen to 145 pounds. Her blood sugar counts are now normal, and her systolic blood pressure has dropped twenty points. She fully intends to maintain her revised lifestyle and continue losing weight until she reaches her maintenance goal of 125 pounds.

Lynn could not be more pleased by her mother's progress, nor could Donna's doctor or Michael, who is happy to see his wife's restored health and renewed vigor. Inspired by her slimmed figure, Donna has further enhanced her appearance by coloring her gray hair to a shade close to the eye-catching blond tresses of her nubile years.

Back in the early seventies Donna worked at Atlantic Glass Company, which was where she met Michael. She left Atlantic when she became pregnant, later returning to the working world when Lynn started school. She was hired by the County of Atlantic, working in its Mays Landing offices for many years, retiring just a few months ago.

Thinking back now as she and Patrick approach Newark on their way to the airport, Lynn remembers her father's initial astonishment at the news of her phenomenal ATM experience and his caution-constrained excitement as she described the several bankers' unflagging assurances that the deposit to their bank account was genuine and the money is theirs. She recalls his reaction with pleasure. Yet her mother, always the more demonstrative of her parents, seemed by contrast surprisingly . . . what? . . . unemotional? unenthused? placid? even apathetic? Lynn still cannot pinpoint her mother's response to her glad tidings, other than that it was disappointing. But she was even more struck by Donna's peculiar receipt of her announcement that she planned to fly to Madeira to locate her anonymous patron. Her mother's breath caught in her throat. Her eyes shot wide open in what could only be perceived as shock or fear. Lynn had grasped her hands, momentarily afraid Donna was about to faint.

"What's wrong?" Lynn had asked, watching her mother struggle to control her breathing and regain her composure before answering.

"It's nothing, dear," Donna replied finally. "I'm just concerned for your safety. Such a long trip alone."

"I'll be fine, Mom. You needn't worry," Lynn had replied, but she found the incident puzzling. Donna's near collapse seemed so out of proportion to the circumstances. She had actually appeared horrified when Lynn mentioned Madeira, her discomfiture all the more perplexing by comparison to her insipid response to Lynn's so much more dramatic news of newfound fortune.

Lynn still had no idea what prompted her mother's dismay about her journey to Madeira, but it was difficult to believe that simple maternal concern for the welfare of her fully grown and thoroughly competent daughter could explain it.

Now, Patrick turns off the New Jersey Turnpike at Exit 14 and follows airport signs toward the departing passenger terminals, finding TAP Air Portugal listed among the airlines using Terminal B. He eases between a bus and a car to pull to a curbside stop in a no-parking, unloading-only area. He and Lynn have agreed he should not delay his two-and-a-half hour return trip to home and children by waiting for her plane to leave.

"It's not too late to change your mind," he says.

She moves into his embrace. "I have my tickets, my passport, the credit card, a hotel room in Funchal. I'm not going to quit now. Don't worry, sweetheart. I'll be fine. Grab my bag from the trunk and give me a kiss."

Lynn waves good-bye as Patrick drives slowly away. A porter reaches for her bags, but she waves him off. One is only a small carry-on. The larger one has wheels. She needs no assistance handling them. She wonders if she'll ever start acting like someone who has five million dollars in the bank.

Instructions that came by priority mail with her ticket call for Lynn's arriving three hours early for her international flight, at 4 p.m. for a 7 p.m. departure, which she considers a ridiculous waste of time. She arrives at 5:10 p.m., and, from the look of the check-in area, so does everyone else. TAP Air Portugal's four ticket desks are directly opposite the Terminal B door through which she entered. She joins the zigzagging waiting line of baggage-toting travelers, the kind bank lobbies feature. Lynn finds them annoying, preferring a little human disorder to feeling as if she is in a cattle chute.

Signs above each of the four check-in desks toward which the back and forth queue eventually leads designate them as Economy Class. Lynn sees that her ticket says Class K. A fifth desk has a sign labeling it Navigator Class. Patrick has arranged for her to fly coach. No doubt the forty or so passengers ahead of her in line are doing the same, she thinks. Only one person waits at the Navigator Desk, which leads her to conclude that Navigator must be first class. Still, she would like to verify that she is in the correct line now, rather than find she was not after having inched slowly forward through the entire proceeding.

"Excuse me," Lynn says to a man directly in front of her. He turns and smiles pleasantly. "My ticket reads Class K," she tells him. "The sign up front says Economy Class. Would you know if I'm in the right place?" He studies his own ticket, which also reads Class K. The overnight flight they are waiting to board is the first leg of Lynn's trip, TAP Air Portugal Flight 1332, scheduled to leave Newark International at 7 p.m. and arrive in Lisbon at 6:45 a.m. Sunday. She transfers to her Madeira flight in Lisbon.

"We're in the same boat as well as the same line for the same plane," he says. "Mine is K too. I imagine we're all right." He points out what she has already observed: no one now waits for the Navigator Class ticket agent, which presumably indicates that is not the line for coach. Lynn smiles and thanks him, and he turns away. But after they move a few paces forward, he turns back to her and resumes their conversation, asking if she is traveling to Lisbon on business or for pleasure.

"Not pleasure. Not business exactly, either, in the sense of representing some company," Lynn replies. "I guess I would categorize it as personal business. How about you?"

"I'd say the same," he answers. He introduces himself. "My name is David Kubasik, by the way."

"Lynn O'Brien."

"Nice to meet you. Yes, I'm also traveling on personal business," he tells her. "Not in Lisbon though. I fly on to Madeira from there."

"So do I," Lynn says, surprised by the coincidence. She is even more astounded to learn they are staying at the same hotel.

"You wouldn't believe the nature of my business in Madeira,"

David comments. In light of the bizarre reason for her own trip, Lynn laughs aloud. She realizes her mirth must seem inappropriate to him, but he laughs along with her good-naturedly all the same.

"All right," she says. "I'm curious. What is it? Why are you going to Madeira?"

David leans closer and whispers, "Someone in Madeira deposited ten million dollars in my checking account."

Chapter 4

Nordin Mohamad and Rhali Bhatia carefully observe David and Lynn from a position half a dozen places behind them in the waiting line.

"Who is the woman?" Mohamad asks in heavily accented English.

"I do not know," Bhatia responds in kind.

"Of course you do not know. We have not seen her before. A chance meeting, perhaps?"

"If you knew I did not know, why then did you ask me if . . . ?"

"Noooo!" Lynn screams, seizing the attention of everyone in the area. Bhatia stops speaking in mid-sentence. He and Mohamad view Lynn's belated attempt to stifle her outburst with one hand while she clasps David's arm with the other. She leans close enough to kiss David but instead whispers something into his ear. They burst into animated conversation and fairly dance about right there in line.

"Chance meeting, indeed," Bhatia scoffs. "I know two lovers when I see them." Mohamad reserves judgment, studying the actions of David and this woman they have not heretofore seen during their surveillance of the American scientist. He must admit that the two seem overjoyed at being together. They smile, they laugh, they touch, they babble incessantly and with marked exuberance as they advance together in the line.

"Observe their delight in each other," Bhatia says. "This is no random encounter, Nordin. We wondered why he is going to Lisbon. Now we know. He is embarking on a tryst, an assignation, he and his sweetheart on holiday, flying off together for a romantic interlude in Portugal." When David takes Lynn's arm and approaches a ticket agent with her, Bhatia's smile is smug with triumph. "Adjacent seats, no doubt," he gloats, nudging his companion. Mohamad rewards the nudge with a rib poke of his own, but he is forced to agree. Their quarry is not the reclusive, dedicated, wholly absorbed, single-minded research scientist they had thought him to be.

Nordin Mohamad and Rhali Bhatia are security agents of General Habib Aláz, military ruler of Telám, an oil-rich North African nation about the size of Pennsylvania, slightly smaller than neighboring Tunisia and located between that country and Libya on the Mediterranean Sea coast.

The two foreign agents are burly, swarthy men who might be taken for bodyguards, nightclub bouncers, professional wrestlers, NFL linemen. Mohamad is somewhat more mammoth than his associate and distinguishable as well by his thicker, surely several times broken nose and bushier black eyebrows. Bhatia, by contrast, is three inches shorter at 6'2", twenty pounds lighter at 260, and has a more angular face. He wears a small sapphire earring in his left ear.

They have been stalking David Kubasik for the past ten days, assigned by General Aláz to abduct him and spirit him to the presidential palace in Ractá, Telám's capital city. They have no idea of the reason for their mission. They are attempting to carry it out, unsuccessfully thus far, solely because they have been ordered to do so. Their target has unwittingly avoided abduction as the result of his peculiar work habits and the tight twenty-four hours per day security of his Princeton University laboratory.

Because David is so engrossed in his research, he spends practically all his time at the lab, has rarely left it in recent days, even has taken to sleeping there. Mohamad and Bhatia have found no opportunity to seize him, indeed were unable to get anywhere close to him. General Aláz cautioned them not to create any kind of public spectacle in abducting David. There must be no witnesses to their actions, he had commanded, nothing and no one that might lead to their apprehension by police or reveal their identities as agents of Telám, constraints that have further complicated their assignment.

Foiled from accomplishing their mission and fearing the consequences of failure, Mohamad and Bhatia were elated when they learned David would be traveling to Lisbon, information they obtained by means of super-sensitive electronic eavesdropping equipment they used throughout their surveillance. Attending the listening device also rewarded them with the discovery of David's ten million dollar windfall, which they harbor no doubt is somehow linked to General Alaz's interest in him. How the money relates they do not know, do not want to know, are happy not to know. No questions asked. No reasons why. They care only that David is en route to Lisbon, where, they are certain, they can easily snatch him, whisk him aboard a waiting Telámian government plane and deliver him to the general. And, as it has turned out, his pretty paramour with him.

★ ★ ★ ★ ★ ★ ★ ★ ★ ★

Lynn's scream, "Noooo!" has riveted the attention of everyone within earshot. Embarrassed, she attempts, too late, to stifle her outburst with one hand while she clasps David's arm with the other. She leans close enough to kiss him, but instead whispers into his ear, "This is impossible, David. The same thing happened to me, only in my case it was five million dollars." The two burst into animated conversation, describing to each other the circumstances of their discoveries and their interactions with banking officials since receiving the money. Each new revelation by one to the other is accompanied by shared laughter, grasping of hands, excited embraces as they move forward in line.

"Next, please!" an open ticket agent calls, and David starts toward her to check in.

"Come with me," he invites Lynn, and she walks forward with him. He is assigned seat 14-H. "Is the seat adjacent to mine available?" he asks.

The agent checks her computer. "That would be 14-J. Yes, it's still open."

"Lynn?" David asks.

"Definitely, I would like that seat, please," Lynn tells the agent. They learn that their flight will leave from Gate 66 and that boarding will begin at 6:15 p.m.. The TAP Air Portugal representative points the way to that gate. With time to spare before they board, David asks if Lynn would like to have a drink, some coffee, a bite to eat. They go to a bar in the terminal and continue their discussion, wholly unaware of dark eyes monitoring their every move.

Boarding begins. Lynn and David shuffle toward their seats, Row 14, Seats H and J on the titanic but jammed Airbus A-310, brightly painted in Portugal's national colors: red and green on the otherwise white aircraft. No sooner are they seated than they resume their spirited conversation, each marveling at the almost inconceivable realization that they are living the same fantasy, that they met as they did, that they can share the search for their unknown benefactor, who, they conjecture, must surely be one and the same person. Perhaps together they can determine why they have been so financially favored and explore what unknown factors they must have in common to effect this remarkable bond between them.

"Tell me about yourself," David says. Lynn tells him that she is married to Patrick O'Brien and they have two children: Kerry, age fourteen, and Sean, twelve. "Wow! I'm surprised at your children's ages. You must have married when you were very young."

Lynn nods, smiling at his compliment's implicit meaning that she looks too young to have children their ages. "I was nineteen.

Patrick was twenty-one," she reveals, going on to tell David about her parents, that she is an only child, that she grew up in South Jersey. She married less than a year after finishing high school, later continuing her education and earning an associates degree at Atlantic Cape Community College when her children were toddlers. She had taken evening courses while Patrick tended to Kerry and Sean. She also attended a number of seminars since then and took specialized courses enabling her to pass qualifying tests for her several aerobics and personal trainer certifications.

"So you're a personal trainer?"

"Uh-huh, certified by ACE and AFAA. The American Council on Exercise and the Aerobics and Fitness Association of America," she clarifies, changing David's puzzled expression to a comprehending smile. "Only for about a year now. I have eight regular clients so far. I do my personal training at a health club where I work as an aerobics instructor. Been there nine years. Part-time." Lynn further explains that she took up jogging as a temporary measure to whip her body back into shape after Kerry was born. "Before long I was running regularly and then competitively, and from there became interested in aerobic dancing." One thing led to another, she informs David, eventually blossoming into a fitness training career as an instructor of aerobics and its evolving, more specialized aspects like spinning, treadmill, weight training, stair climbing and others.

"What does your husband do?" David asks.

"Patrick is with Atlantic Glass Company. He's been there since he finished high school, working at the company's original plant in Weymouth, New Jersey. His father worked there for years too. So did *my* father. My mother too for a while. Patrick started as a stock clerk and worked his way up through most of the plant's departments. He's now their assistant plant manager.

"When I finished community college, Patrick enrolled at Stockton State College. He went through six years of night school for his BS in Business Management. He's a fine man, my husband." She pauses briefly, wondering if there is a point in further extolling Patrick's virtues, his being a loving husband and father, a good family man, a hard worker. She asks instead, "Does any of this seem to have anything to do with you?"

David is thoughtful for a moment, then slowly shakes his head. "No, nothing I can detect. You and your family seem to have a lot of connections with that glass company where your husband works, though."

"Atlantic. That's true, but it's not so unusual, David. Before the casino industry came to Atlantic City we didn't have a lot of major employers in our area. The glass company was always one of the better ones. They've really grown, even since Patrick started with them, opening more glass production plants, getting into plastics. Atlantic is now a division of Pristina Corporation. Pristina's a subsidiary of Titan, Limited."

"Titan is the British company?"

Lynn nods. "Headquartered in London. Do you think our family's involvement with Atlantic is significant?"

"I don't know. I don't see how. Do you?"

"Until now I hadn't even considered that it might. But it must not be a factor, since there's no connection between Atlantic and you. What about you, though, David? Tell me something about yourself." Lynn has already made some observations about him. He is close to her age, she thinks. He's very tall, about Patrick's height, but slimmer, maybe 185 or 190 pounds. His light brown hair, casually brushed and bordering on unkempt, is thick and full. His eyes, also brown, are alert and intelligent, intense and penetrating when he is concentrating or thoughtful, warm and friendly, sparkling and animated in his conversation with her.

"Sure," David says. He tells her he is thirty-seven years old, that he grew up and went through grade and high school in Moorestown, New Jersey, which he has always considered home and to which he returned to live a few years ago after more than twelve years away. He says that he attended Rice University, majored in biology and chemistry and graduated at age eighteen.

"You graduated from college at eighteen?" Lynn asks incredulously. David merely nods affirmation. "How old were you when you finished high school?"

"Fifteen."

"And when you started?"

"Twelve."

"You must have been a brilliant child."

"Well, I learned to read when I was three years old, so I was placed in accelerated education programs starting when I was five. I was good at math; understood college level mathematics while I was in grade school."

"That's amazing. So, after graduating from Rice, you did graduate work?"

"Yes. I have a master's in molecular biophysics and biochemistry from Princeton and a doctorate from Emory University."

"A Ph.D. I'm impressed, David. What was your doctoral dissertation subject?"

"Mitochondrial diseases. That's still my field. When I finished my formal education at Emory I was asked to join their research staff. It was a marvelous opportunity. Emory's people did the groundbreaking work with mitochondrial DNA mutations. My focus is on GOA."

"GOA?"

"Gunsenhouser's Optic Atrophy." Lynn's palms are upturned, her shoulders hunched and questioning. She had never heard of the condition. "It's a rare and quite debilitating optic nerve disorder," David clarifies.

"So you, uh, do research on . . .?"

"Gunsenhouser's."

" . . . on Gunsenhouser's at Emory. Isn't Emory in Atlanta?"

"It is, but I've left there. I moved my work to Princeton a while back."

"So you could come back to Moorestown?"

"That's right," David says appreciatively. She is a quick study, this young woman he has just met. She doesn't miss anything. "That was really my main reason for leaving Emory. I had presented a paper at the 2003 International Conference on Mitochondrial Disease in Philadelphia, which led to a speaking engagement at Princeton. Then Princeton invited me to move the locus of my research there. I was reluctant to leave my friends and associates in Atlanta, but I couldn't pass up the opportunity to return home."

"So was the old hometown still the same?"

"Well, my parents still live there, and it's great to be able to see them fairly often."

"Friends? Girlfriends?"

"The girls I knew had either married or moved away. I didn't have that many close friends, really. I was always years younger than my classmates. A couple of my unmarried neighborhood buddies are still around. I enjoy seeing them occasionally, but we don't really have much in common any longer. In any case my work absorbs practically all my time. My days in the lab usually run late into the evenings. Most of my workweeks go right through the weekends. Pretty much a one-dimensional life, huh?"

"Oh, I don't know," Lynn says. "I mean, it sounds as if you could be missing out on some everyday things, but your work must be very important."

"Well, yes, that's true, Lynn. I can hardly regret the fact that my research has become my whole life. I've discovered how we can deal with Gunsenhouser's. I'm on the verge of developing a way to prevent and cure it. I just need a little more time and a lot more money."

"Money? How much money?"

"About ten million dollars."

"David, do people know that?"

"Sure. My research progress was announced in the relevant journals and science magazines. All the articles about my work mentioned my need for funds. I've submitted grant applications to obtain funding, of course, and I'm certain to get it eventually, but it's a waiting game right now. You're thinking someone may have sent me the ten million dollars so I can complete my work?"

"It makes sense, David."

"That was my first thought too when all those dollars showed up unannounced in my bank account. But now I learn you also received money, also from someone in Madeira, likely, it would seem, the same person."

"Which casts doubt on the notion that what you got was meant to fund your work?"

"Kind of does, doesn't it?"

"Not necessarily, David."

"No, there must be just one person involved, but I suppose he could have sent my money for my research and yours for some entirely different reason."

Lynn sighs. "I don't think you should be here, David. You should have just used the ten million and not delayed finishing your work."

"I struggled with the idea, Lynn. I wanted to use the money and plunge right ahead, but no one came forward to say they gave it to me for that purpose. No one has given me any kind of explanation. I can't bring myself to spend the money until I know who sent it and why."

"No one could understand that better than I do. I know exactly how you feel," Lynn commiserated.

Chapter 5

Mohamad and Bhatia are seated in Row 18, four behind Lynn and David and at an advantageous angle that permits a good view of them. But what with the chatter of boarding passengers, the fast-food drive-through speaker tinniness of flight attendant safety instructions, the captain's descending sing-song announcements, and finally the roar of jet engines, the agents are unable to hear anything of the couple's unceasing conversation.

"They have much to say to each other," Bhatia comments. "They never stop talking." He cranes his neck to get a better view past the bulk of his partner. "Do you see? He sits very close to her."

"Yes, and you sit very close to me," Mohamad grouses, leaning his weight into Bhatia to push him some inches aside. The effort gains almost no additional space between them. Individual passenger room on the Airbus is hardly adequate for someone of Lynn's size. It is completely insufficient for giants like the two Telámians, which Bhatia petulantly points out.

As the plane cruises north along the U.S. coastline, four screens descend from the passenger cabin's ceiling in the section where the agents and Lynn and David sit. Mohamad shifts from one position to another in his seat, trying in vain to find some semblance of comfort for his elephantine legs and size fifteen feet while he watches Lynn and David. Bhatia, on the other hand, reclines his seatback as far as possible to lie in relative comfort studying the closest of the screens. Over and over it displays the plane's altitude, its position, how far they have gone, the remaining distance to Lisbon, the temperature outside the aircraft, all this alternately in Portuguese and in English, using the metric system and Celsius measurements for Portuguese segments, miles and Fahrenheit for English. The monitors also periodically show a graphic of the plane's progression above the earth, using an airplane image against a background of land or ocean below it, trailed by an ever-lengthening red line originating at the flight's Newark starting point.

"We are almost over Boston, Massachusetts," Bhatia says.

"What?" Mohamad asks.

"Boston, you see?" He points to the monitor. "Why are we flying north? Surely Lisbon is south of *New Jersey*, never mind Massachusetts." Mohamad merely grumbles in reply. Bhatia considers and posits, "Probably something to do with the curvature of the earth or perhaps the prevailing winds." He stares in fascination as the red flight path curves even farther north and eastward past Boston and out over the Atlantic Ocean, which reads *Oceano Atlàntico* on the Portuguese language pictorial.

Bhatia returns his seatback to upright when flight attendants bring them drinks and then dinner. The men are pleasantly surprised by the superior taste and quality of their meals, having expected less of airline fare. After dinner and another dozen or so reviews of the long red line and in-flight statistics, a movie comes onscreen, *Jefferson City*, starring Natalie Forthright as the scheming seductress Sweet April Lee. Bhatia sighs contentedly and again reclines his seatback to enjoy the American-made film in as relaxing a fashion as he can manage.

"You are not watching Kubasik and his woman," Mohamad complains about ten minutes into the motion picture.

"No, I am watching the movie. Hollywood," he enthuses.

"Is that our assignment?" Mohamad demands.

"Tell me, Nordin," Bhatia counters, "can you hear what Kubasik and his girlfriend are saying?"

"No."

"Can you read their lips?"

"No."

"No," Bhatia echoes. "Relax. Watch the film. Take a nap. There is nowhere they can go." Mohamad intones a wordless basso grumble but soon abandons his pointless vigil, beckons a flight attendant to them and orders two more drinks. "Tell me what has happened so far in the film," he says.

Lisbon's lights glimmer in the pre-dawn darkness below as the plane begins its landing approach six-and-a-half hours and five time zones distant from Newark. Daylight has dawned as the aircraft comes to rest at *Portela* Airport, about five miles north of the Portuguese capital. They arrive ten minutes ahead of schedule at 6:35 a.m.. Mohamad and Bhatia follow Lynn and David as all passengers shuffle from the plane toward a checkpoint where Portuguese customs officials examine passports. This single check is all that most of the passengers are subjected to, no customs declarations or anything more involved than just a quick comparison of faces versus photos and stamping of passports. The procedure is brief and simple for Lynn and David and every other passenger disembarking in front of Mohamad and Bhatia. Not so, however, for them.

The uniformed guardian of his country's main gate glances at their passports. He studies their faces, pauses at Mohamad's pugilism-punished proboscis, Bhatia's sapphire earring, runs his eyes up and down the two colossal men. The corners of his mouth first descend from his initial tourist-welcoming smile, then curl upward into a suspicious sneer. No one so perfectly matching the terrorist profile he has been trained to watch for has ever attempted to pass through his checkpoint. He lifts an intercom transmitter from his desk and barks something in Portuguese. In seconds two uniformed policemen, holstered pistols, sheathed nightsticks and canistered mace dangling from their broad black belts, appear at his side. They order Mohamad and Bhatia to come with them.

An older, higher-ranking cynic greets them in a brightly lighted room containing one desk, behind which he sits, and two more chairs on which he commands them to sit.

The official scans their passports. "You are Telámian?" he asks. His tone drips skepticism.

"Yes," Mohamad answers.

"Not Libyan, Algerian, Iraqi, Iranian, Syrian, Lebanese, Afghani?"

"Telámian." Spokesman Mohamad sounds unflustered, assertive but not confrontational. He too has been trained for this. Bhatia knows that inwardly his companion is as panicked as he that David Kubasik will elude them as a result of this unforeseen but inescapable interruption of their pursuit. The Telámians are not aware that David and Lynn are flying on to Madeira. Spying on their always sheltered subject back in Princeton had unveiled only the Newark to Lisbon portion of David's travel. Bhatia visualizes the lovers lifting their luggage from the airport carousel, traipsing through the exit doors, kissing in a taxi as they drive off and disappear into the modern metropolis that is twenty-first century Lisbon. He also envisions General Aláz's fury at his and Mohamad's failure, expulsion from their jobs, blacklisting, banishment and poverty. And that is if they are lucky.

Mohamad declares they are tourists. Yes, they visited the United States. No, they had no business there. They were merely tourists. They intend now to tour Portugal. The questioning and Mohamad's careful responses continue for close to fifteen minutes, drawing to a close soon after the interrogator learns they work as security guards on the staff of their country's president. They produce identification to substantiate that fact. Their ID's are in Arabic, indecipherable by the official, but they look authentic and bear photographs unquestionably their own, and their passports are valid. Finally, they are photographed, fingerprinted and cleared after an unsuccessful computer search for adverse information concerning them.

"Welcome to Portugal," their inquisitor snarls and releases them.

The Telámian agents walk at a moderate pace until they enter the airport terminal proper and are no longer visible from the passport review zone. Once inside, Mohamad utters, "Aieee!" a subdued scream he can barely contain. He takes off at a trot, the fastest gait he dares employ, afraid to call further attention to himself and his companion by sprinting madly through the terminal. Bhatia stays beside him. They come upon an escalator. "Rhali, you check the baggage pickup area. I'll search outside. Meet me here when you finish."

Bhatia agrees, descends the escalator and inspects the baggage carousel room. Lynn and David are nowhere in sight. A sign points to the airport's rental car desks. He hurries to study the faces of everyone waiting for service. No luck. He dashes back to the escalator and returns to the main floor. Mohamad is just arriving also. He looks desperate. "They are not outside," he snorts.

"Nor on the lower level," Bhatia pants. The two men gaze at the escalator. They turn to each other and leap on the upward-flowing stairs. A short distance from the top they spot Lynn and David entering Terminal A's Gate 15 waiting area. Bhatia utters a sigh of relief that sounds like a prayerful chant, but Mohamad cuts it short by pulling him toward a nearby airport monitor. He searches for Gate 15 among the listed departing flights, and there it is: TAP Air Portugal Flight 1625, departing Lisbon at 8:50 a.m. from Gate 15.

"They are going to Madeira," he cries. "Why did you not know Kubasik is flying to Madeira?"

"I? I? It is we, Nordin, we!"

"We must get tickets for that flight," Mohamad screeches. Abandoning caution, he outright gallops toward the ticket counter."

"But . . . but . . . wait!" Bhatia protests. Mohamad ignores him and does not stop running until he reaches the ticket counter.

"Nordin, Nordin, come to your senses!" Bhatia shouts, grabbing the larger man's arm to tug him away from the counter. "We cannot take the Madeira flight."

The ticket agent whom Mohamad has approached agrees. "Oh, no, *senhores*, Madeira Flight 1625 is completely full. We cannot add a single passenger."

"It's all right. Thank you," Bhatia calls back over his shoulder. He turns to his partner. "Nordin, have you forgotten? General Aláz's plane is here waiting for us outside the terminal."

Mohamad's jaw drops. He thumps his forehead twice with a soccer ball-sized fist. "I am a fool," he mutters.

Bhatia laughs. He nudges Mohamad. "Huh? Huh?" he encourages until he gets Mohamad to smile sheepishly. "Can you picture the general if he learned we took a scheduled flight to Madeira and left his plane sitting on the tarmac here in Lisbon?" He roars with laughter, but Mohamad does picture the scene and finds entirely no humor in it.

"One day your laughing head will roll, Rhali. This is not amusing. What will we tell the general?"

Bhatia shrugs. "I think we will be all right. We can report that we did not know of Kubasik's plan to travel on to Madeira because his girlfriend must have made those arrangements. The general will not care anyway so long as we deliver Kubasik to him. We simply fly to the island ourselves and capture our elusive prey at last."

"Yes, yes, that is good, Rhali. The woman arranged their Madeira flight. Of course. And now we follow them to Madeira and grab them at the airport there. That will be even easier than it would have been here, had we not been detained by those imbeciles at the airport entrance." Bhatia suffers his giant compatriot's grateful hug, and they lumber out of the terminal to rendezvous with General Aláz's Lear jet crew.

★ ★ ★ ★ ★ ★ ★ ★ ★ ★

When Lynn and David had arrived in Lisbon from Newark they checked an airport monitor to find the gate number for their connecting flight to Madeira. They found that TAP Air Portugal Flight 1625 was on time for its scheduled 8:50 a.m. departure and would leave from Gate 15. Because their seat assignments had been made back in Newark and their bags were checked through to Madeira, they had nothing to do and time to spare before boarding.

David spied a money exchange booth and stopped to trade some dollars for Portuguese *escudos*. Although Lynn planned to cover major expenses with her million dollar credit card, she too bought some *escudos*, Madeira's currency as well as mainland Portugal's, for tipping and other situations where cash might be required. After their brief pause at the money counter they sauntered to the terminal's coffee shop for a leisurely cup of the beverage, the local form of which Lynn found to be at the outer edge of her taste buds' bitterness tolerance: sippable, barely drinkable. Half a cup remained behind when they proceeded to the waiting area for their flight, across the width of Terminal A and up an escalator one level above where they arrived from Newark.

Boarding begins. They climb a portable staircase to the plane, another Airbus, this one an A-319, which, though smaller than the A-310 used for their Trans-Atlantic flight, affords them additional leg room and is generally more comfortable. They place their carry-on bags in an overhead compartment and buckle up in preparation for take-off. Lynn observes that the plane is only half-full when the passengers who had been waiting with them are all seated. Ten minutes later, though, another sizable group boards, German tourists, and they are followed by the last minute arrival of Madeira's national soccer team, returning from a match in Oporto.

The A-319 has overhead monitors like the A-310's, providing

similar information about speed, distance, altitude, time of day and temperature. It also displays the same kind of graphic of the plane with a red line trailing it from Lisbon to Madeira, in this case a six hundred mile, one hour and forty-minute flight. Lynn and David are temporarily talked out. She naps briefly while he reads an airline magazine and watches a video about Madeira.

Lynn and David land in Funchal at *Aeroporto da Madeira*, the runways of which extend out over the Atlantic Ocean on massive concrete columns. They get their baggage, hail a cab and ride to the Hotel Savoy, located on the Madeira capital's *Avenida do Infante*. Lynn is dazzled by the flower-adorned city's beauty, its palm tree and purple-blossomed jacaranda-lined avenues. She is surprised too by Funchal's size and metropolitan bustle. David tells her the video he watched on the plane called Madeira a floating garden and stated Funchal's population at about 120,000 of the island's quarter-million residents.

Lynn points to some men untangling strings of lights on a sidewalk. "That's the sixth group of workers I've noticed putting up lights in trees since we drove into town."

"Christmas lights," David explains.

"In October?"

David nods. "The video on the plane showed Funchal scenes at Christmastime. Every tree in the city is decorated with lights. I guess they have to start preparing now. Christmas and New Year's Eve here are supposed to be spectacular. People come from all over Europe. The harbor fills with cruise ships and yachts."

Lynn spots the Hotel Savoy on their left. The taxi passes right by it. She looks back, wondering if she might have been mistaken. She wasn't. "David, we just passed our hotel," she blurts in alarm. Overhearing, their English speaking cab driver explains that left turns are permitted only at intersections. He turns left at the next street, then right onto one that circles back to *Avenida do Infante*, returns to the hotel's entrance and makes his legal right turn into its driveway entrance. David pays the fare, but Lynn insists on tipping the driver before he is able to do so, both of them using *escudos* astutely, having mastered the exchange rate back at the airport currency exchange kiosk.

★ ★ ★ ★ ★ ★ ★ ★ ★ ★

Nordin Mohamad and Rhali Bhatia had relaxed in cushioned, Lear leather luxury for most of the short hop from Lisbon to Funchal. That is, they relaxed until the pilot told them there would be a short delay in landing. Then they panicked. "A delay? Why?"

"Because we did not file an advance flight plan that included a landing in Madeira."

"Why not, you idiot?"

"I am the idiot? You are the idiot," the pilot rejoined. "But for your blundering we would not have come here at all. I informed *Aeroporto da Madeira* of our need to land while we were en route. We must circle until we receive clearance to land." Mohamad uttered a curse. Bhatia asked how long it would take. "Not long," the pilot answered.

Mohamad drew his cohort aside. "Not long," he scoffed. "If we lose Kubasik because of this, you and I will not have long." He executed a series of throat-slitting gestures to illustrate their fate if their mission should end in failure.

The Lear was forced to circle twice before receiving clearance to land. TAP Air Portugal Flight 1625 arrived on schedule while the Telámians were making their first aerial circuit of the island. Bhatia attempted to calm Mohamad by accentuating the positive: Kubasik and the woman were only a few minutes ahead of them and would be delayed at the baggage carousel. But his friend was not to be mollified. Fixated on the aircraft's door Mohamad awaited its opening with all the patience of a Brahma bull kicking and butting its chute, raging to charge into a rodeo ring, hurl off, and, if possible, gore the vile human clinging unnaturally to its back.

The agents vault from their plane and bound through the airport terminal in time to see Lynn and David escaping in a taxi. Mohamad and Bhatia jump into the next cab in line at the curb. "Follow that cab," Mohamad orders. The driver screeches off in pursuit, beaming with exhilaration as he keeps his vehicle scant yards behind the other's tail. Only when Bhatia settles their fare in the Hotel Savoy's driveway does he realize that the cabby does not speak English. "No *Inglês*?"

"*Pouco*," a little, the cabbie replies and demonstrates. "Okay. Coca-Cola. How much? Follow that cab."

Bhatia laughs. "Thank you, Hollywood," he says.

"Hollywood," the driver enthuses, pleased to realize his English vocabulary includes that additional word.

Bhatia joins Mohamad in the lobby, across which Lynn and David stand at the front desk, checking into the hotel. A bellman and several hotel guests enter an elevator with the couple, quashing any immediate opportunity for the Telámians to accomplish their abduction. While Lynn and David go to their separate rooms, rather than to the joint accommodation Mohamad and Bhatia mistakenly believe they share, the agents walk out front into the hotel garden to avoid hotel security's scrutiny.

"I saw a car rental agency up the block," Bhatia says, meaning they had better rent a car. Mohamad's left eyebrow rises, but only fleetingly. They can hardly hail a taxi while clinging to two struggling abductees. Soon Bhatia returns with their rental, which, Mohamad sees with trepidation at the prospect of eventual expense accounting, is a Mercedes sedan. Bhatia again soothes his concern. "Our justification is that we did not want to arouse suspicion by loitering in the lobby or on hotel grounds. Watching from the car for them to leave the hotel is much safer, and of course we need a roomy vehicle for conveying Kubasik and the woman back to the airport."

★ ★ ★ ★ ★ ★ ★ ★ ★ ★

Exhausted, Lynn sleeps through the afternoon and into the evening when the ringing telephone beside her bed wakes her.

"Hi, it's David. Sorry to wake you, but it's six-thirty, and I'm starving. I've been reading about local restaurants. One of the island's best is nearby. I was hoping you might join me for dinner."

She should call Patrick to tell him she arrived safely, but it's only one-thirty at home. He's at work. She'll call him later. "I'm hungry too," she says. "Give me a half hour or so to freshen up." They agree to meet in the lobby at seven-fifteen.

Lynn arrives downstairs a few minutes late. David was prompt and has learned from the concierge that *Quinta Palmeira*, the restaurant he chose because of its appealing description and its *Avenida do Infante* location, is not just nearby but right next door to their hotel. They leave the lobby with eight or ten other guests, all of whom walk through the garden onto the sidewalk and to the same destination as they. Lynn is fascinated by Funchal's sidewalks, which are cobble stoned, but not with the bulk cobbles of city streets. Rather they are made of small, tile-like but sturdy cobblestones, white, with a gently twisting pattern of black cobbles woven intricately through them, mile after mile of stone after stone. She comments to David that the job of laying them must have taken years.

Quinta Palmeira is a beautiful restaurant, just off *Avenida do Infante*, down a staircase to a garden-encircled courtyard. Its floor duplicates the sidewalks Lynn admires. Tiki hut-like umbrellas stand above each dining table. One wall is made completely of unobtrusive green latticework, hardly noticeable because the outdoor room's other border is a semi-circular stand of tall lush green tropical plants. Here and there throughout the foliage-defined room, small tables hold candles, floral-encased by birds of paradise, antherium and other exotics Lynn does not recognize. The decorative candle and flower arrangements greatly enhance the restaurant's ambience, while white lights strung throughout the tiki umbrellas gently illuminate the space.

Waiters in white jackets and black pants service the tables. A macaw whistles intermittently. Lynn mistakes its call for a signal originating from the kitchen, meant for the waiters. David has also wondered about the sound and located its true source. He sees Lynn's confusion and calls her attention to the bird, correcting her impression so graciously that she does not feel a tad foolish for her silly error, one she knows would ordinarily embarrass her.

Their dinners are wonderful. After a bean soup appetizer Lynn has medallions of veal in a mushroom and red wine sauce with tiny roasted potatoes, carrots and Brussels sprouts. David, more adventurous, has read about a fish caught only in Madeiran and Japanese waters, a scabbard fish Madeirans call *espada*. He orders *espada* in a banana and passion fruit sauce. It is delectable. At their server's suggestion they select a bottle of *Vinho Verde*, green wine, so called because, like *Beaujolais Noveau*, it is young and meant to be savored without aging. They find it light, fruity, delightful. For dessert David has crêpes suzette. Lynn chooses an almond ice cream, *Quinta Palmeira's* own, made on premises. It is served with two delicate cylindrical cookies and crowned by hot chocolate sauce. They both order coffee. Lynn asks their waiter if they have decaf. He assures her they do, but both are served espresso, half a cup each, which, if not filled to the brim with milk, Lynn believes will keep her awake for a week.

After dinner they slowly climb back up the steps to the street, warmed and cozied by the exquisite cuisine, paying little attention to their surroundings. They do not notice the Telámian agents or their Mercedes waiting at the top of the staircase, parked directly on the sidewalk, which attracts no attention whatsoever in Funchal. The city, as is true also of Lisbon, has not nearly enough parking spaces available for the number of vehicles on its streets. Both the police and the driving public, as a result, are remarkably tolerant of the most outlandish parking practices. Too bad for Lynn and

David in this instance, as the agents easily seize the unwary couple and shove them into their waiting rental car.

One of Mohamad's enormous hands stifles Lynn's scream while the other holds a small knife at David's throat. Lynn sees the knife and falls silent. David does not move a muscle. Bhatia speeds them to the airport and General Aláz's waiting Lear jet.

Chapter 6

In the car as they zoom to the airport, Mohamad says, "I am going to release you lovebirds now if you promise you will not attempt anything foolish. Do you promise?"

Lynn nods. She sees David do likewise. *Lovebirds*, she realizes the monster has called them. She is about to amend his misconception, but David's eyes and a slight shake of his head stop her. Maybe he senses a possible advantage in deluding their abductors, she thinks. Perhaps there is one. Despite her own fear she finds herself worrying about David. He is a scientist, an intellectual, so out of his element in this situation. Not that she isn't, but she prays this seemingly gentle man will not be foolhardy on her behalf. He appears in control of himself, though. If he is frightened, it does not show. If angry, that is no more apparent to her.

Mohamad releases them and is momentarily silent while he closes and pockets his knife. Lynn studies him. The man needs no weapon. He is a mountain. The mountain speaks. "I am sorry to have treated you both this way. My partner and I apologize for our behavior."

"You apologize?" Lynn has to vent.

"Yes."

"You are sorry?"

"Truly."

"Well then, maybe you will return us to our hotel, or instead we will be satisfied if you leave us right here."

Mohamad turns to David. "Your woman is feisty as well as beautiful."

"Where are you taking us?" David asks.

"Ractá."

Ractá? His disclosure solves nothing for Lynn until David explains, "Ractá is the capital of Telám." Telám, she knows, is somewhere in North Africa.

"Why?" she asks.

Bhatia is enjoying what he can hear of the conversation from the driver's seat. He turns his head and contributes, "I have sometimes wondered that."

Lynn is puzzled, but the man mountain beside her bellows with laughter. "You must excuse my foolish friend," he says, still chuckling. "He knows quite well that you are questioning why you are being abducted, not why Ractá is Telám's capital. One day his head will roll as a result of his peculiar notion of what constitutes humor. Yes, I can tell you something of why you are here." Lynn and David wait while he frames his response.

"Bhatia and I," – he nods toward the driver – "are agents of our government. We have been following you, Dr. Kubasik, for some days, in the United States and since you left New Jersey, under order of our president, General Habib Aláz, to capture you and bring you to him. Until now we found no opportunity to do so. We have no orders to bring Miss, Miss . . ."

"O'Brien," Lynn says.

" . . .Miss O'Brien to the general, but there proved to be no other way. We could hardly grab you and leave your sweetie standing screaming in the street. As to the general's reason for our mission, we have no idea why he wants to see you. We are merely following orders. But, whatever he has in mind, I can assure you that you are in no personal danger. He has already instructed us to return you to where we found you after you have met with him."

The Lear rockets across the 180 miles between Madeira and the North African coast. "That is Morocco below," Mohamad tells them. Morocco makes Lynn think about *Casablanca*, which makes her think about her recent phone conversation with her niece Molly, which makes her think about Patrick. He must be so worried about her.

The plane hugs the Mediterranean's southern coast past Algeria and Tunisia before finally reaching Telám. A car awaits them when they exit the plane, another Mercedes, this one black, bigger, shinier. In minutes they arrive at the presidential palace. It is an immense structure, turreted like a fortress, cupolaed like a mosque. They drive through a high, arched, armor-clad gate in a wall that appears thick and sturdy enough to be impervious to any kind of attack short of nuclear.

Mohamad and Bhatia lead them to a dimly lighted library where General Aláz rises from a leather easy chair to greet them. He switches on additional lighting and introduces himself, pumping David's hand. "Dr. Kubasik, it is my pleasure to meet you," he says. "And your lovely lady." He bows to Lynn and actually clicks his heels. She wonders if she should curtsy but does not risk trying it. He thanks Mohamad and Bhatia, who salute and march from the room, closing the door behind them.

He is an imposing man, the general, tall, muscular, dark. Lynn thinks him probably in his mid-forties. He is crowned with a mane of ebon hair that he wears brushed straight back but which, as Lynn can see, lifts itself from his scalp, refusing to be controlled. His deep brown, almost mahogany eyes are shaded by thick, heavy eyebrows and are so deep-set in his dusky face that they appear to be as black as his hair. He wears a military uniform with gold buttons. Five-star epaulets adorn each of his shoulders.

"Please, take a seat," he invites Lynn and David. They settle into the room's two other leather chairs, which face the general's. "You must forgive me for the manner in which I have, uh, summoned you here. I mean you no harm. On the contrary I am most eager to befriend you and to make you as comfortable as possible during your brief stay with us." Lynn focuses on *stay*; finds *brief* the key word. She studies the room. It is cool and comfortable, its air conditioning refreshing after the humid, eighty degrees or higher temperature outside in the Telámian night. Yet a fire blazes in the library's fireplace, its logs crackling as merrily as a New Hampshire White Mountains hostelry's in January.

The general follows Lynn's glance. "I cannot abide television, but I love looking into a fireplace," he tells her. "Here one cannot expect the kind of chill evening that calls for a hearty fire. We get no such nights. So . . ." He executes a grand, sweeping gesture toward the flame, then reaches behind him to tug twice on a red velvet cord hanging against a wall. The library's door swings open and two young women roll serving carts to them, one bearing an assortment of wines and liquors, the other piled with food. General Aláz waves the women off before they can begin to serve, which Lynn sees is clearly their intent. "Have a drink, some food, while I explain why you are here," he says.

"Thank you," David responds. Lynn marvels at how readily he has accepted the outlandish state of affairs in which they are embroiled. "What would you like, Lynn?" She would like to go back to Madeira, but she emulates David's equanimity and accepts a glass of decanted, origin-unspecified, pleasingly light red wine and several tiny sandwiches, hummus and olives in pita bread. She settles back in her chair to hear how in the world their captor can possibly justify the way they have been treated.

"I lived in poverty as a child," Aláz begins, "as did almost all my countrymen other than our political leaders and government bureaucrats. At sixteen I joined the guerilla fighters attempting to overthrow our repressive government. In time I rose through the ranks of what became an army equal in size to the government's regiments. For years we battled them back and forth across the land, accomplishing little other than keeping our people impoverished. Telám sits atop an ocean of oil, but our primitive petroleum industry and commerce in general were in collapse from the constant disruption of military encounters.

"Eventually I found myself in command of our troops, and I determined to end the senseless turmoil. I proposed to our military opponents that, instead of fighting each other, we join forces, oust the politicians and take control ourselves. Our combatants, equally as miserable as ourselves, agreed. We declared our newly formed junta in command of the country, and I assumed the presidency. I still prefer to be addressed by my military title, however.

"Since the fighting stopped four years ago, oil production and export have more than quadrupled. New equipment has been purchased, additional wells drilled, and the industry's methods have been modernized. More people are now employed in petroleum-related jobs, and their increased purchasing power has begun to improve the fortunes of other business sectors. I have been working to secure foreign investment in Telám and attract multi-national businesses, with some limited success.

"We are also in the initial stages of trying to develop tourism," Alaz continued, "but it will be some time before we can properly accommodate visitors. Given a few more years I believe our efforts will be fruitful. However, not everyone shares my optimism. There is much impatience. Too many people are disappointed with their continuing plight, and unrest has become rekindled. New opposition groups have formed to fan the flames of discontent. At the same time, there are those among my administration and military who lust for greater power and wealth of their own.

"What I am trying to convey to you is that at this critical moment in my nation's history, I personally cannot afford any display of weakness. Any sign of it would be seized upon and exploited by friend and foe alike. And in the face of all this, Dr. Kubasik, I have recently been diagnosed with a disease of the eyes that will likely lead to blindness."

Suddenly Lynn realizes why they are here. She sees that David is not surprised. He has already discerned the general's motivation. "Gunsenhouser's." He states it as if making a diagnosis, softly, factually, sympathetically.

"Yes," Alaz confirms. I learned of your research, but I could not come to you, and I dared not trust the security of our communications systems. Yet I had to speak with you personally. Is it true that what you are doing promises a cure for this terrible affliction?"

"I can't yet demonstrate it, but yes, it's true," David replies. "My work promises to be the culmination of the research efforts of many scientists worldwide. We have known for some years precisely the mitochondrial DNA mutation that causes the malady. In fact I was fortunate enough to be associated with Emory University researchers when we developed the definitive method of detecting it.

"For the past decade I've been part of a cooperative international study of Gunsenhouser's. We have assembled a great body of information concerning diagnosis, genetic mapping, treatment, why some people with abnormal DNA are not affected, why some patients' vision is later restored. My own work carries the research to its conclusion: prevention, effective treatment and a lasting cure."

As David explains his work, Lynn speculates that perhaps it was General Aláz who wired the ten million dollars to him so he could complete his research. If so, did he also send my money? she wonders. David must be thinking along similar lines. He does not ask the question outright, but instead tells the general that he is unable to resume his efforts until he secures substantial additional funds.

"So I understand," the general says. "But why do you need these funds, if I may ask?"

"Certainly. What I have done is design the equipment

necessary for effective treatment. The money will fund its physical development, its actual creation."

"Ah, I see. So we have arrived then at the main reason I wanted to speak with you, Doctor. I am prepared to offer you the money you require."

Lynn checks David's reaction. Looking not at all surprised, he smiles slightly and nods. "It is a substantial sum, General. Somewhere in the neighborhood of ten million dollars."

A very nice neighborhood indeed, Lynn can't help thinking but resists verbalizing. So if Aláz is willing to contribute ten million dollars, that must mean he did not send the money David already received. Nor hers, she is now sure. David's eyes meet hers ever so briefly but long enough for the couple to forge a silent pledge not to reveal that he has already received the funds he needs from someone else.

"I will wire the money to your bank account anonymously," Alaz offers. David, revealing nothing of his earlier windfall, is properly appreciative of the general's offer. While Lynn sits mutely admiring David's aplomb, the two men discuss a host of further details. As their interchange winds down, David furnishes his bank's name and address and his account number. Finally, after again apologizing for their ordeal and swearing them to secrecy about his medical condition, General Aláz says, "You must both be exhausted after such a long and trying day." He tugs once on the velvet cord behind him and tells the woman who responds to the bell, not one of the two who appeared earlier, that his guests are ready to go to their room.

Room! Not rooms, Lynn realizes. Well, of course, why would lovers want separate rooms? She turns to David who surely recognizes her apprehension. He does not seem to share it, however. Indeed he appears quite content with the arrangement.

In their bedroom the woman escorting them offers sets of silk pajamas, which they accept with polite thanks. Lynn's own nightclothes are in her Madeira hotel room. She can't ruin the dress she wears, the best garment she brought with her, by sleeping in it. She accepts the pajamas with gratitude and grace. So does David.

While he goes into their adjoining bathroom to change, Lynn surveys their accommodation. A king-size bed dominates the luxurious space. Fine netting encloses it on all four sides, suspended from the ceiling of the room, Lynn is surprised to see, rather than draped from the bed's overhead rails as one would expect. Mosquito netting, she decides, observing that the room's wide French doors and windows are not screened. Two walls are mirrored from floor to ceiling. The others are painted a pale blue, one of them containing the windows and wide French doors which open onto a charming balcony. A gentle breeze rustles the door's curtains, inviting Lynn to step outside. The night has been cooled by the Mediterranean, of which the balcony offers a lovely view. She watches the lights of small boats bobbing by in the distance and listens to the soft song of the peaceful surf.

"Hi, coming to bed?" David asks, joining her on the balcony.

"You can sleep on the sofa," she says.

"There is no sofa," David points out.

Lynn had ascertained that fact immediately upon entering the bedroom. There is furniture other than the bed: a dresser, two bureaus, several chairs, none of them sleep-worthy, but no sofa.

"Well then, how about the floor?" Lynn suggests. It is tiled, dark blue, quite pretty and burnished to a mirror-like shine, but she is not serious about his sleeping on it.

"If you insist . . ." David murmurs.

"No, David, I couldn't make you do that. This is a big bed. You sleep on one side, way over there. I'll stay on the other, way over here. All right?"

"Oh, good. Thanks, Lynn."

"But no fooling around, David," she cautions.

"Of course not. What kind of man do you think I am?"

"Like every other, I suspect," Lynn says. "Just stay on your side."

David is lying along the seaward edge of the bed when Lynn finishes in the bathroom. "You look lovely in your pajamas," he whispers, his voice taking on a mischievous edge.

"Never mind. Behave yourself," she admonishes lightly. After a moment his continuing chuckle makes her look across at him. He lies on his back, an index finger pointing to the ceiling above the bed. It is mirrored. He waves to her in the mirror. Lynn giggles too, understanding now why the mosquito netting is not draped across the top of the bed. She reaches to turn out the light and lies in uneasy embarrassment until she hears David's breathing lengthen. She closes her eyes and is asleep in seconds.

Lynn awakes to the soft light of dawn flowing into the room and reflecting off the floor's deep blue tiles and from the mirrored walls in muted pinks and rose. Her head is on David's chest. One arm is wrapped around him. She springs upright.

"Good morning," David says. "I didn't want to disturb you." She sees the fault is her own. He is on his edge of the bed, having honored her wishes. She obviously rolled across during the night, reached for him as she always does for Patrick, and assumed one of their accustomed husband-wife sleep positions.

They breakfast with General Aláz in a room larger than Lynn's combined living room and dining room at home. Their host calls it his breakfast nook. Relative to the immense dining room adjoining it, though, it is merely a nook. Like David's and her bedroom several floors above, this space overlooks the Mediterranean. Lynn wishes she had brought her camera but then supposes that Mohamad and Bhatia would have confiscated it back in Madeira anyway.

She and David leave the palace in what looks to Lynn like the same black Mercedes they rode in last night, but with a different driver. Their two captors accompany them to Ractá's modest airport, where the Lear jet's crew awaits their four passengers. The pilot taxis out to the runway and takes off immediately. No waiting for air controller clearances here, nor are they delayed in Madeira this time, landing without incident on the welcoming island.

Mohamad and Bhatia escort Lynn and David into *Aeroporto da* Madeira's terminal. Again they apologize profusely for their role in the abduction and bid the couple farewell, wishing them good luck and a long life of continuing love.

Chapter 7

Mohamad and Bhatia wave a final farewell to Lynn and David before turning to walk back toward their plane. But they only pretend to be leaving. In reality they are staying in Funchal. General Aláz, a thoroughly suspicious man, has instructed the pair to keep tabs on David while he is in Madeira and wherever else he and his lady travel until he is safely back home in the States. When the agents are certain that is so, then, and only then, they are to return to Ractá.

Lynn and David, unaware of the foreign agents' deception, hurry to a waiting taxi, eager to get on with their search for the source of her five million dollars and the first ten of his twenty million. In the cab Lynn whispers softly enough to avoid being overheard by the driver, "So you will have twenty million dollars, David. Why did you accept the general's money when you already have what you need?"

With a slight shake of his head and a finger to his lips he gestures for her to wait for his answer until they leave the cab. They pass the Savoy and circle back to make the legal right turn into the hotel entrance. Meanwhile a rented Mercedes coasts to a stop across *Avenida do Infante*. From its comfortable confines Mohamad and Bhatia watch the American couple enter the hotel together, talking, as always, completely unaware they are being observed.

David answers Lynn's earlier question. "I agreed to accept General Aláz's money because it seemed more prudent back at the palace to let him believe he has all my attention. Also it's a kind of insurance. If he reneges or if someone reclaims the first ten million, I'll still have the money I need. That's all that matters to me. I'll be happy to refund whatever amount remains when my work is completed."

It is almost four o'clock when Lynn and David arrive in the hotel lobby, too late for conducting business today in Funchal. Banks have closed. Other offices are ready to shut down operation, their employees logging off computers and locking file cabinets, eager to return to home and family as soon as the clock's big hand reaches twelve.

The main item on Lynn's and David's agenda, of course, is to meet personally with the director of *Banco Espirito Santo*. That will have to wait until tomorrow. Lynn wants to shower and change clothes. "I might like to lie down for a few hours too, David, since we won't be able to get much of anything done anyway." David says he may do the same. They agree to meet in the hotel lobby at 7:30, go to dinner and brainstorm ideas of other positive actions they might be able to take besides seeing the bank director, in the likely event that official will persist in his refusal to reveal the name of the person who wired money from his bank to each of them.

David has just come down to the lobby when Lynn steps off the elevator at exactly 7:30. "You look lovely," he says. She accepts his compliment with a gracious smile but does not thank him verbally, wishing not to encourage any further deepening of their personal relationship. She believes David realizes how she feels. Still, being thrown together in these exotic surroundings with so much already in common between them creates a circumstance that cries out for caution.

Lynn scans the lobby. "Do you think anyone else is lurking about, planning to grab us again this evening and give you another ten million?"

He laughs. "I hope not."

"Do you have a place in mind for dinner?" Lynn asks.

"I do. We have a reservation for 8:30, but first I want to stop at the front desk. It occurred to me that we might be able to learn something helpful from the U.S. Embassy or Consulate here in Madeira. Someone on the hotel staff must be able to tell us where the appropriate agency is located, if indeed there is one."

Lynn's eyes brighten immediately. "That sounds good, David. Officials there should know something about Americans living here on the island." She considers the notion further. "Maybe U.S. citizens are required to register with them."

"And provide addresses and information about assets and income."

"Wouldn't that be a break? Do you think we can get access to such records?"

David shrugs. "If they do exist we may not be entitled to see them. Still, even if we don't have the standing to see official documents, somebody on the embassy or consulate staff might be willing to share his or her personal knowledge on an unofficial basis. It's worth a try, don't you think?"

"Absolutely. It's a great idea," Lynn enthuses.

They inquire at the Hotel Savoy's front desk for the location of the American Embassy. The clerk does not know where it is or even if there is one. He refers Lynn and David to the hotel concierge, who turns out to be a suave gentleman named Nuno Alves.

"There is an American Consulate right here in Funchal," Alves tells them. He reaches for a note pad, jots the address, tears off the page and hands it to David with a flourish. The consulate is located at *Rua Luis Camões*, Building B., *Ed. Infante*, Fourth Floor. "It is open Monday through Friday from 9 a.m. to 1 p.m.," the concierge adds. Lynn and David thank him profusely for his help.

"Nine to one. Nice hours," Lynn remarks as they leave the lobby.

"Aren't they? Time enough, though, for us to visit the consulate when we finish with Mr. da Silva in the morning," David comments.

"Enrique da Silva, the *Banco Espirito Santo* director. I spoke with him by phone from home. I should have realized you probably did too." Lynn marvels once again at how alike their common experience has been.

"I had the impression that Mr. da Silva wanted to be helpful, despite his refusal to identify the depositor who sent us, or at least sent me, money. All he told me, though, was that it's a man," David recalls.

"I did learn one other thing," Lynn says. "He told me his depositor lives on Madeira but not in Funchal."

"He did?" David's surprise, as with all his emotions, is as transparent as a child's. "I'm impressed, Lynn. He wouldn't tell *me* that much. Did he say anything else."

"No, nothing more than that."

Outside the hotel Lynn expects David to hail one of the waiting taxis. Instead, he says, "We're kind of early for our reservation. Would you like to walk? It's a beautiful evening."

"That would be nice, but do you think we're safe?"

"I feel sure we are. Everything I read about Funchal praises its safety."

They tread gingerly from one stepping stone to another through the Savoy's garden and out onto *Avenida do Infante's* sidewalk. The Madeira evening is lovely, Lynn thinks: temperature in the low seventies; a light salt breeze drifting in off the Atlantic in cool intermittent puffs. Perfect! The street is alive with traffic, pedestrian as well as vehicular. Its bustle allays her concern for their safety. "Where are we going, David?"

"A place called the Cliff Villa."

"And of course you, who have never been to Madeira, know the way."

He shrugs. "I checked a city map. The restaurant looked easy enough to find. It's not far, maybe a fifteen minute walk."

They go on in silence for a time. Lynn enjoys the feeling of moving along under her own power after hurtling about in jet planes, taxis and luxury automobiles the past couple of days. She and David have talked at such length that she feels no uneasiness now at their silent strolling. She finds a cadence that offsets his long strides, three steps of hers to two of his. She admires the lush foliage of hotel and private gardens that border the intricately cobbled sidewalk as they pass one magnificent property after another.

"I don't suppose you've had a chance to call your husband," David says.

"Not yet. The time difference. I plan to call him tonight at eleven. We should be back at the hotel before then, don't you think?"

"Yes, I'm certain. We'll catch a cab back in plenty of time." David steers her into a left turn a block too soon, but they find their way to the avenue he seeks and stroll *Estrada Monumental* until they pass Reid's Palace Hotel and arrive at Cliff Villa Restaurant just before eight o'clock. Every table is taken, but one will be available for them at the time promised. They wait at the bar.

Lynn feels David's and the bartender's eyes on her. "Sorry," she says, turning away from photographs hanging on the wall beside her. "What did you ask?"

"What you would like to drink," David answers. The barman stands by, his serene smile belying the pace his duties demand. "How does *Vinho Verde* sound, Lynn?"

"Wonderful."

David nods, and the barman springs into action.

"What are you looking at?" David asks.

"Movie star photos on the wall here," Lynn says.

David leans closer. "That's Natalie Forthright in the one shot," he says. "Isn't that Roger Moore with the young man?"

"Uh-huh." Lynn reads the caption. "He and his son," she says.

"And the person in the third picture?"

"Albert Finney."

"Presumably they've all dined here?"

"I guess. The photos are all dated in the late nineties," she observes.

"And signed, I see. We're in good company."

The bartender removes their wine bottle's cork. David performs the sniff and taste ceremony. He watches Lynn smile as their glasses are filled. "What?" he asks.

"I'm thinking what fun it will be to tell my niece Molly about these movie star photographs." She explains her niece and nephew's fascination with movie trivia and how Molly quizzes her every time they talk. "These are sure to stop her."

"Is that fair? She couldn't possibly know about them."

"No, she couldn't, but I don't mind being unfair. I need every advantage I can get. I haven't been able to stump her for months. The game here will be seeing how many hints she needs to guess all their names."

Lynn is pleased that their table proves to be in the Cliff Villa's outer dining room, which features tall windows overlooking the surrounding gardens and the ocean beyond. It's too dark outside to be able to see much, though. Boat lights are visible in the distance; some of the gardens are partially illuminated, but reflected candle glow from restaurant tables is the featured presentation in the darkened windows at this time of night. This is the place to come for lunch, she thinks. The view must be spectacular.

David sits opposite Lynn for a moment, decides they are too far apart for their conversation not to be overheard by nearby diners, and moves to a chair beside her. Their server rearranges his place setting, takes their order and fetches an ice bucket for their half consumed Green Wine. Over Lynn's wine-basted fillet of pork with date and walnut stuffing and David's *bacalhau*, dried codfish pie, they discuss tomorrow's visit to *Banco Espirito Santo*.

David suggests that if Bank Director da Silva refuses to identify his depositor he might be willing, as an alternative, to pass along one of David's business cards to the man. "I can give him my room number at the hotel. Maybe our benefactor will call me after learning we've come all this way to meet him."

"I don't know about that," Lynn says after considering the idea. "He took steps to remain anonymous. Knowing he is actually being sought might drive him deeper under cover."

"And make him harder to locate than if he's unaware we're here searching for him," he completes her thought. "You may be right."

"Or it might prove to be a good idea, David, but I think it does have that risk. Hmm, I wonder . . ?"

"What?"

"There's also the possibility that da Silva might call to warn him about us anyway after our meeting tomorrow."

David weighs that eventuality, nodding all the while. "If he thinks that alerting a wealthy depositor will ingratiate him I think he *will* call."

"And we both got the impression that da Silva seems an ingratiating kind of person."

"True." David pauses, takes a bite of his codfish pie and a sip of wine. "Or da Silva might well hesitate to let his depositor know we're in Madeira, afraid he will be blamed for our getting this close."

They explore the pros and cons of how best to handle Bank Director da Silva, finally deciding to get a first-hand sense of the man at their meeting before trying to determine what tack to take with him.

"Any other ideas we can consider, Lynn, besides visiting the bank and the consulate?"

"What do you think about going to the local real estate tax office?"

"And?"

"Seeing if we can learn the location of American-owned properties with high assessments," Lynn explains.

"Maybe he's not American. Witness General Aláz's patronage."

"If he's not an American, the consulate won't be of any help either. Don't you think, though, that odds are he's from the States?" she asks.

David nods tentatively. "I suppose, and we have to start somewhere." He jots the real estate tax office idea on his short To Do list, which now comprises bank, consulate, tax office. "Do you have anything else?" he asks.

Lynn shakes her head. "Do you?"

"One thing. I'd like to call on whatever ophthalmologists are located here in Funchal to find out if they have any Gunsenhouser's patients. If so, we can follow up with them. One might be our benefactor or know who he is."

"That's a great idea, David. Whoever sent us money surely had a strong motive for doing it. In my case we don't have a clue what that motive can be. But someone who faces blindness and has the financial wherewithal to prevent it has all the reason in the world to send *you* money, just as we've seen with General Aláz." *Ophthalmologists* becomes the final addition to David's list.

Lynn is back in her hotel room at ten-thirty, gets ready for bed and places her too long delayed phone call home.

Patrick answers the phone on its first ring. "Hello."

"Hi, honey, it's me." Lynn's cheerful tone reflects her joy in hearing his voice.

"Lynn! Lynn! Are you all right?"

"Fine. I'm fine."

"Where are you?"

"I'm at the hotel, the Savoy."

"I was about to try calling you there. Where have you been? Why haven't you called before now?"

"I'm sorry if I worried you, Patrick. I . . ."

"Worried?" he snaps. "I've been scared to death. I was sure you would call yesterday to let me know you arrived safely."

"Oh, I wanted to, sweetheart, but . . ."

Again Patrick doesn't let her finish. "Wanted to? You wanted to? Why didn't you?"

"I couldn't call because, uh, I was . . . I wasn't here last night."

"You weren't there? Where were you?"

"I was in North Africa."

"North Africa?" Patrick shouts. "Is there something wrong with our connection? Did I hear you say you were in North Africa last night?"

"Calm down, Patrick. I'll explain, but first, are you glad to hear from me?" He sighs loudly but doesn't answer. "I'm happy to hear your voice, Patrick, but I hope you'll lower it a little."

"Yes, yes, I'm glad to hear from you, Lynn. Of course I am. Now tell me what you're talking about."

"I will if you'll give me a chance. You see, last night after David and I had dinner . . ."

"David?" Patrick is yelling again. "Who the hell is David?"

"A man I met at Newark Airport. You won't believe it, Patrick. Somebody also deposited millions of dollars in *his* bank account."

"Somebody gave him five million dollars too?"

"No, not five. Ten million."

"Oh, ten million. And he doesn't know where it came from either?"

"No."

"You're right, Lynnie. I am having some trouble believing this. You just happened to bump into this guy at the airport."

"Yes."

"That was some coincidence."

"Well, it was, but we were both getting the same plane."

"Uh-huh. Let me ask you: did you tell him about coming into your five million dollars before he told you about his ten million?"

"Uh-uh. He told me first."

"All right. So why did you have dinner with the guy?"

"David. David Kubasik."

"Yeah, with David."

"Well, we have so much in common, and . . ."

Patrick interrupts. "You went with him to North Africa, didn't you?"

"No. Well, yes, but it wasn't as if I accepted his invitation to take me there. We didn't go voluntarily. We were abducted."

"Abducted? Somebody kidnapped you? Were you hurt?"

"No. I'm perfectly all right."

"Tell me what happened and how and who did it and why, Lynn. This conversation is making me crazy."

"Okay, okay, here's the way it was. When David and I left the restaurant after dinner, these two foreign agents threw us into a Mercedes. They took us to the airport where we all boarded a Lear jet and flew to North Africa. We met with the leader of a country there, and today the agents brought us back to Madeira."

The sound of silence, punctuated by an occasional crackle of static on the line, is all Lynn hears for the longest time. "Patrick?" she says finally.

"I'm here," he mutters. "That's some story, Lynn. Is that all of it?"

"Well, yes, in a nutshell, sweetheart."

"Foreign agents abducted you."

"Yes. Mohamad and Bhatia."

"What?"

"That's their names: Mohamad and Bhatia."

"These two guys just snatched you off the street and threw you into a Mercedes?"

"Yes, David and me."

"Did he try to stop them?"

"Who, David? No, he's not James Bond. He's a scientist. They're both very big men, and besides, Mohamad had a knife."

"My god, Lynn, but, but you weren't harmed?"

"No."

"Did the other man threaten *you* with a knife?"

"Bhatia? No, he was driving."

"Because if somebody laid a finger on you . . ."

"Well, of course they laid fingers on me, Patrick. Mohamad threw me into the Mercedes."

"But he didn't hurt you."

"No."

"Why did they abduct you?"

"Because I was with David. They really only wanted him, but they said they couldn't leave me screaming in the street. They thought we were lovers."

"Why would they think that, Lynn?"

"They mistook our meeting for a lovers' rendezvous."

"Meeting? Your meeting with this David Kubasik in Newark, you mean?"

"Yes."

"The foreign agents were in Newark?"

"Yes, they were following David for days, waiting for an opportunity to grab him, but they weren't able to do it until yesterday here in Funchal."

"Were they after his ten million dollars?"

"No, in fact their leader offered him ten million more."

"What? And another five for you?"

"Don't be silly. I don't have anything he wants. It's David he needs."

"But he already gave you five million?"

"Who?"

"This leader."

"No, he didn't."

"He didn't?"

"No, of course not."

"And he didn't give your, uh, purported lover his first ten million?"

"No. We're going to start our search tomorrow for *that* man."

"Who, you and David and Mohamad and Bhatia?"

"Just David and me. Mohamad and Bhatia are back home in their country."

"What country are you talking about anyway, and what's this leader's name?"

"Well, I, uh, I can't tell you those things, Patrick."

"Why not?"

"We promised."

"You and David."

"Yes."

"Promised each other?"

"No, promised the gen . . ., promised the leader." When Patrick pauses to gather his thoughts, Lynn says, "Patrick, you know I trust you implicitly. I thought you trusted me too."

"I did. I do. I mean, I've always trusted you, Lynn. You know that. Right now, though, it's kind of a tall order. Was this leader some kind of terrorist?"

"Um, no, I don't think you could call him a terrorist. A rebel maybe. A junta leader. He's the president of his country, and, um, a general?" Lynn hurries on, escaping more questions. "Anyway, he was nice. He treated us very well, Patrick. You just have to trust me. What went on yesterday had absolutely nothing to do with me, with you and me. I just happened to be there. I'll explain it all when I get home."

"When will that be?"

"I don't know, but I'll call you every night until then, and I'll leave as soon as possible. Can I talk to Kerry and Sean for a minute?"

"They're at Theresa's, Lynn. I stayed home waiting for your call. I'm going to dinner there too."

"I'm glad. Is everyone all right?"

"We're all fine."

"Good. I love you. Tell the kids I send my love, and don't worry. I'll be all right. I'll call you tomorrow."

"Okay." Lynn hears only doubt and confusion in her husband's voice. Not a trace of reassurance.

"Bye, sweetheart," she whispers.

"Good-bye, Lynnie."

Chapter 8

A short line of hotel guests wait to be seated in the Savoy's dining room when Lynn arrives there Tuesday morning. She checks her watch: 8:07 a.m. "My friend already has our table," she tells the captain as she eases past the queue at the entrance. She and David agreed last night to meet inside at 8:00 a.m. She knows he has been waiting for at least seven minutes, and, sure enough, there he is, waving from a table in the rear of the room. It is a huge room, overflowing with early morning diners. Every one of a hundred tables is occupied, while dozens of additional breakfasters busily load their trays at two large buffet service areas. Each buffet consists of several food-laden tables. Still other guests fill juice glasses and select fresh fruit at counters strategically positioned throughout the room.

"Good morning," David greets her, standing to seat her in gentlemanly fashion.

"Good morning, David."

"One of us should stay here so we don't lose our table," he recommends.

"So I see." A steaming pot of coffee rests on their table, along with cream, sugar, silver, cloth napkins. "You get your breakfast. I'll have some coffee," she says.

Minutes later, David returns with a breakfast of eggs, bacon, sausage, potatoes and toast, along with a delicious-looking, honey-dripping bear claw pastry.

"Hungry?" Lynn asks.

David blushes but grins amiably. "A little juice and fruit and I'll be set," he replies. He soon comes back again, deposits an overflowing bowl of fruit beside his breakfast tray, and lifts his glass of juice for her to see. "Passion fruit," he announces.

"Wow! Not your average continental breakfast, is it?" Lynn exclaims.

"Sure isn't. Let me see, I guess I have everything," he says, reviewing his selections as Lynn leaves their table "Hurry back," he calls after her.

Lynn cruises the buffet, chooses a roll, finds the same mouth-watering pastry David picked up, opts for the passion fruit juice over the orange, pineapple and grapefruit on offer, and fills a hefty bowl like her breakfast partner's with a colorful assortment of fresh, mouth-watering fruit. "This is an amazing breakfast. I'll eat here anytime," she tells him.

They arrive at *Banco Espirito Santo* at 9:20, time enough for Bank Director da Silva to settle in, perhaps have his morning coffee. "May I help you?" a front desk receptionist asks in English. Her smile, though attractive enough, is practiced, too tentative to be welcoming. A wariness is evident in her eyes. She is prepared to gird against any requests she deems unworthy. With the most cursory of glances, she recognizes Lynn and David as Americans.

David bids her good morning. "We would like to speak with Bank Director da Silva," he says. Simultaneously he hands her a note on which he has written his and Lynn's names, beating the woman to the punch before she can begin some canned verbal brush-off resulting in a waste of time dealing with a series of lesser bank luminaries. "*Senhor* da Silva knows us," David tells her.

"Certainly. Have a seat. I will be right back," she responds, while her narrowed eyes and further strained smile add, "to throw you out, I hope." But she returns in mere seconds, all graciousness. Miss Congeniality. "*Senhor* da Silva will see you now, sir, madam. Please follow me."

Bank Director Enrique da Silva's affability and smile, in contrast to those of his first line of defense receptionist, are open and genuine. He is impeccably dressed in a fashionable five hundred dollar black suit, a lavender shirt, a perfectly coordinated tie containing the suit's, the shirt's and other complementary colors. He wears slim, soft, black Italian leather shoes. Altogether, he is more Madison Avenue than Wall Street, more GQ than Business Week, but it is the twinkle of curiosity in the Portuguese gentleman's eye that surprises Lynn. He looks open, playful, not at all guarded as one would expect of a person who knows he is about to be put on the spot.

"Mrs. O'Brien, Dr. Kubasik, welcome. I never expected to meet either of you. Yet here you both are. I am amazed. How in the world did you find each other?" He shakes David's hand with verve and bends to kiss Lynn's, a first for her. She is charmed. Both she and David return his infectious smile.

David explains how he and Lynn came to meet. Da Silva wants to know more about them, and he listens with rapt attention to the brief biographical highlights each offers him.

"Fascinating," he comments when they finish. "Am I correct in concluding that you did not know each other before meeting at the airport?"

"That's right," David replies. Lynn nods confirmation.

"And besides both of you having been favored with a fortune, are there other common factors in your backgrounds?"

"No," Lynn answers.

"Not that we've determined," David adds modifyingly.

"This is such fun," da Silva remarks. "You have a fairy godfather, so to speak, and I am one of his helpers." He asks them to relate the circumstances surrounding their receipt of the money and is openly enthralled by their similar ATM adventures. "Now you have come all the way to Madeira to find your benefactor?"

"Yes," David says.

"Believing, I suppose, that the same person is the source of both your, uh, endowments?"

"It seems likely to us," David says.

"Is one person the source?" Lynn brazens.

"Ah, yes," da Silva replies, I will not deny it. But, of course, that is the only information I can give you."

"One wealthy American man who lives on the island but not in Funchal?" Lynn ventures..

Da Silva's grin tells Lynn that he has not missed her insertion of an additional fact about his bank's important depositor. "Yes," he grants with a smile, "but why have you come to find him? Surely you no longer doubt that the money is yours, and you are well aware your benefactor insists on remaining anonymous. Why not just accept those realities and enjoy your money?"

"We can't. We must know who he is and why he has given us all this money," Lynn answers. David's open handed, palms up gesture tells da Silva that she has said it all.

"Then why come to me? I've already told you both by phone that I am not authorized to help you. Quite the opposite, in fact. In accordance with our depositor's proscription, everyone associated with our bank is expressly enjoined from revealing his identity. You have come all this way in vain, I'm afraid, if you are relying on us to give you the information you seek."

"That's too bad," David says. "I was hoping you could tell us if he is ill."

"Ill? Our depositor?" Da Silva's pupils betray his alarm. Worry lines displace his smile's established creases across his cheeks. "No, what makes you think that?"

"Whoever sent my money, or someone very close to him, has a serious medical condition. I am working on a cure for that condition, and I believe the money is meant to fund my research," David explains.

Da Silva shakes his head. "You are mistaken in thinking this man is ill, Dr. Kubasik. He is in good health, excellent health, in fact, for a man of his age."

Lynn can't help smiling. So. An older man. She sees the flash of a fleeting grin on Bank Director da Silva's lips as well, before he turns his gaze back across one shoulder and peers at her with one eye closed, feigning a scolding, petulant mien. "Ah, I have misspoken. Shame, shame, Mrs. O'Brien."

"Well, now we know he is not a retired thirty year old dot com multimillionaire who cashed out before reality set in," David quips.

"Do you seriously believe the money is for your scientific research?"

"I do."

"Interesting. I have no reason to think our depositor is ill, however. Quite the contrary, as I have said."

"Perhaps someone in his family," David suggests.

Da Silva weighs his words. "I do not know his family," he allows.

"Let me propose a method by which you might help us without violating your depositor's trust," David says.

One fashionably clad shoulder rises and falls. Lynn takes it for a half-hearted shrug. But the banker's curiosity is aroused. "And what might that method be?" he asks.

"I will give you my card, a business card, on which I note my room number at the Savoy. You alert your depositor to the fact that we have traveled to Madeira to meet him. You tell him that I have asked for him to call me. Perhaps knowing we are actually here and that contacting us is at his sole initiative might prompt him to change his mind."

Da Silva considers for a long moment before his head begins to nod, hesitantly at first but soon with some vigor. "I don't want to promise I will do it, but give me your card, Dr. Kubasik. I will consider your proposal." He pauses until David notes the hotel information for him before asking, "Have you taken into account the possibility that your idea could have a converse effect?"

Lynn answers for them. "We discussed the notion that alerting him to our presence might drive him underground."

"Was that *your* notion, Mrs. O'Brien?"

"I believe it was."

"We think alike. Perhaps mistakenly in this instance, however, Dr. Kubasik," he concedes.

"You also might be reluctant to contact him for fear that he will hold you personally responsible for our getting this close to him," Lynn adds.

Da Silva chuckles. "A worthy consideration. *Your* thought, I expect?" he asks her.

"Actually I think that one was David's." The three of them enjoy a good laugh.

"You are true cynics," da Silva declares. They see he means it as a compliment.

Before they leave the bank David asks *Senhor* da Silva for his help in locating Funchal's ophthalmologists and the local real estate tax office. The banker obliges, searching the city telephone directory and finding two such medical specialists. He writes their names and addresses plus the tax office location on a personalized notepad and makes certain David can decipher his script. "If there is nothing more I can do for you this morning . . ."

"I think not," David says, thanking him for his help.

Lynn's eyes meet the banker's. "I hope you will contact our benefactor for us," she says.

Da Silva smiles and nods, but Lynn reads no commitment in his expression. "I hope your search is successful," he says as he walks with them through the bank lobby, "but, in any case, do not let it detract from your appreciation of our beautiful island. You must enjoy yourselves while you are here." He bids them *adeus* and returns to his office.

David waves down a passing taxi. "The American Consulate," he tells the driver and reads off the address from his note. The cabby executes a series of deep, bowing nods to indicate he knows the consulate's location. They arrive there in minutes, enter an empty office and approach a counter at the back of the room. An American flag stands in a corner behind it. The rear wall of the room displays the seal of the United States.

A young woman enters from an office behind the counter. There is a door in the opposite wall, presumably opening into a second office. Although she greets them in English, Lynn knows right away that she is a local girl.

David explains that he and Lynn are American citizens visiting Madeira, that they are seeking help in finding an American living on the island, and that they would like to speak with the United States Consul.

"I am sorry, sir, madam, but he is visiting Washington, D.C. this week. Would you like to speak with a consular representative?"

"Yes, that would do nicely," David replies. The young woman disappears into the office from which she emerged.

Minutes later a man about Lynn's and David's age appears, wearing shirt and tie, and wriggling into his suit jacket as he approaches. Lynn notes the lightness of his steps. Quick, graceful, he moves like a dancer. His greeting is polite as he shakes hands with her and David in turn. He introduces himself as Consular Representative Rupert Hankinson and invites them into the office opposite the one from which he came. Inside he waits for them to be seated before moving to his own chair behind the room's single desk. Lynn expects Hankinson to perch cautiously on the edge of his chair, birdlike. Instead he collapses into it, sinks back, raises his arms and clasps his fingers behind his head, thoroughly at rest, his posture suggesting they can have as much of his time as they wish. "What can I do for you?" he asks.

David gets right to the point. "We're trying to locate an American who lives here in Madeira. We were hoping you might be able to help us."

"I see. Can you tell me the name of this person?"

"I wish I could, but we don't actually know his name." Hankinson takes his hands from behind his head, leans forward in his chair, rests an elbow on his desk and his chin in his hand, and looks from David to Lynn and back with a bemused, somewhat puzzled grin.

"You're trying to locate someone you don't know," he says. "Most unusual. Why do you want to find this man?"

"We both received rather sizeable sums of money from someone here in Madeira, money that was sent to us anonymously. We've come over here from the States to try to learn who sent it and why."

Hankinson manages to smile and look skeptical at the same time. "Well, I've heard, of course, of scams promising such money but requiring victims to pay taxes or some such fees in advance. I must say, though, that your situation is a new one to me. You actually received such funds? What kind of amounts are we talking about?"

"Millions of dollars," David says.

"Millions? Takes a stretch of the old credulity, doesn't it?" When David does not answer Hankinson asks, "Does this money involve illegal drugs?"

"No, of course not."

"Anything else of an illicit nature?"

"No."

"Do you represent any official branch of government? Police? FBI? CIA? Welfare authorities?"

"No, we're just private citizens." They show him their passports and business cards as David explains further. "We know our benefactor is a wealthy American man living in Madeira, somewhere other than in Funchal."

"An older man," Lynn interjects.

"An older man," David echoes. "We thought it likely that consulate records might be able to aid us in our search. Do Americans living here register with you?"

"Yes, most of them do, which is true at our embassies and consulates throughout the world. People generally want their presence and whereabouts known, you see, in the event that they need to be contacted in an emergency. We also like to copy their passports in case they lose them. Makes them easier to replace. Same thing with visas. Of course *we* don't issue visas to Americans living here. They get them at the Portuguese Embassy in Washington before coming over, but a clear copy of a lost visa speeds up the process of getting a new one."

David listens politely if impatiently until he gets the chance to ask, "Can you provide us a list of Americans living here, perhaps sorted down to just male millionaires past the age of . . .?" He turns to Lynn. "What do you think, Lynn, maybe age fifty?" She was thinking age sixty adequate, but she nods, and David finishes his request to Hankinson, "male millionaires past age fifty."

"No, I'm sorry, but I don't believe I can do that." Lynn is sure she must appear as disappointed as David does when the consul's assistant looks from one to the other of them. "You see, the Privacy Act prohibits us from divulging the whereabouts of any U.S. citizen without that person's expressed consent," he says. "By extension it seems to me that the intent of that constraint would apply at least as strongly to a group of Americans as it does to any individual in that group."

David can't fault the man's logic. Lynn, though, is a bit less willing to capitulate to mere logic. "You have our passports and business cards," she says. "We are who they say we are, and our reason for traveling all the way here is exactly what David has told you. We're American citizens seeking our government's assistance, the provision of which, I might add, is your agency's sole reason for existence. Now, you said you are prohibited from divulging the whereabouts of a citizen without that person's expressed consent. I assume that means you are allowed to contact someone by phone for authorization to release information about his location?"

"Precisely."

The huffiness of his reply is wasted on Lynn. "Well then, by extension," she argues, with a touch of sarcasm and no attempt at hiding her annoyance, "we request that you call everyone in the group David described for authorization to release information about their locations."

"That is preposterous," Hankinson objects.

"Nevertheless, it is your stated procedure," Lynn replies. "So what we want you to do is sort your records of Americans down to male millionaires over age fifty, and when you have called every one of them you can give us a list of those who authorized your release of the information we need."

On *Rua Luis Camões* outside the consulate, despite his disconsolation at their quest's lack of progress, David can't resist laughing at Lynn's performance. "I don't think you made a friend in there," he suggests.

"The jerk," Lynn summarizes.

Hankinson had refused to do what she asked. He told them he would present their request to his superior, American Consul Jeffrey Egan, on his return from Washington. Of course, that effectively negated any consular assistance to them since Egan was not expected back for over a week.

David hails a passing taxi and gives the driver the address of Funchal's real estate tax department office. They would visit there next, then call on each of the two ophthalmologists in town this afternoon.

Although Madeirans and mainland Portuguese are noted for courtesy, which from their experience before today Lynn and David would readily avow, the woman with whom they speak at the tax office is even more imperious than Bank Director da Silva's receptionist. She gives them short shrift, telling them they have no standing that entitles them to the information they seek, even if she had it, which she states she does not. Tax records for parts of the island outside Funchal reside in each town's local government offices. The records keeper instructs them to go to the proper tax office and make their inquiries there. However, if they do so armed with as little factual information as they have presented to her, she offers no hope they will learn anything whatsoever.

"Whew!" Lynn whistles afterward.

"I'll say," David agrees.

It is almost noon, and they are in downtown Funchal, not far from the *Sé*, Funchal's Roman Catholic Cathedral, which David knows is in a neighborhood abounding in restaurants and *pastelarias*, informal eating establishments offering coffee and pastries as well as alcoholic beverages.

Deciding to reinforce their resolve with some lunch and a drink, they come upon an appealing restaurant called The Golden Door on *Avenida do Infante*, two blocks from the *Sé* in the direction of their hotel. Its ground level dining room appears inviting enough to Lynn, but before they entered she noticed that outdoor dining is featured on a second floor balcony. When after a moment no hostess comes to seat them, they find their own way upstairs. Several tables are empty. A smiling waitress tells them to sit wherever they like.

"Great day for eating outside," David comments.

"And have you noticed, David, there don't seem to be any bugs in Funchal?"

"But there are flowers everywhere, Lynn. There must be plenty of insects."

"I guess, but if so they're much better behaved than those at home. I slept with my balcony door open to the ocean air last night without a single pest flying in."

"Maybe they're too busy with the flowers to find time for bothering people."

"But flies? Mosquitoes? I haven't seen even one."

David just shrugs. "Me neither," he agrees.

A boy deposits a basket of rolls and a bowl of what looks to Lynn like a thin pâté on their table. Julienne carrots and sticks of celery surround it. The waitress takes their drink order – rum and passion fruit juice for both of them – and hands them luncheon menus to study.

Lynn samples the pâté. "Mmm, tuna. It's delicious." David joins her and they polish it off along with all the vegetables and half the rolls in the few minutes they wait for drinks. "I wonder if they charge for appetizers like this that people don't actually order?" she asks.

"Oh, I'd bet on it," David answers, "but meals here are so reasonably priced it really doesn't matter."

They leave the restaurant about forty minutes later, their spirits revived by pleasant lunches and two drinks each. David ordered a sandwich. Lynn asked for vegetable soup. What the waitress brought her did contain a small quantity of vegetables but was otherwise the same potato and cabbage-based broth she is served everywhere she eats soup in Madeira. Apparently the base of all island soups is ubiquitous. Order bean soup, you get some beans in potato and cabbage soup. Pea soup comes with a few peas. Now ditto the vegetable soup: potato and cabbage with a few veggies. It's always delicious, though, whatever it is called. Lynn resolves to see if she can duplicate its base when she gets home.

In a taxi once again, they ride this time to the office of Funchal ophthalmologist *Doutor* Fernando Fonseca, hoping all the while that medical professionals do not follow the custom of island retail shops by closing their offices from one to three o'clock. Luckily, Dr. Fonseca, for one, does not. Several patients wait to see him. David tells a receptionist that he and Lynn are not patients, nor do they have an appointment to see the doctor.

"Please give him my card," David requests. "He will know who I am."

"He is with a patient," the woman objects.

David smiles agreeably. "I know," he says, "but I would like you to take my card to him now. I assure you he won't mind." Obviously reluctant to interrupt the doctor at his work, the receptionist nevertheless complies with David's request.

"Man, you can be pushier than I am," Lynn whispers when she is gone. But seconds later Dr. Fonseca appears. He is younger than Lynn expects. She thinks he looks no more than thirty-five years old, if that. Beaming as he extends a hand to David, he gushes, "Dr. Kubasik, I'm honored to meet you." He asks David why he is here but does not wait for an answer before ushering him and Lynn into a private room.

"I'm sorry to interrupt you and your patient, Dr. Fonseca," David apologizes.

"Quite all right. I just finished administering drops. Have to wait for her pupils to dilate anyway. Why are you here in Madeira, and what can I do for you?"

Lynn is duly impressed that David's name is so instantly recognized and highly regarded this far from home. After introducing her David asks Fonseca if any of his patients have Gunsenhouser's Optic Atrophy.

"No. I haven't seen any Gunsenhouser's cases here."

"If you did, doctor, where would you refer them?"

"Well, um, I think I would ask *Doutor* Vitór da Cruz here in Funchal to confirm my diagnosis and recommend where to refer the patient."

"I see. We're planning on Visiting Dr. da Cruz today also."

"Oh? I can call him if you like; save you a trip."

"Thanks, but that's not necessary. We have the time, and I would like to see him in person if I can."

"Surely. On second thought I wouldn't want to be responsible for his missing out on meeting you. I know I'd hear about that if he learned you had been here."

David explains why he is looking for Gunsenhouser's patients in Madeira. The ophthalmologist shakes his head. "You mean to tell me someone here on the island sent you ten million dollars so you can build your equipment? I can see why you think it might involve a Gunsenhouser's victim and why they'd give you the money too, I guess, if they're able to afford it." He glances at a wall clock. "I'd better get back to my patient. Good luck with your search. I wouldn't waste a lot of time with it, though, if I were you. Your work is too important, but who knows that better than you do? It was a pleasure meeting you, Dr. Kubasik. You, too, *Miss* O'Brien." Lynn doesn't bother to correct him.

Dr. da Cruz, the second eye doctor they visit, is sixtyish, graying, and as elated to meet David as was his colleague, although with his more heavily accented, even somewhat halting, English, he has difficulty expressing his enthusiasm as clearly as did the younger man. He is between patients when they meet him. Otherwise their conversation varies little from David's talk with Dr. Fonseca. Da Cruz has no Gunsenhouser's patients either. To David's question of where he would refer such a patient, he says that he would send a local resident to the Oliveira Ophthalmic Institute in Lisbon. If the patient was American, Fonseca would recommend Wills Eye Hospital in Philadelphia; if British, Moorfields Eye Hospital in London; if German, the University of Essen *Augenklinik.*

It is close to three o'clock when Lynn and David leave Dr. da Cruz's office. David is discouraged. He has crossed off everything on his *To Do* list. They have exhausted all their ideas, done all they had planned to do without any of it proving successful. Lynn feels the same as he does, but she tries to hearten him. "We'll go to dinner and talk it through again," she says. "We'll come up with other ideas. I'm sure of it. Meanwhile Bank Director da Silva might decide to follow up with the phone call we're hoping for."

"Maybe."

"Hey, do you feel like shopping? I have this million dollar credit card calling to me from my pocketbook, and all the shops reopen in a few minutes."

"I hate shopping, but how about this? I'll walk around with you until five o'clock. Then I want to swim in the hotel pool for an hour or so before dinner."

"I'll skip the swim. Otherwise, it's a deal. Agreed?"

"Fair enough."

"Let's go back to the cathedral," David suggests. "Every street in that area is lined with shops."

Chapter 9

At seven p.m. Lynn and David take a taxi to a restaurant in Monte, a picturesque village in the hills above Funchal, known for its gracious white-stucco church *Nossa Senhora do Monte*, Our Lady of the Mountain, and its popular snowless sled ride. The restaurant they choose, *A Seta*, is frequented by locals as well as tourists and has a markedly different feel from the more elegant places they've visited in Funchal. No romantic, candlelit tables for two here, *A Seta* offers family style dining and features *espetada*, flame-seared beef on skewers suspended from wrought-iron hooks above each table. Lynn and David get to enjoy folk dancers and *fado*, fate, music, Portugal's melancholy brand of blues, along with their *espetada* and a bottle of the *Vinho Verde* they hope they'll be able to find locally when they return home.

Lynn is happy with the pretty silver bracelets she wears, purchased this afternoon in Funchal along with Patrick's Casamira ties, Kerry's pashima and Sean's sweatshirts, gifts already packed away in her suitcase back at the Hotel Savoy. David is relaxed after his hour-long swim in the hotel pool with its waterfall fountain and lush, greenery-filled little island. He is pleased also with Concierge Alves's recommendation of *A Seta*.

Their spirits were first buoyed during their cab ride to Monte. By chance their cab driver was a gregarious type who spoke excellent English and was unusually knowledgeable about the island. On a whim, really more like a flash of inspiration, Lynn told the cabby that she and David were interested in finding a vacation home on the island in a community of particularly fine homes. She asked if he knew of a peaceful town or village where the residents are professionals like doctors and lawyers, business executives, perhaps some wealthy Americans, people owning luxurious homes and villas like the one they are seeking.

"Garajau is the place for you," the driver pronounced.

David grasped Lynn's idea right away. They would locate a real estate agent, pretend to be interested in buying an expensive Garajau property, and try to learn of wealthy Americans living in that area. Finding their benefactor in that manner would be a long shot, but the man might reside there. If not, he could well be part of the social network of Americans who do live there. "Can you recommend a real estate agent who knows that area well, someone who can help us find the kind of upscale property we're looking for?" he asked the driver.

"You should see Umbelina Gorgé at Moreira and Gorgé Realty," the man replied. Her office is on *Avenida Zarco* near *Mercado dos Lavradores*, the Workers' Market. Lynn and David decide to visit *Senhora* Gorgé tomorrow morning.

The front desk has messages for Lynn when she enters the Savoy on their return from Monte. She has had three phone calls, all from Patrick. Upstairs in her room, ready for bed, she dials home at exactly eleven o'clock. Patrick is waiting beside the phone. "Hello," he says before Lynn even hears it ring.

"Hi, sweetheart."

"Lynn, are you all right?" His tone dampens the pleasure with which she has looked forward to talking with him. "Where have you been all day? I called you three times," he complains.

"I know, Patrick. The front desk clerk gave me your messages. Is something wrong at home?"

"No, not here. It's there that I'm worried about. Where were you all day? I called at ten this morning, five this evening and nine-thirty tonight. You're never there."

"Did I come over here to sit around the hotel, Patrick? I was out trying to find our mystery man, of course."

"Nine-thirty at night?"

"Well no, not at nine-thirty. I was at dinner then. I got back to the hotel just after that time."

"Dinner with David, I suppose."

"Yes, with David."

"At the hotel?"

"What's the difference where we ate, Patrick. No, not the hotel. As a matter of fact it was at this charming little restaurant in Monte." She realizes her own annoyance will only make matters worse but can't help resenting his attitude. He ignores her pique.

"Monte? Where is Monte?" he asks.

"In the hills outside Funchal."

"How nice for you both. I guess you did lunch together too?"

"People do have to eat."

"May I ask where?"

"I don't know. The Golden, uh, something or other."

"Did you breakfast together also?"

"Yes."

"What, you called down for room service?"

Now Lynn is angry. "Yes, we did, and the cutest little waiter brought up our trays, so we invited him to jump into bed with us. Oh, I guess that explains why I missed your first call." Her husband does not respond as she expects. She hears him breathing heavily, the way he sometimes does to control his temper, but he says nothing. After a moment she continues, modulating her tone from sarcastic to soothing. "We had breakfast early this morning in the hotel dining room. Then we spent the day trying to find our man. We met with the bank director and from there went to the American Consulate. We checked the local real estate tax office and visited two doctors in the city, ophthalmologists." She pauses, waiting for a question or comment.

Finally, Patrick speaks. "So have you found him?"

She knows he means their benefactor. "Not yet."

"What was the point of seeing the eye doctors? Did David break his glasses?"

"The man we're looking for might have Gunsenhouser's."

"Gunsenhouser's?"

"It's an eye disease."

"And then you went to dinner?"

"What?"

"You went to dinner after you saw the doctors?"

"Not right away. Don't you want to know about the eye disease?"

"Not really."

"Or about our meeting with the bank director, why we went to the consulate, what we were doing at the tax office?"

"No. You already told me you didn't find the guy, so what's the point? Did anything at all get accomplished?"

"The bank director might contact the man and ask him to call us."

"Might?"

"He said he would consider it."

"So did you go to dinner after you saw the doctors?"

"It was too early for dinner. We went shopping. I bought a few inexpensive bracelets for myself and two ties for you. I picked up a couple little things for Kerry and Sean."

"David went shopping with you?"

"Yes, I didn't want to wander around the city by myself."

"Then you went to dinner?"

Lynn sighs. "Not yet. I came back to my room for a while. I sat on the balcony watching boats on the ocean and admiring the flower gardens below. People were diving into the water from a cliff by Reid's Palace Hotel across the way. And there's a replica of the Santa Maria, Columbus's ship, here in Funchal. I watched it sail by."

"Was David with you?"

"No, of course not. I was in my room. He was swimming."

"Swimming? In the ocean?"

"Uh-uh, in the hotel pool."

"What will you be doing tomorrow, other than breakfast, lunch, dinner and sightseeing with David?"

She ignores his acerbity. "We're going to Garajau."

"Why? What's there? Wherever it is."

"It's a village where there are a lot of expensive homes and wealthy residents, the kind of place where our man might live. We hope to find him or someone who knows him."

"Is it safe, your wandering all over the island as you are?"

"Quite safe, Patrick. There is very little crime here. The people are friendly and helpful to tourists. They realize the importance of tourism to their economy."

"Will you be gone all day?"

"I don't know how long the Garajau visit will take."

"Will you be trying anything else?"

"Not unless we think of something more. Right now we're out of ideas. Anyway, I'll call you tomorrow."

"Please, and, Lynn, be careful."

"I will. Are the kids at home?"

"Yes. They're waiting to talk to you."

Lynn's conversations with Kerry and Sean are warm and loving. The children are their usual accepting, non-contentious selves, no different at this distance than if she were back in New Jersey welcoming them home at the end of a school day. She feels better talking with them. But not for long.

Patrick gets back on the line. "Hold a second," he says. She hears him tell Kerry and Sean to go finish their homework before dinner. "There's one thing that's really bothering me," he tells Lynn.

"What?" she asks, but she is sure she knows what it is.

"Night before last, when you were in Africa, where did you sleep?"

This is precisely what she expects him to ask. "In the presidential palace," she answers. She was glad yesterday when it didn't occur to him during their phone conversation, but she knew then that the question of sleeping arrangements at the palace would not long elude him.

"Uh-huh. Stop me if I'm wrong, but didn't you tell me the foreign agents thought you and your friend and dining companion David were lovers?" He is not wrong, so Lynn doesn't answer. "So I assume that the unnamed leader of the anonymous country also thought you were lovers?"

"Uh, yes. That's true. He did."

"So it seems reasonable to conclude he wouldn't offer you separate bedrooms. Why would he think that lovers wanted separate rooms?"

"He didn't."

"You both slept in the same room?"

"Yes," Lynn admits.

"Tell me he slept on a couch."

"Well, uh . . ."

"He didn't sleep on a couch?"

"There was no couch."

"A chair? The floor?"

"No, Patrick."

There is a moment's silence on the line before she hears him hang up and their call disconnects. After a while she puts her telephone back on its cradle. She turns off the light, walks out on her balcony, and sits in one of its two chairs. She should be mad at Patrick, she tells herself. But anger at her husband is not what she feels. How can she? What is he guilty of? Loving her? Worrying about her? Of distrust, yes, and wrongfully so, but how can he know that? She has not betrayed him as he thinks, but she has hurt him. What she feels is guilt, frustration, loneliness, homesickness. She begins to cry and finds a measure of relief in surrendering to the flow of her tears.

Before long Lynn finds herself shivering in the cool night air. She goes back inside, closes the doors and lies down on her bed. She does not fall asleep until just before dawn.

Chapter 10

When Lynn and David finish breakfast Wednesday morning, they leave the Hotel Savoy and walk across *Avenida do Infante*. Mohamad and Bhatia slouch down in their seats to avoid being seen by the Americans, who, they are shocked to see, are coming directly toward them. Mohamad raises his head cautiously when he is certain they have passed, just in time to see the American couple enter the car rental agency where Bhatia got their own vehicle.

"That was a close call," Bhatia whispers.

"They are renting a car," Mohamad says. "We did well to refuel ours yesterday. If they are not taking taxi cabs today as they have until now, their destination must be distant. Somewhere outside Funchal, I would wager."

"Sightseeing, I hope. Why do they never relax and enjoy this beautiful island?" Mohamad does not answer, knowing the question is rhetorical. Bhatia has already asked it numerous times.

"I think you should turn us around and park opposite the rental agency so we can see them as they exit," Mohamad says.

"We can see them from here."

"They will be in a car. We don't know what make or model it will be. We might miss them."

"If we turn around we will be facing east."

"So?"

"I think they will be going west."

"You are a soothsayer? Why will they go west?"

"There is more to see going west than east."

Mohamad sighs. "Why is that?"

"Simply because more of the island is west of Funchal than east of it."

"No it isn't. We are in the middle of Madeira relative to east and west."

"I do not believe so," Bhatia says. He begins unfolding a map of the island.

"Never mind the map," Mohamad says. "They will drive away while you study it. If you insist on facing west, just back up closer to the agency."

"You are joking! We will be killed backing up in this traffic."

"You may be killed if you don't shut your mouth," Mohamad threatens. Bhatia uses a driveway to begin a risky and surely illegal U-turn across traffic. He stops with their right wheels well up on the sidewalk and most of the car off the avenue. "You are facing east," Mohamad says.

"To satisfy you."

"Perhaps you are right in thinking we should face west."

Bhatia performs a madcap maneuver similar to his first, this time facing west when he stops on the side of the street where the car rental building is located. "They will not be driving a Mercedes," he ventures.

"Really? What do you predict, oh wizard?" Mohamad scoffs.

Before Bhatia comes up with his answer they see Lynn and David emerge from the agency's driveway in a dark blue Volkswagen Passat. "Probably a blue VW Passat," Bhatia says. They watch the Americans exit the rental lot and turn right. "Ha! They go west, just as I thought," he observes smugly. He starts the Mercedes and follows at a safe distance. At the first intersection David turns right, and at the next corner right again.

"Ha, yourself!" Mohamad gloats. "They go east."

Bhatia falls into traffic five cars behind Lynn and David. They drive out of Funchal and travel along the island's southern coast, eventually curving southeast toward Garajau. Bhatia has no difficulty following them while remaining safely out of their sight several cars back on the busy road. Once, though, he is forced to pass the couple when they stop abruptly at a fork in the highway. Bhatia must choose quickly. He decides to go left, coasting to a stop where the Mercedes can remain inconspicuous.

"They study a map," Mohamad says. "Because you have turned left, they will doubtless turn right." They do. Bhatia takes pursuit. Mohamad checks a signpost at the fork as the pursuers pass to its right. "Garajau, twenty kilometers," he reads aloud.

"What is in Garajau?" Bhatia asks.

"I should know? You are the clairvoyant, not I."

"I hope they find whatever they look for so ardently. Then they can go home and so can we," Bhatia mutters.

"Why do you complain? We have been living royally in this wonderful climate with flowers everywhere one turns, a room at the Savoy, swimming in the hotel pool, fine dining, tropical drinks and music at the Alameda Bar when the Americans retire each night. I hope they stay here for months. Why are you so eager to return to Ractá?"

"Women."

Mohamad breaks into derisive laughter. "Women?" he mocks, laughing all the harder. "I have seen your women. You should pray that Kubasik travels to Tibet or perhaps Peru, somewhere far, far away from the women in your life while we follow him."

"You are a fine one to talk about women," Bhatia thrusts, "you who have never been with a woman as far as I know."

"And how little you know, my friend," Mohamad parries.

"What? Are you saying you have a woman?"

"I am saying nothing. But if I were saying something, I might mention a pretty little serving girl at General Aláz's palace who has an eye for me."

"An eye for you?" Now Bhatia is laughing.

"Yes," Mohamad insists.

"An eye? You had better hope she is blind in it," Bhatia snickers, unable to resist taunting his companion but careful enough to duck an anticipated slap on the back of the head for his flippancy. But he is in luck. The blue Passat slows. The Telámians watch its occupants scrutinize buildings in what seems to be the commercial center of the region. The Passat's brake lights flash. The Americans point and talk and nod, evidently having reached their destination, which they demonstrate by parking, climbing from their vehicle and entering a storefront office. A sign pronounces it *Moreira and Gorgé*, followed by a Portuguese word they cannot translate, but the dozens of photographs of homes and villas in its window are evidence enough of its function.

"A realty office," Bhatia says.

"Aha!" Mohamad exclaims. "You sound puzzled, my friend, but now everything they have been doing makes perfect sense. They are buying a home in Madeira."

Bhatia is skeptical. "Why do you think that?" he asks.

"Did they not visit a bank yesterday?"

"Yes."

"To discuss obtaining a mortgage."

"Well . . ."

"And they went to the American Consulate."

"To?"

"To inquire about where they should search for property. Perhaps to discuss requirements for registering with their consulate after they have made their purchase. Did we not also watch them call upon Funchal's real estate tax office? Real estate, Rhali. Real estate."

"Why did they visit eye doctors?" Bhatia asks.

"References."

"References?"

"Yes, references. Testimonials. The Americans were obviously referred to see those particular doctors because they are Garajau residents who can verify what the lovebirds had been told about the area being a desirable one in which to live."

"Hmm," Bhatia murmurs. "The bank, the real estate tax office, the consulate and now visiting a real estate agent certainly make your case. I think you are correct, Nordin. Perhaps about the doctors too, although their connection seems rather flimsy."

"Admittedly that aspect is more conjecture than are the other elements. But you think the overall theory is sound?"

"How can it be denied? Here we are waiting for them to come out of a real estate office in Garajau."

"Accompanied by a realtor, I would bet."

"Ah, now who is the prophet?" Bhatia teases.

Five minutes later Lynn and David leave the office with a smiling, solicitous woman dressed in a business suit. She ushers them into her car, a green Peugeot, climbs behind the wheel, waits for a bus to pass, and drives off in the same direction the pursued and pursuers had been heading.

For the next five hours Mohamad and Bhatia trail the Americans and the realty woman, who visit nine magnificent villas in the Garajau hills.

At the fourth of these prospective properties, Bhatia parks the Mercedes a carefully calculated distance from the woman's Peugeot while they wait for the trio to inspect the fourth palatial home they enter.

"Look at this place, Nordin," Bhatia urges. "It is a mansion."

"As were all the others," Mohamad says. "Wouldn't you love to own any one of them?"

"Yes. I wish we could have seen the interiors. Oh, to live like that!"

"Indeed, but it would cost a fortune. These must all be million dollar properties."

Bhatia utters a loud sigh. "Probably even more than that, but Kubasik can easily afford one with the money he got from General Aláz."

"We would do well not to dwell on the general's beneficence to Kubasik."

"You are right. Or on these splendid villas, for that matter." Bhatia's stomach grumbles. "I hope they stop for lunch soon. I'm starving."

"I have been noting places to eat as we travel," Mohamad says. "There are many that seem promising in the region."

Fortunately for the hungry agents, the realtor's next stop is at a restaurant. They wait several minutes to make certain the woman and her prospective buyers find the menu and surroundings satisfactory before themselves locating another eating place. They bolt their lunch and hurry back to establish their stakeout across the parking lot from the Peugeot.

By the time the Americans finally leave Garajau to return to Funchal, they have seen five additional residences and spent a long half-hour conversing with the real estate broker at her office. Mohamad and Bhatia follow their Passat back to the capital city, check where they park and continue around the hotel lot to a safely distant spot in which to leave their Mercedes.

★ ★ ★ ★ ★ ★ ★ ★ ★

Lynn could barely keep her eyes open by the time she and David returned to their hotel. Having gotten so little sleep last night because of her upsetting telephone conversation with Patrick, and after the exhausting, frustrating day in Garajau, she was ready to collapse. She had fallen asleep on the drive back to the hotel while David was still bemoaning the complete failure of their scheme. They learned nothing of any value from the real estate broker. *Senhora* Gorgé talked all day about the joys of living in Garajau. She praised the class of people residing there without ever naming one of them, despite Lynn and David encouraging her to do so by means of every prompting ploy they could devise, short of an outright demand for names. And she had shown them through nine exquisite properties. In one day! Lynn found the ordeal thoroughly tedious. So much so that she had begged off dinner with David, slept until 10 p.m., and ordered from the hotel's room service menu when she felt more revived.

At eleven o'clock she takes a deep breath and dials her home phone number, ready to agree to anything her husband wants her to do, prepared even to abandon her search, leave Madeira, fly home, and let happen what will. The phone rings once, twice; she grows apprehensive. He always answers on the first ring. Three times. Is he refusing to talk with her? Four times. Patrick's recorded voice comes on. "Sorry," he says, "we are not at home right now. His message suggests an alternate number to call. Lynn recognizes it as Theresa's phone. He and the kids must be at his sister's house.

Lynn dials Theresa's number. Her niece answers. "Oh, hi, Aunt Lynn," Molly says. "I've got one for you. In the movie *The Day The Earth Stood Still* . . ."

Lynn interrupts. "Molly, Molly, I can't do that right now, sweetheart. I'm not at home. I'm calling from Madeira. Is your Uncle Patrick there?"

"No, he's not here, Aunt Lynn."

He's not there. Where is he? she wonders, but asks instead, "Are Kerry and Sean at your house?"

"Uh-huh, and my parents, Danny and me. Do you want to talk with Mom?"

"Please."

Molly yells, "Mom, it's Aunt Lynn on the phone. She's calling from Madeira."

"I'll be right there," Theresa shouts from a distance.

Then Lynn hears her nephew Danny trumpet to his sister, "Hey, Molly. Madeira? That's where Natalie Forthright is hanging out with some old geezer millionaire, isn't it?"

Natalie Forthright is in Madeira? Lynn remembers seeing the actress's photograph on the wall at the Cliff Villa restaurant. That picture was taken some years ago, but she's in Madeira now? And with some old geezer millionaire? No doubt the actress has millions of her own dollars as well, Lynn thinks.

Lynn's sister-in-law interrupts her musings. "Hi, Lynn. Sorry I didn't answer right away. I was in the kitchen cooking dinner. I guess Molly told you that Patrick is not here?"

"Yes, where is he, Theresa?"

"He's on his way to Madeira."

"What?" Lynn is aghast.

Theresa hurries on. "He's driving to Newark now, and he flies to Lisbon at seven o'clock. He'll arrive in the morning. He said to tell you he decided to go over there after his conversation with you yesterday. He booked his trip last night but couldn't get a seat on a Lisbon to Madeira flight. He'll stand by in Lisbon, hoping to get on one of two planes that go from there to Madeira tomorrow."

"I can't believe it," Lynn says.

"Are you upset that he's coming?"

"Oh, no, Theresa. I couldn't be happier. I'll be so glad to see him. I'm just shocked that he's actually doing it."

"Well, you know Patrick. A man of action. Are you having any luck finding the person you're looking for, Lynn?"

"No, I've been trying all day, every day, but I feel like I'm getting nowhere." Lynn almost says *we* instead of *I*, but she catches herself in time. She doubts that her husband told his sister about David.

"Maybe Patrick will be able to help," Theresa says.

"I hope so." After the two women talk for a few minutes, Lynn asks to speak with Kerry and Sean. They each tell her they're having dinner at the Conlin's, doing homework with their cousins and staying over until Lynn and Patrick come home. They're content with the arrangement, but Lynn is pleased that both of them ask her to hurry home.

When Theresa gets back on the line to say good-bye, Lynn asks if she can talk to Danny. Her twelve-year-old nephew, a big boy whose voice already shows signs of changing, greets her in his younger, first tenor-like voice, "Hi, Aunt Lynn, how come you're talking to me?"

"Why do you ask that, Danny? You know you're my favorite nephew." The boy's laugh is deeper, older sounding, a foreshadowing of the baritone he soon will be. "But Danny, I'm curious: what did you say a while ago about Natalie Forthright?"

"She's over there where you are, in Madeira."

"I thought that was what I heard you say."

"Yeah, she's with some rich old guy named Jonathan Kingsley. They're, uh, they're lovers," he adds shyly, "according to Hollywood gossip."

Jonathan Kingsley! Lynn is stunned by her nephew's news.

Theresa gets back on the phone. "Jonathan Kingsley is in Madeira at the same time as you, Lynn? Isn't that something? Small world. And with that young movie star. The old fool!"

Lynn knows, of course, that Jonathan Kingsley was romantically involved with Natalie Forthright at one time. Who didn't know it then? He and the actress had caused a sensation at that year's Academy Awards Presentation when Natalie bent to kiss Jonathan passionately on national television before hurrying up the aisle to accept her award for best supporting actress.

Lynn could still picture her father and Patrick roaring with laughter in front of the Gallagher's TV when they saw their staid and proper employer, the man who founded and headed Atlantic Glass Company, make a spectacle of himself before the whole world.

After that fiasco, Lynn and Patrick had gone to see *Checkered* a few weeks later at the Tilton Theater in Northfield. Lynn thought the movie, which had been well-rated by critics but not nominated for best picture of the year, was predictable, standard police-movie fare. Patrick enjoyed its action sequences, and, like every male who saw Natalie Forthright's debut film, was struck by the actress's sensual beauty. "You have to give old Kingsley credit," he had said. "She is one great-looking woman." He and Lynn agreed that Natalie's compelling performance as Policewoman Holly Armstrong deserved the Oscar it won her.

However, the award ceremony and the kiss that titillated America that night and in magazine and wildly speculative tabloid newspaper reports for weeks afterward took place years ago. Lynn could hardly imagine that the pair's unlikely relationship still endured after all this time.

Lynn dials David's room as soon as she hangs up from Theresa. He answers promptly. She's glad he is still awake. He says he has been watching BBC News and asks her to hold while he lowers the TV's volume. "What's up, Lynn?"

"David, you remember my telling you that my husband works for Atlantic Glass Company?"

"Yes, and so did his father and your father, as I recall. Your mother did too at one time, right?"

"Right. You remarked that our family seemed to have a lot of connections with Atlantic."

"Yes. Why are you bringing it up now? Is it important?"

"Well, a man named Jonathan Kingsley was the founder of Atlantic Glass."

"Uh-huh?" David prompts..

"He's here in Madeira. Natalie Forthright is with him."

"The movie star?"

"Yes."

"Wow! Come to think of it, we saw her photo here in Funchal the other night."

"Yes, taken some years ago. David, do you know Jonathan Kingsley?"

"When you put his name beside hers I do. Natalie Forthright and Jonathan Kingsley. Sure! He was the older man she kissed on the Academy Awards show. Know him personally, though? No, I don't. Why?"

"I think he might be the man we're trying to find."

"Really, Lynn? How about if I come over to your room or you to mine to discuss this?"

"Not now, David. It's late. We can talk about it at breakfast. If you and he don't know each other, I'm probably wrong about the whole thing. I don't have any reason to think Jonathan Kingsley would send me money. It's just that he happens to be here; the money came from here; he knows my husband, my father, Patrick's father, maybe my mother too. But if there's not some reason why he would send money to you . . ." A gasp stops

Lynn in mid-sentence. She catches her breath. "David, maybe he has Gunsenhouser's."

"Or maybe Natalie Forthright does," David suggests. "That could explain why he is being so secretive."

"It certainly could," Lynn agrees. "Imagine the publicity if the press got wind of that."

"I think you're on to something, Lynn. We certainly can't ignore all the coincidences involved here. Let's follow it up first thing tomorrow. We'll try to locate Jonathan Kingsley and see what comes of it. There's nothing else on our agenda anyway."

"There is one thing."

"What's that?"

"My husband is on his way here."

"He is? That's great. I'll be happy to meet him."

Lynn is not so sure about that.

Chapter 11

The next morning, Mohamad and Bhatia sit in their rented Mercedes, parked once again across *Avenida do Infante* from the Hotel Savoy. They eat doughnuts and drink coffee while they watch the hotel driveway for Lynn and David's blue Passat to appear.

"We sit in a car eating doughnuts and getting powdered sugar all over us while the Americans enjoy bacon and eggs, exotic fruits, tropical juices, freshly baked rolls and exquisite pastries in a luxurious dining room," Bhatia bewails.

"These doughnuts are delicious," Mohamad avers.

"We burn our fingers holding scalding coffee in plastic foam containers. They, on the other hand, sip theirs from delicate china cups, pouring as many refills as they fancy from a pot dedicated solely to them."

"Too much caffeine is not healthful."

"I tell you, it is not fair," Bhatia rails. "We pay for our lodging just as they do. We are entitled to the same breakfast as they. It is included in the price of our room."

Mohamad is about to reply when, without warning, someone raps loudly at the passenger side window beside his right ear. Both men jump. Some of Bhatia's steaming coffee erupts from his cup and splashes to the floor, barely missing his leg. Mohamad's hand flies toward the knife in his pocket. His eyes meet the intruder's, and he consciously wills his hand to stop. He sees that the man, who misses none of this, appears to find it amusing. The stranger reaches into his own pocket. Mohamad expects to face a handgun. Instead the interloper flashes some sort of badge. He wears no uniform, but the badge looks official. The Telámians quickly regain their aplomb. Bhatia thinks they are about to be chased or issued a parking ticket. Mohamad opens the window.

"Good morning, Nordin, Rhali. Let me in. We need to talk," the man demands. He reaches down to pick up an attaché case that has been resting against his leg on the sidewalk.

"You seem to have the advantage of us," Mohamad replies. "You know us. We do not know you." Yet the man does seem vaguely familiar to both Mohamad and Bhatia, a face they have seen somewhere, sometime.

"My name is Ben Saber. I'm with the CIA." He gives Mohamad a better look at his United States Central Intelligence Agency shield, which does indeed identify him as Benjamin Saber, its photo matching the forty-two year old, olive complexioned, six foot, one hundred eighty pound man standing beside him. Same brown eyes. Same black, brush-cut hair. "Now would you knock off the bullshit and open the door?" Saber says. "You're wasting our time."

★ ★ ★ ★ ★ ★ ★ ★ ★

At breakfast Lynn rehashes last night's phone call home and tells David everything she can remember about Jonathan Kingsley. She has never met him, but having listened for years to the tales of her father, her husband and her father-in-law, all Atlantic Glass Company veterans, she is a wellspring of information about the man.

"Jonathan Kingsley is about the same age as my dad, maybe seventy years old. He was married, but his wife died about ten years ago." Lynn pauses, thinking back. "Yes, that would be right. My son Sean was about two years old at the time. The Kingsleys had one child, a daughter. I don't know much about their family. Mr. Kingsley's business life is what I've always heard about.

"He started his company in the mid-sixties when he opened Atlantic Glass's first plant, the one where Patrick works, in Weymouth, New Jersey. Later, he built or acquired other glass products plants in Pennsylvania, Ohio, New York, Massachusetts. Then in the early eighties when plastic substitutes for items formerly made exclusively of glass became widely available, the glass industry was hit hard. A slew of companies did not survive the plastics revolution in consumer products.

"Mr. Kingsley, though, was shrewd enough to foresee the changing marketplace. He bought out a small plastics manufacturer in Sussex County, Delaware. That plant flourished, so he added others and before long Atlantic had developed a plastics division. Meanwhile, he refined his glass lines, focusing on items not so amenable to plastic substitutes.

"Sometime later in the eighties he purchased a Portuguese firm, *Lisboa* Glass, now *Lisboa* Plastics and Glass, which is located somewhere just outside Lisbon. After that he traveled often to Portugal, which must explain how he comes to be in Madeira."

"Makes sense," David says. "He probably brought his wife with him to Lisbon on business trips and vacationed with her here."

"Maybe. In any event it seems Natalie Forthright has been here with him."

"Yes. I wonder how they ever came to meet."

"I can tell you how that happened. Atlantic eventually was bought out by Titan/Pristina."

"Yes, the British firm, so you told me earlier."

"Right. Well, *Checkered*, the movie for which she got her

best supporting actress award, was a Celestial Studios Film. Titan/Pristina also owns Celestial. I know something about the corporation because of my husband working for Atlantic. Patrick is in Titan/Pristina's employee stock purchase plan, so he always gets a copy of their annual report. Their management likes to spice up the financial statements with movie star photos and tidbits about Celestial's future film releases. They're also big on flying the CEO's of their subsidiaries to Hollywood for major business meetings. Patrick says they like to dazzle the yokels with glamour. The first time they invited Mr. Kingsley out to the coast he wangled an introduction to Natalie Forthright, and they started seeing each other. Naturally something like that spread through the employee grapevine like wildfire. Everybody at Atlantic heard about it. Then there was the media furor over their Academy Award kiss. Millions of people witnessed that.

"Mr. Kingsley didn't stay with Atlantic for long after Titan/Pristina bought him out, no more than a year or two. He's been retired for five or six years now."

"Do you think he lives here in Madeira?" David asks.

"I don't know. He might, or she might, or maybe they just visit."

"Do you know much about Natalie Forthright?"

"No," Lynn answers, "I don't, but I read a brief article about her in our newspaper's Sunday supplement recently. It said she earned close to twenty million dollars for the movie she just finished shooting, but she usually makes only one or two films a year."

David emits a low whistle. "I guess once or twice a year should do it then," he says, shaking his head in wonderment at the unconscionable figure.

Lynn sees that David has finished breakfast, his meal easily as copious as yesterday's. She gulps her last mouthful of coffee.

"Ready to go?" she asks.

"Yes. Let's see if we can learn anything from our friend the concierge."

Senhor Alves ushers them into his office. He confirms that Natalie Forthright is reported to be in Madeira. He does not know for a fact that she is, but, if so, she is no doubt staying at Jonathan Kingsley's villa.

"Kingsley lives on the island?" David asks.

"He does."

"Do you know where?"

"Of course," the concierge replies. He furnishes the millionaire's address as readily as he had supplied the American Consulate's location two days ago. "Mr. Kingsley lives west of Funchal, near *Câmara de Lobos*. His villa is on Route N101, which we locals call Old South Road. Its actual name is Rua da Torre, Tower Road. The villa is situated on a seaside cliff between *Câmara de Lobos* and *Cabo Girão*.

"*Cabo Girão?*"

"Yes. *Cabo Girão* is Europe's highest seaside cliff. If you reach it you have gone too far. The villa is east of it. After you drive through *Câmara de Lobos* watch for a road sign saying, '*Cabo Girão*, 5 kilometers.' Mr. Kingsley's villa is opposite that sign, up the hill on the ocean side of the road."

David wants to drive to Jonathan Kingsley's villa right now. Lynn, though, is torn. She is as eager as he to confront Kingsley but does not want to be away from the hotel when her husband arrives. However, because Patrick was unable to book a flight from Lisbon to Madeira in advance, what time he will get to the island is uncertain. Then, too, she considers, when he does arrive he will probably try to dissuade her from visiting Kingsley and insist she call off her quest just as it seems most promising. She decides to leave a message for Patrick and go with David.

She hands her note to *Senhor* Alves and asks him to be sure it is delivered to her husband when he arrives. At the mention of her husband she sees a different sort of smile appear on the man's face. A knowing, insolent smile, the kind of offensive expression any woman would recognize, replaces his standard deferential, fawning mien. She does not have to wonder what he is thinking. He is transparent. She has a husband and a lover, ergo she is a wanton, available sex object, fair game for any man, especially him. Boldly, imperiously, she stares him down with the kind of withering look no man would fail to recognize. Forget it, Charlie! Never in a million years. He takes her unspoken message along with the written one she hands him, saying only, "Of course, Mrs. O'Brien." She feels his eyes on her back as she crosses the lobby to David.

★ ★ ★ ★ ★ ★ ★ ★ ★ ★

While they wait for the American couple to finish breakfast and leave the hotel, Mohamad and Bhatia attend CIA Agent Saber's every word as he explains his presence in the back seat of their rented Mercedes.

"We know you are Telámian agents carrying out an assignment for General Aláz," Saber says. "You were sent to the United States to escort David Kubasik and Lynn O'Brien to Ractá. You took them to the palace on Sunday for a face-to-face meeting with the general. On Monday you brought them to Madeira, and you have kept them under surveillance since then. We have learned that both of these Americans received millions of dollars from General Aláz. What we are not certain of is why they were paid such large sums of money. But we have our suspicions. Feel free to stop me if I'm wrong or if you have questions."

Escorted them to Ractá? If he thinks they went voluntarily, Saber is wrong about that. The woman was also paid money? Is he correct about that? No, she is merely Kubasik's lover. How does he know of the secret meeting at the palace? What are the suspicions of which he speaks? Mohamad's head is spinning, but he says nothing.

Bhatia asks, "Are you speaking in a royal mode, using 'we' as would a king or a queen?"

"What?" Saber says.

Mohamad intervenes. "Rhali asks, in his inimitable fashion, about whom you are speaking when you say 'we'."

"We? I mean the CIA, the United States Government, and I."

"Ah," Bhatia utters.

How did Saber learn of the palace meeting? Mohamad wonders for a second time.

"How did you learn of the palace meeting?" Bhatia asks. Mohamad cringes. How can Rhali ask such a question? Saber will never answer it.

But he does. "An informant," Saber says.

An informant at the palace? Mohamad wonders.

"An informant at the palace?" Bhatia asks.

Mohamad cringes. Surely the CIA man will never reveal such information. He will think us fools for asking it. But Saber is not fazed. "Yes," he answers.

Why is he telling us such things? Mohamad wonders.

"Why are you telling us such things?" Bhatia asks.

"I need your help."

"You need our help?" Mohamad asks.

"The CIA needs our help?" Bhatia questions. Both of them have turned toward Saber.

"You're looking at me instead of the hotel."

"Oops, sorry," they say, swiveling back to resume their watch.

"Here is what I want you to do. Nordin, when we see Kubasik drive out, you come with me. We're going into the hotel. Rhali, you follow their car. I want to know where they go." He reaches into his attaché case and produces a cell phone. "Use this phone." He hands the instrument and a business card to Bhatia. "Call me at this number when they reach their destination." He points to one of two telephone numbers he has written on his card.

"How will I know when they reach their destination?" Bhatia asks.

"They will stop."

"Ah. But they may stop one place, start up again and go to another place."

"Call me whenever they stop and whenever they go on," Saber says.

"Ah. And what is this second number you have given me?"

"That's for the phone you will be using."

"Ah."

Mohamad's eyes are rolling throughout this exchange. He jumps in before Bhatia comes up with any further inanities which may well cause Saber to pull a pistol from his attaché case and shoot them both. "Why should we do what you say?" he asks Saber.

"Money."

"Ah," Bhatia intones yet again.

Mohamad rises to his full seated height, assumes an imperious comportment, and, voice dripping disdain, says, "You expect to bribe two loyal Telámian agents who are conducting a mission on behalf of General Habib Aláz himself?"

"Yes," Saber replies easily.

"How much money?" Bhatia inquires.

"Fifty thousand dollars."

Does he mean fifty thousand each, Mohamad wonders.

"Do you mean fifty thousand each?" Bhatia asks.

"Yes, twenty-five thousand now. Twenty-five thousand when our mission is completed. American dollars. Cash."

"We will do it," Bhatia blurts.

"Wait just a minute, Rhali," Mohamad cautions. He is as excited as his comrade. His heart pounds, too, at the prospect of receiving so much money. Oh, what he could do with fifty thousand dollars! Fortunately for Mohamad, though, excitement does not make him reckless. On the contrary, the loud, pulsating sound of blood racing through his arteries only serves to remind him how singularly imperative is the regular beating of the vital organ pumping it. And betraying General Aláz is no prescription for continued coronary well-being. "Fifty thousand dollars is a substantial sum, Mr. Saber . . . "

"Agent Saber," the CIA man interjects.

"Agent Saber," Mohamad corrects himself.

"The sum is a hundred thousand dollars," Saber points out. "Fifty thousand each."

"Yes, yes," Mohamad acknowledges impatiently, "one hundred thousand. What I want to know is what exactly we must do to earn it."

"You must help me get transferred from Ractá to Langley."

What does he mean, transferred from Ractá? Mohamad wonders.

"What do you mean, transferred from Ractá?" Bhatia asks.

"I've been stationed in Ractá for five years now. Before that I spent five years in Rabát. Before Morocco my assignments were in Libya, Kuwait and Tunisia. I've spent the past twenty years of my life in this part of the world. I want to go home."

Mohamad and Bhatia look at each other. Both are nodding. Wishing to leave Ractá is something they understand. "I knew I had seen you somewhere before," Bhatia volunteers.

"As did I," Mohamad says. "We must have passed by you in the city."

"Probably so. I've also seen both of you, but, of course, I knew your identities, whereas you did not know mine."

Mohamad wonders what Saber's cover is in Ractá, and he asks the question before Bhatia can beat him to the punch, although he does not expect the American agent to divulge that carefully guarded information. But Saber readily tells them he is manager of the Hotel Riviera. The Telámians are impressed. The Riviera is the city's most luxurious hostelry. This is a distinction easily achieved, however, in the CIA man's opinion. He considers Ractá's few other hotels fleabags. And Saber knows hotels.

Born in the United States (Saratoga Springs, New York) of an

American mother and a French father, Saber grew up in France. His father, Guy LeSabre, was a Parisian hotel director; his mother, a teacher: of French in the U.S.; of English in France. Starting at age fourteen Saber worked summers in five-star hotels his father managed, each year in a different capacity. By the time he was ready to begin college he could handle any position in the hotel business. He also was fluent in English and French. At age eighteen he left France to attend college in the States. At twenty-one he changed his legal surname from LeSabre to Saber.

His major in International Studies, along with his bilingual facility secured the interest of a CIA recruiter with whom he interviewed during his senior year of college. Saber joined the Company that summer and spent the next two years learning Arabic and studying Islamic culture. Now, after twenty years in the Middle East, the veteran CIA operative has had his fill of field work. He wants to go to the CIA's Langley, Virginia, headquarters and settle into some upper level staff slot. He believes he has earned it.

"Let me clarify our position," Mohamad says. "You say you and the CIA need our help?"

"Yes."

"You want us to help you return home?"

"Yes."

"And what does the CIA want?"

"To know what General Aláz is up to with the American couple."

Mohamad feels his fifty thousand dollar expectation evaporate like desert dew. Bhatia appears poised to cry. "We do not know what the general is up to," Mohamad confesses.

"I know you don't," Saber says.

"He does not entrust us with such information," Bhatia adds.

"I know. Nobody learns anything from Aláz, but that doesn't matter. We can't touch him anyway. However, we can surely nab his co-conspirators. We'll find out from the Americans what they and the general are cooking up." Mohamad and Bhatia sigh in relief. Saber does not expect them to possess the information he seeks.

The CIA agent continues. "Whatever it is they plan, I'm going to track it down and kill the deal. And you can bet with Aláz anteing up so much money, it's big."

His conclusion rings true with the Telámians. They both nod tentatively. "What do you suspect it might be?" Bhatia asks.

"Let me ask you," Saber says, "do you think the general would deal in military arms?"

Mohamad and Bhatia glance at each other and answer together, "Yes." They both nod.

"Missile delivery systems?"

"For sure." They continue nodding.

"Nuclear secrets?"

"Absolutely." Still nodding.

"If he could, would he manipulate world oil prices?"

"Without a doubt." Vigorous nodding.

"There you have it," Saber says. "You help us find out what Kubasik and O'Brien plan to do here in Madeira. I nail them, and when they are under arrest you get your money. I get my transfer to the States." He shrugs. "Case closed. Simple as that."

Bhatia is sold. He looks to his comrade. Mohamad remains skeptical, fearful of the consequences. "What if there is no arrest?" he asks.

"Why would there be no arrest?"

"I don't know," Mohamad answers with a shrug. "Perhaps, for example, the Americans prove not to have committed the crimes of which you suspect them?"

"Don't worry about that?" Saber says. "They're guilty of something big."

"But what if?" Mohamad persists.

"Well," Saber considers, "I suppose if our mission doesn't result in any arrests I wouldn't be able to justify paying you each a second twenty-five thousand dollars."

"But we would not have to refund the fifty thousand you are giving us in advance?"

"No way. That's your money right now for services to be rendered."

"I see. I believe that is fair, don't you, Rhali?" Mohamad asks.

"I do." Bhatia says.

"Still, to betray General Aláz . . ." Mohamad begins.

Saber interrupts. "What did the general instruct you to do here?"

"Follow the Americans."

"That's what you will be doing."

"Until Kubasik is aboard a plane back to the U.S.," Mohamad adds.

Saber shrugs. "My sentiments exactly," he says.

"So we will only be doing what the general ordered us to do?"

"Right," Saber says.

"Just as we would be doing anyway," Bhatia adds encouragingly.

"But with an extra fifty thousand dollars in your pockets afterward," Saber points out.

"Or at least twenty-five," Bhatia says.

Saber nods. "Right, at least twenty-five. In all likelihood, though, it will be fifty."

"And the general will not learn of our sudden good fortune or its source?" Mohamad asks.

"Never," Saber assures him. "No one will know except you and me. Even my CIA superiors won't know. I have funds allotted for circumstances such as this, money to be used at my discretion for information or assistance from local sources. I must account for it, of course, but only to the extent that I report payments for information and assistance. No one is identified by name. Keeping sources confidential is crucial to our operations."

Mohamad considers: follow the American couple and earn an easy twenty-five or fifty thousand dollars, or follow the American couple and get nothing. "We will do it," he says.

Chapter 12

Mohamad and Bhatia agree none too soon to join forces with Saber. They spot David and Lynn's car across *Avenida do Infante*. The three of them drop down in their seats to avoid being seen. Carefully elevating their eyes to window level they watch David find an opening in traffic, make a brisk left turn out of the hotel driveway, and aim the Passat westward.

When the unsuspecting Americans have passed, Saber and Mohamad scramble from the Mercedes, and once again Bhatia takes pursuit. He falls into traffic several cars back. Content that his quarry has not observed him, he grins with satisfaction at his stalking prowess. Then, blissfully considering his and Mohamad's unbelievable windfall, the wholly unanticipated, fantastic fortune they have received from Saber, he reaches below his seat and his grin blossoms into a joyous, radiant smile. He caresses the large, expandable folder containing its wondrous cache of hundred dollar bills. Five hundred of them! Fifty thousand dollars! Half Mohamad's; half his! And just as much more to come later! Hot damn!

Saber and Mohamad return to the Savoy. "Let's go up to your room," Saber says. "I need some privacy to make a phone call." Upstairs the CIA man calls his immediate superior in Langley. He utters a curse while the recorded voice he wants to hear in person instructs him to leave a voice-mail message.

"This is Saber," he tells the machine. "Please call immediately. Highly important. Madeira 351 (91) 222 031, Room 601." He hangs up, shaking his head. "I never catch those guys at their desks," he tells Mohamad. "Always have to talk to machines. Hot shots are all too busy wasting time in stupid meetings or playing grab-ass with some secretary. Voice-mail," he scoffs. "What the hell is voice-mail anyway? Friggin' oxymoron."

Completely unfamiliar with voice-mail, oxymorons, hot shots, time-wasting meetings and any kind of grab-ass, secretarial or otherwise, Mohamad nevertheless nods sympathetically, presuming Saber's complaint calls for some such response.

"You hungry?" Saber asks.

Mohamad shrugs. "I had a doughnut and coffee."

"So did I. Wasn't much of a breakfast. Do me a favor? Call room service and order us a big lunch. I must use your bathroom."

Forty minutes later, their leisurely room service lunch consumed without Saber receiving a return call from Langley, his cell phone rings. He answers it, "Saber. Uh-huh. Uh-huh. Where? Right. And where is that? I see. Yes. Yes. Across from a highway sign? What does it say? Okay, you stay there and watch for them. Your buddy and I will meet you there, unless they leave the villa to go somewhere else. If that happens call me right away. You got it? What? We're in your hotel room. I'm waiting for a phone call from the States. We might be a while. You'll get back to me if they move, right? Good."

Saber pockets the cell phone. "Bhatia," he tells Mohamad, who nods, having figured out that much. "He said Kubasik and the woman stopped at a villa along the coastal highway west of — he checks his note — *Câmara de Lobos*. They went inside the place. Bhatia cruised past a couple of times searching for a name or address, but there is none. There's a sign opposite the villa saying, '*Cabo Girão*, 5 kilometers.' You have any idea where that is?"

"No," Mohamad answers.

"No matter. We'll find it. Bhatia said we just go west and stay on the coastal road."

Another half hour elapses before Saber finally gets his call from Langley. He reports that he is in Funchal, has made contact with the Telámian agents who have been following David Kubasik and Lynn O'Brien, and has secured their help in uncovering what the two Americans are plotting with General Aláz, why they are here in Madeira and who else is involved in the conspiracy. Saber is aggravated at the beginning of his phone conversation by the inordinate and probably unnecessary length of time he waited to receive the call, but he is smiling when he hangs up.

Mohamad observes his new associate's change of disposition. "They are happy with your progress?" he ventures.

Saber chuckles. "I'm practically on my way home. Come on, big guy," he says, patting Mohamad on the back, "let's get out of here and into some international intrigue."

They strut through the Savoy's lobby, bound for Saber's rental car, a red Fiat, parked nearby. As they pass the front desk they happen to overhear a man announce his name to Concierge Alves. "I'm Patrick O'Brien," the man says. Saber stops so abruptly he stumbles, almost falling before Mohamad steadies him.

"Are you all right?" Mohamad asks.

"Fine, fine," Saber answers, embarrassed by his clumsiness but excited by what he has heard. "Did you hear what he said?" he whispers to Mohamad.

"Who?"

"The guy at the desk."

"Yes, I believe he said he is Patrick O'Brien."

"He's the husband."

"Husband?"

"Lynn O'Brien's husband."

"Miss O'Brien has a husband?" Mohamad is incredulous. No, he thinks. Saber is mistaken. She has a lover but not a husband.

"Miss O'Brien? No, she's not Miss O'Brien. She's Mrs. O'Brien. Let's hear what the husband's got to say." Saber sashays to the end of the front desk, picks up a newspaper and pretends to read while he eavesdrops on Patrick and the concierge. Six-foot, five-inch, 280-pound Nordin Mohamad knows better than to try to appear inconspicuous. He simply stands beside Saber, who feigns reading the Portuguese language newspaper.

Patrick tells Concierge Alves that he is Lynn O'Brien's husband and that he will be staying with her in the room she already has.

"Yes, Mr. O'Brien," Alves says smoothly, "we have been expecting you." He retrieves Lynn's note and hands it to Patrick.

So, Saber thinks, the husband is in on the plot with his wife, Kubasik, General Aláz and whoever lives at the villa Bhatia is watching.

So, Concierge Alves thinks, here is the big, strong husband. The lover appears to be no match for him. What will happen here? And what must that sex kitten be like to manipulate two men as she does. He drifts momentarily into related fantasies.

Mohamad is puzzled. So, Saber is correct, he thinks. This man is Miss, Mrs., O'Brien's husband. She has a husband as well as a lover. The husband expects to stay with her in the hotel room she already has. But no, she does not have her own room. She is staying with Kubasik. Hmm, she and Kubasik must have learned that her husband was coming and booked a second room so he would not know his wife has been sleeping with a lover? Is that it? Yet she has gone off with her lover but left a message for her husband? This is all very confusing. What could her message say? Mohamad wonders. 'Sorry, dear, I have gone off with my lover? See you later?'

Patrick reads Lynn's note. Dear Patrick, it says, sorry I missed your arrival. David and I had to leave the hotel to follow up a promising lead. Please wait for me there. I'll be back as soon as possible. Love, Lynn.

Wait? I should wait for her? She should have waited for me, Patrick thinks. He takes several deep breaths to control his anger. Concierge Alves recognizes it anyway and moves safely back from the front desk. "Do you know where my wife might have gone?" Patrick asks after a moment.

"Yes, sir," Alves answers in his typically helpful, revelatory fashion. "She and Dr. Kubasik have gone to the villa of Jonathan Kingsley."

Alves sees that his piece of information stuns Patrick. So does Saber. So, even, does Mohamad when Patrick shouts in disbelief, "Jonathan Kingsley. Whaaat?"

"Uh, yes sir, Jonathan Kingsley," Alves confirms, his back against the wall, as far away from Patrick as he can manage to move.

Saber immediately speculates that Jonathan Kingsley must be the Madeira connection in General Aláz's plot with Kubasik and the O'Briens.

Mohamad is puzzled. Who is Jonathan Kingsley? he wonders, and why did the mere sound of his name so upset Mr. O'Brien? Could it be that Mrs. O'Brien has yet another lover?

Concierge Alves wonders how the O'Brien-Kubasik love triangle ties in with Jonathan Kingsley and Natalie Forthright. He volunteers to Patrick, "Natalie Forthright is with Kingsley at his villa."

"Natalie Forthright? The movie actress?" Patrick asks in disbelief.

"Yes," Alves verifies. A Natalie Forthright fantasy pops unbidden into the concierge's brain, one of his favorites. He pauses it for later entertainment.

Natalie Forthright? What the hell does Natalie Forthright have to do with this? Saber wonders. Is she in on the plot too? Does it involve Hollywood money? And the concierge said she's with Kingsley at his villa. Villa! Ten to one it's the same villa to which Bhatia has tailed Kubasik and the O'Brien woman.

Natalie Forthright? Mohamad is too confused to ponder how all these people fit together. He only hopes that he and Bhatia get a chance to meet the beautiful movie star while they are here in Madeira.

Patrick asks Alves where he can rent a car and if the concierge can provide directions to the villa. As usual, Alves discloses all.

Saber listens as carefully as does Patrick. The concierge's directions to Jonathan Kingsley's villa, other than being more thoroughly detailed, are the same as those Bhatia recited on the phone. Saber congratulates himself on winning his mental ten to one bet.

Patrick tells Alves he wants to go up to his room to clean up before he gets a car and goes to the villa. He waves off a bellman and carries his own small bag.

Saber gestures to Mohamad to come along. They follow Patrick onto a hotel elevator. Other guests are also aboard, so Saber and Mohamad are unable to take any action until Patrick reaches his floor. They follow him to his room. When he opens the door Mohamad shoves him inside, and he and Saber burst in behind him.

★ ★ ★ ★ ★ ★ ★ ★ ★ ★

Lynn and David leave the Savoy unaware that Bhatia is following them, and, of course, oblivious to his having left Mohamad and United States CIA Agent Benjamin Saber behind at their hotel. As she and David drive out of Funchal, Lynn worries about Patrick arriving and finding her gone. Soon, though, her concern gives way to the excitement she and David share at the prospect of at long last confronting the person who has bestowed a fortune on each of them. And, although she finds it impossible to fathom why, Jonathan Kingsley evidently is that man.

She looks across at David. He is his usual placid, untroubled self, whistling some familiar-sounding tune. After a moment she recognizes it as a *fado* melody they heard a young woman sing the other night at the restaurant in Monte. Unlike the plaintive strains of most *fado* music, this song is happy sounding. Lynn thinks its cheerful lilt appropriate to this typically perfect Madeira morning. David sees her smiling. "Nice morning," he comments.

"It's a magnificent day, like every day here," Lynn says. As they drive west on *Rua da Torre*, she is once again struck by the island's beauty. Bougainvillea adorns every property along the winding road with vivid splashes of pink, red and fuchsia. Banana plantations, small farms of several acres each, are terraced in the hillsides, their trees resplendent with hands of tiny bananas. Some of the fruit is covered with plastic bags, individual greenhouses to insulate it from harm in any sudden change of weather. She is surprised to see broad stands of eucalyptus trees, not knowing they were brought to Madeira and mainland Portugal from Australia in the 1840's and are now widely dispersed.

Vineyards are everywhere, all lined with stands of dried heather, bound together to form windbreaks protecting the precious grapes. Their vines tumble down the sides of hills, swarm over *levadas*, mount the walls and line the rooftops of low-lying farm buildings. Birds of paradise, antherium, poinsettias, hibiscus abound in semi-tropical profusion. She sees the familiar flowers of trumpet vines, the largest and most lush she has ever encountered, and wonders if there are hummingbirds here. If so, they feast as well on blue and purple morning glories and scores of other flowers she cannot identify.

David points out African tulip trees, their brilliant orange flowers dramatically framed by luxuriant rainforest-green leaves. Palms, Norfolk pines, avocado, orange, lemon, chestnut and kapok trees border the road. Every building is white; each rooftop orange. The roofs shine so brightly in the morning sun that they seem tiled with sunshine itself. Some of them are ornamented with doves representing the Holy Spirit, others with angelic faces, still others with leaves of oriental origin.

Jonathan Kingsley's walled and tree-lined villa appears suddenly, at the crest of the rising road, perched in solitary splendor atop a seaside cliff, the highest Lynn and David have yet come upon. "I believe this is the place," David whispers in awe. "Jonathan Kingsley's villa."

A narrow road snakes upward to it from the highway. David turns into its entrance, which is directly opposite the sign that Concierge Alves told him to watch for. The road ascends through acres of banana trees and vineyards, working farms that appear to be part of the Kingsley property. Its last hundred or so yards are lined with palm trees. The private drive widens as it approaches the villa, the palms curving farther apart along its edges and then branching off to parallel the villa's high exterior wall. To Lynn and David's left they cluster with African tulip trees and pines, forming a wooded margin perhaps fifty feet wide and extending the full length of the L-shaped main building. To their right the palms tiptoe gingerly in single file along the wall through a wide garden of fierce cacti.

David parks the Passat in the broad driveway outside what is obviously the vehicle entrance. That wide gate and a smaller door beside it appear to be the only means of passage through the ten foot high wall bordering the villa's landward side. Both are as solid as the wall itself, impossible to see through.

"It's breathtaking!" Lynn exclaims. She thinks the Kingsley villa is easily the most impressive of the many imposing residences they have seen this morning and the equal of the finest properties *Senhora* Gorgé escorted them through yesterday in Garajau. Birdsong fills the air, accompanied at this height by the soft cadence of waves crashing on rocks far below them. Though people are at work in the terraced groves and vineyards through which they have driven, none of humanity's noises reach the summit where the villa stands.

Lynn waits beside the car while David approaches the pedestrian door. "There's a bell," he calls to her. "I rang it." She nods and joins him beside the door. No one comes for several minutes. David rings a second time. They wait even longer, beginning to despair of finding anyone at home, but at last they are relieved to hear a male voice call out, "Who is there?"

"David Kubasik and Lynn O'Brien. Here to see Mr. Kingsley," David calls in kind.

"You are *paparazzi*?"

"*Paparazzi*?" David repeats. "No, we are Americans. We have come from the United States to find Mr. Kingsley."

"He is not here."

Exasperated, Lynn speaks up. "Please stop being so rude and open the door," she scolds.

"I'll get it, *Joán*," a woman says. "It's all right. Thank you. You may go back to what you were doing."

The door opens. Lynn's eyes meet those of the young man whose voice they first heard, a tanned and handsome nineteen or twenty-year-old who smiles brightly before turning and retreating down a garden path. David, though, hardly notices the boy. His eyes are locked on the young woman standing before them, who is as raptly staring at him. The two of them seeming to have lost their tongues, Lynn takes the initiative. "My name is Lynn O'Brien," she says. "And this is David Kubasik."

-143-

"Ah, you *are* Americans," the woman says, "not *paparazzi*. I'm so glad. My name is Monica Mancini. What can I do for you?" Lynn can understand why normally glib David is suddenly dumbstruck. He is smitten. Monica Mancini is stunning; a willowy, olive-complexioned brunette. Lynn guesses she is in her mid-twenties. Her face is lovely: her forehead high, cheekbones prominent, the lips beneath an exquisitely sculpted nose full and sensuous, even when smiling as she is now. The color of her eyes is indiscernible behind her sunglasses, but based on Monica's Mediterranean coloring Lynn thinks they will prove to be a dark shade of brown. She wears shorts revealing long, shapely legs and a brief blouse that bares a slender waistline. Her feet are clad in leather sandals.

"We're looking for Jonathan Kingsley," David manages to say.

"He's not here, as *Joán* said. I am Mr. Kingsley's granddaughter. Please come in. Perhaps I can help you." She asks if she can first see some identification. Lynn and David readily furnish driver's licenses and business cards. Monica studies the ID's briefly, smiles at David, nods to Lynn, and returns their documents. She closes and locks the door behind her visitors and leads them toward the villa.

Lynn notes with delight that the path they walk is made of the same tiles she so admired on Funchal's sidewalks and *Quinta Palmeira* Restaurant's floor. She sees that it is one of a series of walkways that angle from various points at the magnificent garden's periphery to converge in a similarly-tiled courtyard. From that central area Lynn is better able to survey the property.

To seaward, tiled steps descend to a lower level containing a long swimming pool. Its azure water glimmers in the sun. Although lined in poured blue concrete, the manner in which its irregular sides follow the contours of the volcanic shelf into which it is carved makes the pool appear a large, naturally formed hole filled with rainwater. Lynn voices her admiration for it.

"Thank you," Monica says. "I love it. My grandfather swims laps in it almost every day. When he doesn't he uses one piece of exercise equipment or another in his fitness center." She points to a building at the right end of the pool which looks to Lynn to be about the size of a small ranch house back home.

"And the smaller building at the other end is a cabana?" Lynn asks.

"Yes. It has showers, a changing room, a sauna." The cabana's thatch-roofed outside bar reminds Lynn of another stool-surrounded tiki place beside a Chesapeake Bay cove in St. Michaels, Maryland, where she and her husband have several times visited. "And the building by the door where you came in is a combination garage and gardening tools storage area," Monica adds.

Like almost every structure Lynn and David saw along the coastal highway, all these on the Kingsley property are white with orange roofs. The villa itself appears to Lynn unusually tall for a three floor structure, perhaps, she supposes, due to its high sea cliff summit site. The longer wing of its L configuration stands on the landward edge of the grounds with the gardens, courtyard, and pool between it and the Atlantic. The shorter wing extends seaward to the edge of the property's higher level, where its walls of windows overlook the ocean in two directions and the pool, fitness center and gardens in a third.

Monica ushers Lynn and David into the villa and leads them through an enormous reception room, its walls ablaze with huge, brightly colored abstract paintings. A concert grand piano stands in the center of the room's mirror-like tile floor, but the space is otherwise sparsely furnished: just a long mahogany table against one wall and a bar along the rear. Two doors, also in the rear wall, no doubt lead to restrooms. To the right a curving Tara-like staircase ascends through the space's vaulted ceiling to the villa's upper floors. This is a setting, Lynn fancies, meant for cocktail parties, balls, receptions, orchestras, elegant women in fashionable gowns.

From the reception area Monica leads her guests down a hall past a library, a music room and a small theater with tiered rows of loveseats. They turn to the right outside the villa's centrally located kitchen, passing a few closed doors, which Lynn decides must open into functional areas like pantries, laundries, perhaps a wine cellar.

Finally, the three enter the immense, sun-drenched main room at the seaward end of the villa's shorter wing, the one Lynn saw from the courtyard. The panorama of sea, sky and rocky coastline to the south and east of the lofty, glass-enclosed space is utterly spectacular. Lynn experiences the sensation of flying freely as a seabird. She is careful of her footsteps and conscious of maintaining her balance as she walks, looking several times toward the nearby pool deck and gardens to reorient herself as earthbound.

Occupying fully half of the villa's smaller wing, the room is easily fifty feet across and more than a hundred feet deep. Its three walls of windows extend from a Persian-carpeted floor all the way to its ceiling. That overhead dwarfs the height of the reception room's cathedral cap because this space's cube extends upward to its own domed, glass overhead, a full level higher than the rest of the two-story villa. It has no middle floor, Monica explains, only a top level that houses her grandfather's master bedroom suite. Massive decks on three sides of his suite are accessible from this lower level as well, by means of two circular staircases, one on either side of the enormous, windowed room. The suite-level decks shade the space when the bright Madeira sun is highest in the sky.

Monica seats Lynn and David on one of a grouping of plush, silk-covered sofas at the room's ocean end. She pushes a button in a table beside them, and power-retractable windows slide open past strategically placed screening. A refreshing breeze, cooled and purified by a few thousand miles of Atlantic Ocean, streams into the room. She picks up a phone and presses just one digit. "Maria," she says, "I have two guests. Would you make lunch for the three of us? Oh, and a bottle of *Vinho Verde* would be nice. Monica sees the others' smiles, and adds, "Make that two bottles please, Maria."

After leaving the menu choices up to Maria and thanking the woman in advance, Monica takes a seat opposite Lynn and David. "All right," she says, "now tell me why you have come to see my grandfather."

Over lunch Lynn and David tell Monica that each of them discovered millions of dollars anonymously deposited to their bank accounts. They relate how they and officials at their respective banks traced the source of the money to Madeira. They recount the circumstances of their chance airport meeting. They tell her of their abduction from Funchal to North Africa. They detail everything they have done since their return to Madeira to try to find their mutual benefactor, explaining that their search finally led them here to Jonathan Kingsley's villa.

Lynn can see that Monica is enthralled by the astonishing tale. She interrupts them once to verify the amounts of money each received. Lynn repeats that she got five million dollars. David confirms he received ten million. Monica also asks why, to where, and by whom they were abducted. David says that, regrettably, he and Lynn were sworn to secrecy and cannot discuss their abduction. Otherwise, Monica listens to their account in spellbound silence, occasionally sipping her wine; hardly touching her lunch.

"That's an incredible story," she pronounces when they finish.

"Yes," Lynn agrees, "and all of it true."

"And you think my grandfather sent the money?" Monica asks. She directs her question to David, whose eyes, Lynn observed, rarely strayed from Monica's pretty face throughout their luncheon discourse.

"We think so," David answers.

"Do you know if he did, Monica?" Lynn asks.

"No," she replies. "If so, he said nothing to me about it. I believe we'll just have to ask him."

"Wonderful! That's what we've been hoping to do," Lynn bubbles.

"Are you expecting him home?" David asks.

Monica shakes her head. "No, but I can contact him." She reaches for the telephone and dials a number. "Hi, Natalie, it's Monica. Can I talk to my grandfather for a minute?" Then, almost without pause, "Granddad, hi. I'm at the villa. Two people are here to see you. They just told me the most extraordinary story." Monica's eyebrows rise in surprise. "Yes, it is about money they received." She pauses, listening. Her eyes narrow suspiciously. "Yes, a man and a woman." Listening again while her grandfather talks, she sits back in her chair, crosses her legs and laughs lightly. "Hold on, Granddad, I'll ask them." She lowers the phone. "Well, it seems you've come to the right place," she tells Lynn and David. "My grandfather said he has been expecting you to show up here. He wants me to bring you to him. Is that all right?"

Lynn dislikes further delaying her return to Patrick, but she cannot stop now. She agrees as readily as does David. Monica informs Jonathan that they will be coming. "Uh-uh," she says, "you don't have any new messages. Did Dr. Oliveira call you, though? Right. The man from the bank? That's it then. No one else called. No, we haven't seen any more *paparazzi* since day before yesterday. I think they've given up looking for Natalie."

Chapter 13

Patrick is startled when Mohamad propels him into the hotel room. However, despite the force of his attacker's unanticipated thrust, he does not fall. His brain and body react instantly, calling up years of football training long ago imprinted on mind and muscle. Instinctively the necessary adjustments flow through neurons and fibers as they once did on gridirons to resist powerful body blocks and high-speed collisions far more challenging than this sucker shove. His surprise instantly becomes fury. He is about to retaliate despite Mohamad's mammoth size, but Saber flashes his ID and shouts, "CIA, O'Brien, don't give us any trouble."

Mohamad admires Patrick's nimble recovery and his readiness to strike back against patently overwhelming odds. He stands quietly, prepared for anything, until Patrick vents his anger by spouting curses and punching the air with his back to his adversaries.

"Why the hell is the CIA pushing me around? Am I under arrest?" he demands to know.

"Not yet, but you will be," Saber snarls.

"Why?" Patrick asks. At once he thinks of Lynn. "Is my wife in some kind of trouble.?"

"You bet your ass," Saber says, "and so are you."

"For what?"

"For conspiring against the interests of the United States of

America," Saber says. "Maybe even for treason."

"I don't know what you're talking about. I haven't conspired with anybody about anything." Patrick slumps down onto Bhatia's bed. Mohamad sits on his own bed. Saber eases into a chair opposite Patrick.

To Mohamad, the husband of pretty Miss, Mrs., O'Brien appears genuinely dumbfounded. But Saber isn't buying it. "Come on, O'Brien, you're wasting our time with your bullshit innocent act," he growls. "We know about the money."

"What money?"

"What money?" Saber mimics sarcastically.

"You mean the money that showed up in our bank account?" Patrick asks. "I have no idea who sent that money. Neither does my wife. That's why she's here in Madeira, to find the man who sent it."

Saber laughs uproariously at the notion of five million dollars materializing in their bank account without their prior knowledge. "Come on, O'Brien, you know as well as I do that your wife already met with the guy who sent the money."

"No she didn't."

"Yes she did. A few days ago in Ractá."

"Ractá? Where the hell is Ractá?"

"Ractá is the capital of Telám," Mohamad interjects helpfully.

"Telám? And where the hell is Telám?" Patrick asks in exasperation.

"You know damned right well where it is. It's where your wife met with General Aláz," Saber answers.

-150-

"This is ridiculous," Patrick says. "I never heard of a General named Aláz. Who is he?"

"Enough of your crap, O'Brien," Saber barks. "Why did he send you five million dollars?"

"Who?"

"General Aláz."

Patrick sighs in frustration. "Well, if Aláz is the man who had my wife taken to North Africa, and she already met with him, he can't be the one who sent the money."

"Why is that?" Mohamad asks reasonably.

"Because she's still searching for the man who sent the money. I came here to help her find him. It's not your general. It's somebody else. Look, I know where Lynn is now. Let me take you there, and we'll straighten this out."

"Oh, we're going there all right, O'Brien, but *you're* not taking *us*. *We're* taking *you* to your wife and her lover."

"Lover?" Patrick yells. "David Kubasik? I knew it. It can't be true!"

"You know your wife has a lover, but it can't be true?" Mohamad questions.

"I mean I can't believe it."

"Oh," Mohamad says, but he is puzzled. How can a man both know that his wife has a lover, yet at the same time believe it not to be true? he ponders. "How then do you know the name of this man you cannot believe is your wife's lover?" he asks.

"She told me his name."

"Oh," Mohamad says again, but he is no less perplexed.

"You know Kubasik's name, all right," Saber says. "You're all in this thing together: you, your wife, Kubasik, Aláz, and this guy Jonathan Kingsley."

"Jonathan Kingsley?" What does he have to do with this?"

"*I* should be asking *you* that, O'Brien, but don't worry, I know the answer. You're all working for Aláz one way or another. Kingsley is your Madeira connection."

"That is so screwed up, Saber," Patrick says. "Are you taking me to Jonathan Kingsley's villa or not? My wife is there. We can clear this up."

"We'll see who's screwed up, O'Brien. Yeah, we're taking you. In cuffs. Put your hands behind your back."

Patrick figures he can take Saber in a tussle but probably not Mohamad and certainly not both of them. Anyway, punching out a CIA agent would land him in worse trouble than he already seems to be in, despite being innocent of any wrongdoing. He puts his hands behind his back as Saber ordered.

Concierge Alves is shocked to see Patrick crossing the hotel lobby in handcuffs, escorted by two men, one of them a giant. Against his better judgment he scurries from behind the front desk to confront them, unable to resist finding out what is happening. Saber flashes his CIA shield.

"Mind your own business, buddy," Saber warns. Alves backs away, watching them go, wondering how all this involves O'Brien's hot little number of a wife. A lover. A husband. Handcuffs. The CIA. A man mountain. Millionaire Jonathan Kingsley. Movie star Natalie Forthright. Oh, the fodder for fantasy!

Saber lowers Patrick into the back seat of his rented Fiat.

Because it is too tight for Mohamad to sit beside their prisoner, he is forced to move up front. He cautions Patrick not to try anything stupid. They start toward Jonathan's villa and are just leaving Funchal when Bhatia calls Saber a second time.

"Kubasik and the woman have left the villa," Bhatia reports. "They have another woman with them."

"Another woman? Who is she? Is she in on the scheme too? Where are they going now?" Saber demands. Not knowing the answer to any one of these questions, Bhatia remains silent. "Okay, never mind," Saber says, "we're proceeding toward the villa. What should we do?" Bhatia tells him Kubasik is driving farther west, and he is following. They decide Saber should call for further directions when he reaches the Cabo Girão sign opposite the Kingsley villa.

★ ★ ★ ★ ★ ★ ★ ★ ★ ★

As she leaves her grandfather's villa with Monica Mancini and David, Lynn suggests that Monica ride in the front passenger seat. She is amused at the enthusiasm with which normally unflappable David endorses the arrangement. Monica, though, objects to taking Lynn's seat up front. "Are you sure you don't mind?" she asks, immediately appending, "Well, I suppose it might be better since I know the way to the *pousada*." She is already in the car before finishing her feeble protest.

"Your grandfather's villa is magnificent," Lynn says when they descend the private road and turn onto the coastal highway, Route N101.

"Spectacular," David contributes.

"Yes," Monica agrees. "We love it."

"Do you live here too?" David asks.

"No, I'm just visiting. My grandfather and Natalie live at the villa. Actually, Granddad is often alone because Natalie's career is so demanding. When she's making a movie on location she can be away for months at a stretch, and she flies back and forth to Hollywood so frequently she can't give up her own home there."

"He must grow lonely," Lynn says.

"Well, my mother and I vacation here, and friends stop by occasionally, but I think you're right," Monica acknowledges, "although he never says so. He tried traveling with Natalie to a film site once and to Hollywood on another occasion, but he didn't stay long either time. Said he felt like a groupie.

"His villa is way too big for him, though, and much more elaborate than he requires." She explains that, despite his wealth, Jonathan Kingsley is a man of regular habits and simple needs. "I believe he would be happy anywhere," she tells them, "as long as he could work out regularly and eat healthfully. Of course he appreciates the villa's fantastic location. Who wouldn't? But except for his swimming pool and exercise room the amenities are designed more for Natalie than for himself.

"The theater, for example," she says, "has a giant-screen TV that he never uses. He seldom watches television other than news broadcasts in the library or up in his suite. His whole purpose in having the theater built was so he and Natalie can watch her movies together.

"Same thing with the reception room. Granddad plays the piano you saw there well enough to accompany Natalie's singing. She's quite good. He loves listening to her. Sometimes he even brings in a backup orchestra for her if she happens to be on the island when the Oliveiras or other friends are visiting." Lynn remembers reading that Natalie Forthright sang professionally before she got into films. "They never have parties worthy of that huge room, though," Monica continues. "I think it's a shame, but Granddad is perfectly content with everything just as it is. He's the one who counts, after all."

"When you took us through, I couldn't help thinking how perfect a setting it would be for a wedding reception," Lynn comments.

Monica's smile is radiant. "It certainly would," she gushes.

Lynn can see that the notion is not a new one to the ringless young beauty who has surely pictured herself sweeping down the reception room's grand staircase in a breathtaking bridal gown to the admiration of hundreds of guests; later throwing her bouquet from the staircase after whirling around the dance floor for hours. For David's sake, Lynn establishes that Monica is not married. She leaves David's marital status unrevealed.

Monica does not miss the unspoken invitation to ask, "How about you, David? Are you married?"

"No."

"Engaged?"

"No. You?"

"No."

Well, there you go: mutually available, Lynn muses, enjoying the satisfied smiles of her impromptu dating service's two satisfied customers.

"I noticed your wedding ring, Lynn," Monica says.

"Uh-huh. Happily married. At least I was when I left home." She tells Monica something about her husband and their children, including the fact that Patrick works for Atlantic Glass Company.

Monica shifts in her seat to face Lynn. "You must know that my grandfather is the former owner of Atlantic Glass?" Monica asks.

"Yes."

"That can't be just coincidence, can it? I mean, your money, your husband, my grandfather, Atlantic Glass?"

"We don't think so," Lynn answers, "but none of us can pinpoint the connection."

Monica nods thoughtfully. "Granddad will clear it up soon enough, I'm sure. Something is wrong between you and your husband since you left home, Lynn?"

"Just long distance misunderstanding," Lynn says, shrugging off the matter. "We'll clear that up soon enough too, I'm sure. Patrick is on his way to Madeira now. He'll be here today."

"Oh? How nice. I hope we all get to meet him while you're here." They fall silent for a moment until Monica announces, "We are approaching *Ribeira Brava*. There's an intersecting road around the next bend. You should turn there, David."

Monica points out a road sign at the intersection indicating the distance to *Serra de Agua* and *Pousada dos Vinháticos*. "The *pousada* is our destination," she says. David makes the turn, pointing the Passat northward. The southern coast recedes behind them as they begin to climb the foothills of Madeira's central mountain range. Monica explains that the mountains traverse most of the island's breadth from east to west, forming a natural divider of its northern and southern regions.

Lynn observes the changing landscape as they rise from sea level. Gradually, the tropical flora gives way to heather, African lilies, hydrangea, and, at yet higher elevation, huge sycamores, poplars, cedars and forests of laurel and mahogany. She listens to David and Monica discuss their respective careers and is surprised to learn that Monica recently graduated from Thomas Jefferson School of Medicine in Philadelphia. In the car's mirror, she sees David's delight at that information and hears him tell Monica in only the most general of terms that he is a research scientist working at Princeton University. Lynn wonders why he does not explain his work in more detail, especially taking into consideration Monica's medical training and scientific knowledge. She also thinks it somewhat odd that a recently educated medical doctor would not have immediately recognized David's name when they first met, whereas the two ophthalmologists she and David met in Funchal were both well aware of his important work and his stature in the medical science community.

David soon changes the subject, seeming to Lynn, although apparently Monica takes no such note of it, as if he does not want to linger on the subject of his research. "I'm curious about the working farms adjacent to your grandfather's villa," he says. "Are they part of his property, Monica? I thought they might be."

"They are," Monica confirms. She tells them that when Jonathan Kingsley was looking to buy a country villa convenient to Funchal, the sales agents with whom he dealt urged him to buy in an area east of the city called Garajau.

"Isn't that interesting?" Lynn interrupts. "We were in Garajau yesterday, believing that your grandfather might live there."

Monica tells them that Jonathan does admire the Garajau region and did consider locating there, but he had envisioned owning a villa on land which grows bananas and grapes, a place with its buildings high above the sea and terraced crops below it. When he could not find what he wanted east of Funchal, he searched the coastline west of the city and discovered his ideal property. He bought the villa immediately and later secured several parcels of real estate below it. The local farmers from whom he purchased his banana and grapes acreage still work the land they formerly owned, Monica explains.

"Working for your grandfather?" David asks.

"Uh-huh." Monica goes on to tell them that the arrangement provides real mutual advantage. The men farm the land. Jonathan pays them the proceeds of their products' sales. He is not concerned about making a profit for himself. The growers keep the money their bananas and grapes earn. This encourages them to work industriously for their own benefit. Jonathan's patronage affords them the added benefit of subsidy in bad times, should such befall them in the form of weather vagaries, pest infestations or other natural occurrences that could bring them personal financial ruin. He also has expanded and modernized their homes.

Monica goes on to say that in return for their improved and sheltered existence, the men and their families perform other functions for Jonathan such as maintenance, cooking, grounds-keeping, and cleaning. His part-time staff consists of three men, their wives, three daughters and two sons, eleven people in all.

Her grandfather dislikes driving, especially on roads as narrow and challenging as the mountain passes of Madeira, Monica tells them. "His maintenance man and that man's son, *Joán*, John, whom you met at the villa gate," she explains, "are both excellent drivers happy to provide the limited chauffeur service he requires. When alone at the villa he rarely goes out of an evening, content to stay at home. This is true of most weekdays as well, with only an occasional trip into Funchal on one piece of business or another. When Natalie is with him, she, too, is content to remain sequestered at the villa most of the time, although that has become increasingly difficult for her to do as her fame has grown.

"When my mother and I visit, though, Granddad always escorts us about the island. He sometimes does the same for the Oliveiras when they stay with him. Otherwise, he has little personal need to leave his property. His pool is useable year round in the bright Madeira sun, automatically heated whenever it falls below seventy degrees. He has his treadmill, stationary bike, Stairmaster, Nautilus, sauna and hot tub, and there's nothing he likes better than hiding out there inside those ten foot walls," Monica finishes.

"You've mentioned Dr. Oliveira several times, Monica," Lynn says. David and I heard his name mentioned recently in Funchal." She stops at that, expecting David to explain that it was during their visit to one of the ophthalmologists that they heard of Oliveira. Curiously, David says nothing.

Monica seems not to notice David's reticence. "I suppose that's understandable, Lynn," she says. "Dr. Oliveira is a prominent physician in Lisbon. I'm sure many people here in Madeira know of him." Lynn notes her generic labeling of Oliveira as a physician rather than the more specific *ophthalmologist*. Monica adds that Oliveira and her grandfather are old friends, that Jonathan often stayed with the Oliveiras before moving to Madeira and that the doctor and his wife regularly vacation at the Kingsley villa. Lynn says nothing more on the subject of Oliveira, sensing that for some reason Monica seems as unwilling to discuss eye doctors as David is to talk about eye research.

David breaks what threatens to become awkward silence. "Lynn and I were surprised to learn that your grandfather and Natalie Forthright are still, uh . . ."

"Together after all these years? I know what you mean. I never expected it to last, either. I suppose you saw their infamous kiss at the Oscars?"

"Yes," Lynn and David answer together.

"I guess everyone thought the same thing then," Monica says. "A beautiful young Hollywood actress; a much older, extremely wealthy man. Who would have guessed that her interest in him was for other than his money or his attraction to her for other than her youth and beauty? But, never mind that he is seventy and she's thirty-eight, they enjoy being together. Everybody's easy presumption that Natalie was probably just a gold-digger has long since become moot. She's earned her own fortune. As it turns out, they actually love each other, which, of course, the two of them have known all along."

High mountain peaks now surround them. "We've reached *Serra de Agua*," Monica says. "There's a tunnel through the mountains you see in front of us. The road we're on goes through it and is the one regularly traveled nowadays. Before we reach the tunnel, though, we're going to turn off to *Pousada dos Vinháticos*. Until about eight or nine years ago the road to the *pousada* was the only north-south pass on this part of the island. One had to drive up and over the mountains. Now everyone uses the tunnel. As a result the *pousada* has become much more remote and secluded. Nobody goes that way anymore. Of course, its resulting seclusion has only magnified its charm. That's what my grandfather and Natalie like most about it."

"Freedom from *paparazzi* annoyance?" David asks.

"Yes. So often photographers won't leave Natalie alone. They can be relentless, especially when she's making a film or one is about to open. Here comes the road we're looking for, David. We bear left, up the mountain."

David makes the left oblique, immediately leaving all traffic behind them.

"What exactly is a *pousada*?" Lynn asks.

"Oh, it's a kind of small hotel, like an inn," Monica replies. "*Pousar* means 'to rest.' So, a resting place. There are a number of them in Mainland Portugal, about forty, I believe, state run. Here in Madeira there are three, all of them in scenic mountain locations, all privately owned, unlike the mainland's. They have maybe ten or twelve rooms each. Granddad rents all the rooms not already booked, so he and Natalie can have as much of the place to themselves as possible. *Pousada dos Vinháticos* is their favorite. There's a vantage point nearby from which you can see all the way to the north and south coasts of the island. Whenever clouds are not blocking the view, that is."

A charming stone edifice of three stories comes into view on the left side of the quiet road, the darkness of its fieldstone wholly different in appearance from the white of most island buildings. However, it does have the ubiquitous orange tiled roof. Behind and to its right the mountains rise steeply, while to its left the land falls away into a deep valley.

A sign in front bears the name of the *pousada* and indicates that it contains a restaurant. A road sign across from it points the way to Central *Serra de Agua*. Perhaps half a dozen tables, a few of them shaded by large umbrellas, line an open deck along the building's left side. Lynn imagines the deck's valley view must be incredible.

"Here we are," Monica announces, "*Pousada dos Vinháticos*."

David parks the Passat, and he and Lynn follow Monica up a set of stone steps to the *pousada's* entrance where Lynn is astonished to see Jonathan Kingsley and Natalie Forthright smiling brightly, waiting to greet them.

Chapter 14

Two weeks earlier, glancing into her mirror while brushing her teeth one morning in the bathroom of her apartment in center city Philadelphia's Rittenhouse Square, Monica Mancini discovered that her eyes were red and irritated. She thought it looked like simple eyestrain, which struck her as odd. Odd because throughout four years at the University of Pennsylvania, three years at Thomas Jefferson Medical School, and months of arduous preparation for her state licensing examination, her eyes had always been fine. Fine despite long hours of staring into computers, microscopes and books as well as at notes, chalkboards, visual displays, charts, graphs and videos with all their attendant vision stress. Stress which, for the first time since she left high school, she had been free of in the past two delightfully relaxing months.

Only slightly concerned – the problem could be the result of the previous night's second-hand smoke and two glasses of wine – she thought she looked a little better after some self-administered eye drops. But that proved to be wishful thinking. The condition was not improved the following morning or again the next. She re-examined her eyes, more closely this time in a magnifying mirror under good lighting. When she saw that her capillaries were dilated, she knew she must seek medical treatment. Her condition was not mere eyestrain. It was something more serious; possibly much more serious.

Through her father's former network of physician friends and her own associates at Jefferson, Monica had access to a wide world of medical resources. She knew that in mere seconds she could obtain a referral to the top practitioners in ophthalmology or indeed in any field of medicine. She was just as certain that she would not do that. She could not. Dared not. Her whole future was at stake, even if what was wrong with her eyes turned out to be far less serious than she feared it might. If any inkling, the slightest hint or whisper that her vision could become impaired should reach the medical community, her career, her lifetime dream would be finished before it started. All the years of study and hard work, the struggle to graduate at the top of her class at Jeff would have been so much wasted time. The final phase of her medical training, for which she was selected from among thousands of worthy young M.D. aspirants across the nation, the world, would be denied her. Just as the door to a brilliant career was about to open, it would be slammed in her face.

There was, however, one doctor to whom Monica could safely turn, and she did so without hesitation. Dr. Edgar Hornbostel is an internist, one of three primary care physicians who comprise Mancini Medical Associates. Dr. Vincent Mancini, Monica's father, founded the Bucks County, Pennsylvania thriving medical practice twenty-three years earlier and served the community until his untimely death. Hornbostel, along with Dr. Ronald Archer, worked with him for eighteen of those years. Hornbostel and Archer brought Doctor Anthony Fitzgerald into the association two years ago, a year after their close friend and longtime partner suffered his fatal heart attack.

Monica values Ed Hornbostel's medical skills, and he is a family friend whom she trusts implicitly. If she asked him to keep a secret he would take it to the grave. He greeted Monica with a hug in his examining room. They had not seen each other since her graduation. "Congratulations, Doctor," he said.

"Thank you, Ed."

"Your father would be proud." Three years had passed since Vincent Mancini died. Hornbostel and Monica were now able to talk about him without collapsing into tears.

The doctor gasped when he examined Monica's eyes. His head jerked reflexively away from hers, and she witnessed his reaction. Shock shattered the gates of his scientific detachment and stampeded across his face. He said nothing for fully two minutes, as much to gain control of himself as to be certain of what he was looking at. Finally, he stammered, "I, uh, I think this is serious, Monica." He was unable to hide the alarm in his voice. "How long, um, when did you first notice, the uh . . .?"

"Three days. Irritation, redness was all I saw at first, Ed, but when it persisted I checked more thoroughly and discovered the dilated vessels, so . . . I called you."

"The dilation could be telangiectatic, Monica. Also, your optic nerve shows some swelling. It's slight, but I do see it." He told her what he was afraid might be wrong.

"I suspected as much," Monica whispered. She found herself holding his hand, each of them consoling the other.

"I could be mistaken," he offered quickly. "I've never actually had a patient present with this, but . . ."

"But the symptoms are textbook?"

Hornbostel nodded. "I'm going to refer you to an ophthalmologist . . ." he began.

Monica interrupted. "No."

He was taken aback. "No? He's a good man, Monica. Very competent."

"I'm sure, Ed, but I can't see him."

"We refer patients to him all the time."

She raised her hand to stifle further protest. "I'm not just being stubborn, Ed." She explained why she could not seek advice or treatment from the specialist he recommended.

Hornbostel listened attentively, and Monica watched his initial frown fade as she spoke. When she finished he nodded slowly. "I understand," he said. "Still, Monica," he insisted, "you must have expert care without delay."

"I know, Ed. I'll get it. Really. I promise. I have a doctor in mind, a man I can trust the way I trust you."

"An ophthalmologist?"

"One of the best," she assured him.

Hornbostel looked at her suspiciously. "Then why didn't you go to him directly?" he asked. "Why did you come to me?"

"He's a long distance away. I wanted your opinion first."

"Will you let me know what he says? Keep me posted on your progress?"

"Of course I will. Meanwhile, I can count on your discretion?"

"Absolutely. This is just between us."

"You won't tell Ron Archer or Doctor Fitzgerald?"

"No. Not even my wife."

"Thank you, Ed."

"Or your mother," he added, aiming for a lighter note on which to end their meeting, but his smile faltered unconvincingly. On the verge of tears herself, Monica hugged him once again briefly before spinning away and leaving the building.

She drove directly to her mother's home, having no intention of keeping any of this from her. Her mother would not be there, she knew, but Monica had her own key, just as her mother carried one for Monica's apartment. The idea had been Kimberly's. "*Mi casa, su casa*," she had said with a questioning shrug, "just in case we need each other?" It was a loving, intimate gesture that Monica had appreciated, but until today neither had shown up unannounced at the other's door.

Helping herself to a sandwich and lemon-lime seltzer from her mother's refrigerator, Monica carried them outside to the garden. She thought about her father as she nibbled her lunch at a tree-shaded table. Three years after his death, memories of her dad still surfaced frequently, most often and most vividly when she was near her mom. She thought now about the summer three years earlier when he passed away.

Immediately after Vincent's funeral Jonathan Kingsley had invited his daughter and granddaughter to come with him to Madeira. It would be good for both of them to get away for a while, he insisted. Kimberly and Monica, both devastated by their loss, returned with him and grieved together through that summer at Jonathan's villa. Monica would be eternally grateful for her grandfather's kindness to them then. For a time he had left daughter and granddaughter to their sorrow. But as soon as he was able to persuade them to venture out, he began squiring them about the island, taking them to dinner, on daily tours of various villages, providing reasons for them to get up, to dress up, to pretty up.

They visited Monte, Santana, Calheta, Machica, took boat trips to nearby Porto Santo Island. From high in the mountains he showed them *Curral das Freiras*, Nun's Valley, where in earlier times sisters of the Convent of Santa Clara hid to preserve their virtue from despoilment by marauding pirates. One day Monica and Kimberly bathed in the volcanic rock natural pools of Porto Moniz, which had been the inspiration for Jonathan's villa pool design.

Monica remembered with a smile how he had made them laugh at Bridal Veil Falls on the island's north coast where he stopped his car beneath the waterfall, delighted as a child by the cascading water thundering on its roof. The daily itineraries he dreamed up occupied their thoughts, dispelling sorrow sometimes for hours at a stretch. Their distance from home with its constant reminders of their beloved husband and father had also been a blessing. So, surely, was the beauty of Madeira and the comfort and solitude of Jonathan's wondrous villa, but it was Monica's grandfather himself who most helped them cope with their loss.

Mother and daughter had stayed until mid-August. Natalie Forthright was making a film on location in England at the time. When shooting was completed she flew to Madeira to be with Jonathan as she always did. Monica and her mother remained only a few days after Natalie's arrival. Despite the movie star's geniality to them and the passage of seven years since Jonathan's wife Roberta died, Kimberly was unable to feel comfortable with her father's lover on the scene full time.

Neither could Kimberly bring herself to return from Madeira to the family home where she and Vincent had raised Monica and shared such happy years. Yet she did not wish to leave Bucks County. She had so many friends and knew so many people there. So she had put their Newtown, Pennsylvania home up for sale and bought the charming, restored nineteenth-century farmhouse near Washington's Crossing where Monica awaited her now.

Kimberly lived alone. Monica had moved to her center city Philadelphia apartment well before her father died. In fact, her annual lease was coming up for renewal next month, but she recently gave her landlord notice that she did not intend to stay. Because of her upcoming relocation to Boston in January, she had accepted her mother's invitation to move in with her until after Christmas.

What will happen now? Monica wondered. Will she be forced to live with her mother, becoming a burden as her sight fails her? She thought about her father's encouragement and inspiration through the years, how his dreams for her when she was a little girl had formed her own as she matured. She thought about her mother's pride in her successes, her academic achievements. Top of her class. Top of the world. She had come so close, so close, but now . . .now . . . what? Stricken. Fallen from grace. Her dreams dashed. Her plans aborted. She had prayed that she might be mistaken, might in her inexperience have failed to recognize that her symptoms also presaged some much more common, more likely, less fearsome condition. But that last ditch hope against hope ended when Ed Hornbostel concurred with her self-diagnosis.

Monica had always been healthy. Suddenly now she was ill, seemingly becoming so overnight, although she knew that her malady was genetic. It had always been there, a dormant predator, hiding, biding its time, patiently waiting to one day spring to life and assail her vision. Now, unforeseen, unexpected, utterly unanticipated, its quarter century of potentiality had actualized.

She had always been strong, confident, brave, optimistic. Now her strength seeped away, her confidence ebbed, her bravery retreated. She felt hopeless for the first time in a life filled with hope, facing a future of failing fortune against which she would be powerless. Filled with frustration and fear, she cried the afternoon away there in her mother's garden.

She had composed herself by the time her mother arrived home, but Kimberly knew something was amiss as soon as she spied her daughter's car in the driveway without Monica sitting behind the wheel.

"What's wrong, sweetheart?" she asked as she flashed through the door. Dropping keys and purse on a hall table, she charged into her living room to embrace Monica, whose composure instantly failed her. "Oh God, what is it?" Kimberly cried. They clung to each other until Monica pulled herself together once again.

"It's my eyes, Mom," she sobbed.

Kimberly looked at her daughter's eyes. "What, Monica? What should I see? You've been crying. Your eyes are red."

"Not just that, Mom. Look again, more closely."

"I see, Monica. Your . . . blood vessels, I guess?" Monica nodded. "They look swollen and sore. What, what is that?"

Monica sat her mother down on the couch and took her hands in her own, feeling Kimberly's tremble as her daughter told her what she had suspected and Dr. Hornbostel confirmed.

"You've seen Ed?"

"Yes. I came here from his office this morning to wait for you."

"How serious is this?"

"It can lead to blindness."

"Blindness? No!" Kimberly shouted. She shook her head vehemently. "No!" she railed. "Something can be done. Something must be done." Her voice dropped to a whisper. "Can anything be done, Monica? We know so many doctors, your father's friends, your own. Surely there is some answer to this. We'll check. We'll find out whom you should see. The best. The top man." Monica shushed her and explained the threat that course of action would present to her career plans.

"But, Monica, your sight is at stake."

"We're going to act, Mom, but not around here. We'll go to Lisbon. Granddad's friend Dr. Oliveira is one of the finest ophthalmologists in the world. And he's our friend too. He's the man I must see."

Kimberly stood, strode directly to the phone, and called Jonathan in Madeira. Just seeing her mother take control and spring into action brought Monica a measure of relief from the depth of her anguish. Kimberly's hair bounced as she crossed the room, its rich brown fullness falling short of the tailored beige suit she wore.

At age 48 Kimberly Kingsley Mancini is a handsome woman with a businesslike, no frills appearance that comes close to being severe, but not so close as to disguise her attractiveness. Monica knows her mother's tailored suits and sensible shoes come off as soon as she reaches home at the end of her workday, in favor of jeans or shorts and bare feet or tennis shoes.

When she and Monica returned from Madeira after their sojourn with Jonathan, Kimberly returned to work at Organ Funding USA, to which she had contributed her talents part-time for several years. She deemed the agency's mission, helping organ transplant recipients meet the enormous cost of their surgery, a highly worthy one. Grateful for the opportunity to lose herself in her volunteer work there, she was more committed to the agency than ever after Vincent's death. So, while completely surprising to Kimberly, it was understandable to everyone else when, just last year, the agency's board of directors offered her the position of executive director.

Kimberly does not need her salary. In fact she contributes more money to Organ Funding USA than she earns from it. But she relishes the challenge of running the agency and derives a great deal of satisfaction from the feeling of self-reliance her bi-weekly paycheck provides.

Monica was nearly her usual self again by the time Kimberly called her to the phone to speak with Jonathan. She would cry no more. She spoke calmly with her grandfather, explaining her illness, accepting without objection his assurances that everything would be all right. She was no longer alone with her fears. Her mother and her grandfather were at her side. If everything could be all right, it would be. If not, her family would make certain that whatever must be would be the best it could be.

Chapter 15

It was 10:45 p.m. in Madeira when Jonathan finished speaking with Kimberly and Monica. Kimberly had given no thought whatsoever to the time of day, the time of night, when she dialed her father's number: five-thirty on her end; ten-thirty where he was. Neither did Jonathan care about the lateness of the hour when, immediately after speaking with Monica, he called Dr. António Oliveira at his home in Cascais, Portugal. Jonathan's hands shook, as much from eagerness to act, he realized, as from distress at the abysmal news he had just received. For a moment he thought his nervousness and haste had caused him to misdial, but then his friend's deep, reassuring, alert and sleep-free voice came on the line.

"António, it's Jonathan. I'm so glad I reached you."

"Jonathan, my good friend, are you all right? Your tone tells me this is no social call."

"I'm fine, António, but my granddaughter needs you."

"Monica? Why? What is wrong with our Monica?"

"She has developed symptoms of an eye disease which she referred to as Gunsenhouser's Optic Atrophy."

"Gunsenhouser's? Good Lord, Jonathan! Is she certain? Has she seen an ophthalmologist? Who made this diagnosis?"

Jonathan recited the symptoms Monica had discovered. "She diagnosed it herself. Her family doctor concurred. I'm not certain they're correct. Monica seems convinced of it, though. But, no, she has not consulted an ophthalmologist. She wants to see you."

"I take it she is not there with you now."

"No. I'm at the villa. Monica is at Kimberly's home in Pennsylvania."

"Jonathan, there are many competent ophthalmic specialists in her area. Wills Eye Hospital in Philadelphia is one of the oldest and finest in the world. She should be examined right away, but, of course," he added, his voice trailing off, "Monica knows that."

"She does, and I'll explain why she won't do it, but first let me ask you, can you see her on Monday?"

"Today is Friday, October 11th. Do you mean this Monday, the fourteenth?"

"Yes."

"Of course I'll see her. Can she come to Lisbon?"

"Definitely. To your office at the institute, right?"

"That would be best, Jonathan."

"I'm going to call her now and arrange it. I'll get right back to you. Okay?"

"I'll wait beside the telephone," Oliveira promised.

Twenty minutes later, Oliveira's phone rang again. "Jonathan?"

"Yes. We're all set, António. Monica made flight arrangements on the internet while I talked with her mother. I just finished booking us into the Tivoli Lisboa."

"Will you come to the institute with Monica and Kimberly?"

"Yes. Natalie may accompany me to Lisbon. She's arriving in Madeira tomorrow. I won't bring her to the institute, though. God forbid that the *paparazzi* should spot her there and plaster our photos in tabloids all over the world."

"But why stay at the hotel? You know you are always welcome at our Cascais villa."

"I appreciate that, António, but this time I thought the Tivoli Lisboa would be more convenient. It's practically next door to your offices."

"True, and maybe that would be better under these circumstances. Will you tell me now why Monica must come all the way to Europe? Her father had many physician friends whom she could consult, and surely during her medical training she came to know many more."

"She believes she can't allow anyone in the U.S. medical community to learn she has this" – Jonathan searched for a word – "affliction. What is the condition she has, António? Does it lead to blindness as Monica fears?"

Oliveira sighed. "Yes, frequently it does, less often in women than in men, which offers some small advantage to Monica. The neuropathy can be quite debilitating. The correct name for it is Gunsenhouser's Optic Atrophy. It is also sometimes referred to as Gunsenhouser's Disease or even GOA. It's a rare condition that attacks central vision. Usually it affects one eye and then the other. It can do damage quite quickly, but in some people it works more slowly, sometimes over a period of years. Some victims recover a portion of their eyesight after being legally blind for months or even years. It's a hereditary condition, linked to a number of genes in the DNA of structures known as mitochondria.

"But if it's hereditary, genetic, how did Monica get it? To my knowledge none of my extended family ever had it."

"No, it did not come from you, Jonathan," Oliveira said. "It does more commonly afflict men than women, but it is passed down only from a victim's mother. If Monica has Gunsenhouser's, she got it from Kimberly, who inherited it from your wife, to whom it was passed down from her mother. Tell me, was there ever any blindness in your wife's family?"

Jonathan reflected. "Not among those I knew, but Roberta had a cousin who was blind from a fairly young age. I never met him or heard of anyone else with serious vision loss."

"This was your wife's aunt's child?"

"Yes."

"He could have been the family's most recent victim. Gunsenhouser's often skips generations. It's there but doesn't manifest itself."

"I'm sure you realize why Monica wants her symptoms kept secret for the time being, António."

"Yes, I should have understood immediately, and of course I will guard her privacy until we establish with absolute certitude that what she has observed is really Gunsenhouser's. When is she supposed to begin her Harvard neurosurgery training?"

"In January. I only hope that this disease doesn't rob her of the opportunity. She was thrilled when her selection was announced."

"And justly so. Their neurosurgery team at Massachusetts General Hospital is probably the best in the world. To be selected to join it is a singular honor. Hmm, January, close to three months away . . ." Oliveira fell silent, mulling something over.

"What is it, António? What are you thinking?" Jonathan asked.

"Maybe Monica's prognosis will not be as bleak as for

Gunsenhouser's sufferers in the past. A few weeks ago a young American research scientist announced in the journal *Ophthalmology* that he has found a way to prevent and cure Gunsenhouser's."

"Can this be true?"

"Well, he has yet to demonstrate the validity of his claim, and, mind you, I have not read his full report, just excerpts and articles about it. But this young man has probably succeeded, as far as he has gone. I happened to hear him speak several years ago at the International Conference on Mitochondrial Disease in Philadelphia and was quite impressed by him. He was well ahead of everyone else in his field."

"What do you mean, 'succeeded as far as he has gone?'"

"Only that he has developed a method to correct the genetic defect that causes Gunsenhouser's and designed the equipment necessary to do it. But to complete his work he needs a great deal of money. Work of such importance as his will surely attract grants, but that will take time."

"How much money does he need?"

"Ten million dollars."

"Ten million?"

"Yes."

"To build equipment?"

"It's my understanding that the basic equipment already exists. He must purchase and modify it."

"I see. How long will that take him once he finds the money he needs?"

"Not long, I would think. Perhaps a few months."

"Who is this scientist?" Jonathan asked.

"His name is David Kubasik. He is at Princeton University."

"Can you check him out further, António? Maybe you could review his full research report, talk to someone in authority at Princeton, whatever you think could help you evaluate his claims and judge the feasibility of his project. I'm inclined to give him the money he needs if you think it makes sense."

"I can have his paper in my hands tomorrow, Jonathan, and I know people I can consult at Princeton. Do you think I would compromise Monica if I talk to Kubasik directly?"

"I think I'd rather not risk that."

"All right. I'll have my recommendation for you on Monday at the institute. We'll talk after I examine Monica. Should I say anything to her about any of this?"

Jonathan considered for a moment. "I prefer you don't for now. But it would be extremely helpful to Monica if you can offer her hope that a cure will soon be found."

"Suppose I just tell her that a number of researchers are close to finding an effective treatment for Gunsenhouser's and that I need a few days to update myself on the status of the most promising work in the field."

"That's good, António. And I'll persuade her to come back to Madeira with me while she waits to hear from you." Jonathan's thoughts shot off on a tangent. "By the way, see if you can find out where Kubasik lives and any other personal information about him that can help me learn where he does his banking. If you think his work justifies my providing him the money he needs, I'll slip away for awhile and arrange a wire transfer from my bank. Anonymously. I don't want anyone learning about Monica's illness by discovering that I'm funding Kubasik's work."

Late Saturday morning Jonathan and his driver were waiting when Natalie Forthright's chartered twin-engine Cessna Citation arrived inauspiciously at *Aeroporto da* Madeira. Her pilot and co-pilot (two engines, two pilots was Natalie's personal rule for charter flights) flew directly to the island from Davos, Switzerland, site of the World Economic Forum's annual meetings. Shooting of her latest film, *Alpine Playground*, in which she stars as avaricious, debauched British heiress Daphne Todd, was completed the previous day. Much of the movie was shot in Davos and its surroundings. As soon as the director called the final scene a wrap, Natalie made two phone calls: one to the aircraft charter office to book her 7:30 a.m. flight; the other to Jonathan.

He had to laugh at Natalie's disguise as she stepped from the sleek aircraft and strolled across the tarmac to where she knew he would be waiting. She wore a baggy lightweight jogging outfit to hide the fabulous figure that required no body double for the nude scenes which invariably find their way into her movies. Sunglasses covered the green Brenda Starr eyes that captivate all her leading men. No lipstick highlighted the fullness of her sensuous lips. But the brunette wig she wore was what really sealed the incognito appearance she sought this morning. Her unmistakable teased and tangled tumble of tawny tresses, always long and feral looking, a tint or two more flaming than auburn, were pinned up completely out of sight.

The radical changes did not fool Jonathan, of course, but no casual observer would know that he, or even she, was looking at Natalie Forthright. Would the relentless *paparazzi* who hound her everywhere she goes be misled by her masquerade? Probably not for long, Jonathan thought, but, blessedly, none seemed to be on hand this morning.

They postponed their greeting kiss until Joán had driven them well away from the airport. Their one and only public display of affection at the Oscars was more than enough for both of them, thank you very much, America. "Hi, sweetheart," Natalie whispered.

"Hello, beautiful. Who are you anyway?"

"Surprise! I'm your Natalie, you kisser of strange brunettes."

"Ah, I knew I recognized those lips. Welcome home, my baby," he said. She snuggled into his arms.

"What is troubling you, sweetheart?" Natalie asked when they were alone in Jonathan's suite. He had tried not to mar her arrival by disclosing his bad news too soon, but her perspicacity did not surprise him. She was always able to see right through him.

He told her about Monica's illness and explained what he knew of its symptoms and its effects on victims.

"I can't believe it," Natalie cried. "Blind? How can it be? Out of the blue like this? No warning; no history? Oh, how horrible for Monica! She must be devastated. And Kimberly. And you. I'm so sorry, Jonathan. Your sweet Monica. What can we do? Is there nothing that can be done for her?"

"There is hope. Until now there never was. People inherited Gunsenhouser's and never knew they had it until one sad day it showed itself. Victims were subject to its ravages and vagaries while it ran its course unimpeded." Jonathan went on to detail what he had learned from Dr. Oliveira about the promise of David Kubasik's research. He revealed his own plan to fund the completion of the young scientist's project pending Oliveira's approval of it. He explained Monica's concern about keeping her illness from becoming known in the American medical community. "She'll be seeing António to confirm that her symptoms truly indicate Gunsenhouser's. Monica doesn't yet know about David Kubasik's work. António informed me of it. He's reviewing it over the weekend and will tell her about it on Monday if he finds it viable."

"Thank you for sharing this with me," Natalie said.

"Is there anything I wouldn't share with you?"

"No, but I'm afraid Kimberly may be upset that you told me."

"That hadn't crossed my mind," Jonathan said. He shook his head as he considered it. "No, she'll be pleased that Monica has you for an additional ally."

"I hope so," Natalie said. "Will Monica travel to Lisbon to see António?"

"Yes, he'll examine her at the institute on Monday. I'm meeting her and Kimberly at *Portela* Airport." He outlined his plan to escort them to the institute and stay with them at the hotel Monday night.

Natalie had shed her disguise and donned a bikini as they talked. "If you don't mind, Jonathan, I prefer not to go with you to Lisbon. For one thing my presence might further upset Kimberly, which she certainly doesn't need. For another, my being along could bring all kinds of attention to what you're trying to keep hushed. Also I really could use a few days of relaxation here at the villa."

"You deserve it, and perhaps you're right about Kimberly," Jonathan said approvingly. "I'll be back on Tuesday. I hope you can get some time to enjoy the pool before the world finds out you're here. That's where you're headed now, I surmise?"

"Yes. Come join me."

They dined alone at the villa Saturday evening. Jonathan prepared the meal himself, osso buco, Natalie's favorite dish, a rare departure from their standard, almost exclusively vegetarian repasts. He selected *Barbera d'Asti Superiore* wine to accompany it. Natalie fairly glowed with pleasure, refreshed by their afternoon alone at the pool, sated by Jonathan's culinary attentions, soothed by the superb wine. "You're a good man, my sweetheart," she said.

"You liked my dinner?"

"Loved it, but that's not what I mean. I'm thinking how generous you've been to your daughter and granddaughter."

"They're my girls."

"Million dollar trust funds, college tuitions, apartments, homes."

Jonathan shrugged. "I just gave them a boost, helped them get started."

"Now ten million dollars to try to make Monica well."

"I just pray that it does." Jonathan looked away from Natalie's gaze.

She tilted her head to meet his eyes. "Am I embarrassing you by telling you how wonderful you are?" she asked.

He shook his head. "It's not that."

"You should be proud of all you've done for Kimberly and Monica."

Jonathan gauged his feelings briefly. "I guess I am. I know I'm grateful that I've been able to do it."

"But?"

"There is another matter."

"Something you haven't shared with me, Mr. Kingsley?" Natalie prodded lightly, eliciting a smile as he caught her allusion to their conversation earlier in the day.

"I've never told anyone about this."

"But it has been on your mind."

"Yes, for a long time."

"I know," Natalie said softly. "I've watched your thoughts drift off somewhere at times. Perhaps this was where."

Jonathan sat back and sipped the last drops of his wine. "It's time I got the benefit of your thinking on it," he said, "especially in view of the ten million dollars I'm about to spend on Monica's behalf." Natalie knew when it was time to sit quietly and listen, and she did so until finally he unburdened himself of his long-held secret.

Chapter 16

Jonathan was waiting at the gate when Kimberly and Monica's TAP Air Portugal flight touched down in Lisbon at 6:45 a.m. on Monday. Kimberly looked exhausted when arriving passengers emerged fifteen minutes later. He was sure she had a sleepless night en route. The sunglasses Monica wore made it difficult to judge how well she was coping with the calamitous stroke of fate that had so shockingly befallen her. He ran to embrace her, hoping the tear he felt welling in his eye would not flow down to meet her kiss on his cheek.

"Hi, Granddad," Monica said.

"My angel," Jonathan whispered.

Kimberly stood waiting her turn. Each saw the other's pain as Jonathan kissed his daughter. "Hi, Kim," he said.

"Hello, Dad."

He took Kimberly's carry-on bag. "No bag, Monica?" he asked.

Monica shook her head. "I checked two suitcases," she answered.

As they walked toward the baggage return carousel Jonathan told them he had watched them land. "You made record time getting off the plane and through the passport and security checks."

"There wasn't much of a crowd. Our Airbus was only half

full," Kimberly said.

"I guess most of the tours from the U.S. arrive on Sunday mornings," Monica added.

"That sounds right," Jonathan agreed. "In on Sunday, out on Saturday for the one week visitors."

They continued making small talk while they retrieved Monica's luggage. Jonathan expressed surprise that Kimberly had no bags to claim. "Monica brought clothes in case António wants her to remain in Lisbon," Kimberly explained. "I can't stay though, Dad. I'm flying home tomorrow. My agency has its biggest fund raiser of the year on Friday night. I can't miss that, and I need the rest of the week to pull everything together. I've helped arrange these affairs before, so I know how hectic preparations are, but this is my first time actually running the show." Jonathan agreed that a non-profit agency's executive director must be on hand for a gathering of its major contributors. "What time does António expect us?" Kimberly asked.

"He said he'll see us whenever we arrive," Jonathan replied.

Kimberly and Jonathan each wheeled one of Monica's suitcases through the terminal while she carried her mother's small bag. Jonathan asked if they would like some breakfast. Neither woman was hungry. They had eaten on the plane shortly before landing. He told them he had reserved rooms for them at the Tivoli Lisboa Hotel. Knowing the hotel's proximity to the institute, Kimberly and Monica were grateful he had chosen it. The last thing they wanted to do this morning was travel any farther than necessary. He asked if they cared to stop at the hotel to freshen up before seeing António, but Monica preferred not to delay hearing the doctor's diagnosis.

"Maybe we could just drop off my bags," she suggested. Jonathan hailed a cab and asked the driver to take them to the institute after making a brief stop at the Tivoli Lisboa.

"Good morning, Mr. Kingsley, ladies," the receptionist greeted them as they entered the Oliveira Ophthalmic Institute's impressive four story building at 37 *Avenida da Liberdade*. As always, Jonathan had to marvel at the phenomenal growth of his friend's medical practice since he first visited in 1993. At that time, housed in a small office on *Travessa da Queimada* in Lisbon's *Bairro Alto* neighborhood, there was just the doctor, his receptionist, and an optician whose business depended solely on Dr. Oliveira's referrals. But on Jonathan's every intervening annual appointment he had found several additional ophthalmologists and a burgeoning number of support personnel on staff. After two growth-inspired moves to larger quarters, Oliveira bought and fully renovated his present building, enabling him to develop the ophthalmic institute now considered the finest in southwestern Europe. The staff's sixty-two physicians included specialists in glaucoma, vitreoretinal diseases, corneal diseases, neuro-ophthalmology and ocular oncology, as well as cataract and laser corrective surgery, and primary eye care.

"Good morning, Lucy," Jonathan responded to the receptionist's greeting. "How have you been?" Lucia Pimentel had been Oliveira's receptionist when Jonathan first encountered the busy ophthalmologist who was his eye doctor from that day forward and had long since become his closest friend.

"I'm fine, Mr. Kingsley," Lucia answered. "You must be about due for an appointment, aren't you?" Jonathan's annual eye care visits had become quarterly ones in the past two years. Dr. Oliveira was closely monitoring a developing cataract on his right eye. *Ripening* was the word António used to refer to its growth. It was nearly fully ripened now. One was starting on Jonathan's left eye also, but surgery to remove the newer one was still several years in the future.

"I'm scheduled for next week, Lucy," he replied. "I thought António might take a quick look at my eye today when he finishes with Monica."

"Good idea. Don't bother now with any of the paperwork for

Miss Mancini," she told him, gesturing to indicate the hospital admissions type window where two women sat at computers gathering such information from patients waiting to see doctors. A dozen more people in the lobby read magazines or watched TV, waiting to be called. "Doctor is in his office," Lucy informed them. "He said you should come up and walk right in whenever you arrived."

Jonathan led Kimberly and Monica through halls and up an elevator to Oliveira's large, comfortable, well appointed, top floor corner office overlooking modern Lisbon's thriving commercial district. In the past few years the business realities of managing his enterprise had come to dominate the doctor's day. Although he delegated what administrative duties he could, attending the needs of his medical, technical, administrative and maintenance staffs left him little time to practice his chosen profession. The fifty-nine year old ophthalmologist regretted that aspect of his institute's growth. But he exulted in the greater good of being able to provide the best possible vision care to the largest possible number of patients. He still saw some of them personally, like Jonathan and now Monica, and he kept himself scrupulously up to date with the state of ophthalmologic science.

Oliveira rose from his desk to greet the Kingsley-Mancini family with genuine affection. Then, before the purpose of their visit could sully their pleasure in seeing each other, he masterfully shepherded Monica into his examining room. With his arm around her waist he told Jonathan and Kimberly he would discuss his findings with them but preferred seeing his patient alone initially.

Kimberly nervously paced the office. She told Jonathan she wished she were in the examining room to comfort her daughter. She thanked him for arranging to have António look at Monica so promptly. She asked how Jonathan was, fretted about her upcoming fund raiser, inquired about Natalie, even seemed pleased for her father's sake that Natalie had returned and was waiting for him at his Madeira villa. She filled the brief twenty minutes of Monica's examination with non-stop, mostly one-way conversation. Jonathan shared his daughter's anxiety about his granddaughter's health and intuited that a tinge of guilt at returning home and leaving Monica at a time like this was probably intensifying Kimberly's distress.

To their delight and mystification Monica was smiling as she opened the door and asked them in. "My condition is not as hopeless as I feared," she told them succinctly. She took Kimberly's hand as they all sat down opposite Dr. Oliveira.

"Monica has Gunsenhouser's," the doctor pronounced. "Of that there is no doubt. However," he addressed himself to Kimberly, "as I have just told her, several factors are operating in her favor. For one, her symptoms indicate a form of the disease that progresses quite slowly. If indeed it ran its full course to eventual loss of sight, that would not occur for four or five years. I will verify all this with blood tests and genetic analysis, but I have dealt with this strain frequently enough to be certain of what I am saying. Moreover, Gunsenhouser's will soon lose its sting altogether. A host of research projects are addressing mitochondrial diseases in general and Gunsenhouser's in particular. Its cause and progress are well understood. We also know how it can be prevented and what must be done to cure patients already afflicted. We simply need the physical means to make prevention and treatment possible. Several labs are close to reaching that goal. I expect that one of them will soon attain it."

"How soon, António?" Kimberly asked.

"Perhaps six months. Possibly not even that long. Tomorrow I will begin an extensive study of current research to come up with a more precise estimate. Meanwhile, today I want Monica to undergo the additional tests I mentioned."

"Tell them about the way I look, António," Monica said. Oliveira and Jonathan shared smiles at her addressing the doctor by his first name. He had asked her to call him António a number of times when they had met in recent years, but she could not bring herself to do it. Dr. Oliveira was her grandfather's friend, so much older than she, a man who seemed already ancient to the thirteen-year-old she had been when they met. Now elation at her suddenly improved prognosis had vanquished her self-consciousness and *António* just popped out of her mouth.

"Yes, of course," Oliveira said. "What Monica means is that we can improve the appearance of her eyes in a matter of a few days. I'll prescribe an oral medicine to reduce the swollen blood vessels and optic nerve, and there are eye drops available that will eliminate the irritated, bloodshot look with a few simple applications. Her condition will not be observable for a year or longer."

"And by then you think you'll be able to cure her?" Kimberly asked.

"I feel certain of it," Oliveira answered.

"That's wonderful news," Jonathan said.

"I'm so relieved," Kimberly said. She dabbed at her eyes with a tissue.

Oliveira told them he would like Monica to stay in Lisbon for a week or two if possible, until he had the results of her tests and could monitor her eyes' response to the medications she would be using. That amount of time would also allow him to survey and report the status of Gunsenhouser's research. Monica told him she would certainly remain, but her mother could not. Kimberly explained why she had to return home. Jonathan asked if Monica could wait with him in Madeira until António was ready to see her again. Monica said she would like that. Dr. Oliveira endorsed the idea, and Kimberly was further reassured by the arrangement.

Their logistics settled, Jonathan told Oliveira he was scheduled for an appointment the following week but wondered if the doctor might instead check the growth of his cataract today.

"Of course. Come on in, Jonathan. Ladies," he addressed Kimberly and Monica, "would you mind waiting here in my outer office? We won't be long."

When they were alone behind his closed examining room door, Oliveira quickly checked Jonathan's eyes. "There has been very little change since your last visit," he said. "Ask Lucia to schedule you back in a few months, whenever it's convenient for you." He lowered his voice. "Now, about David Kubasik. I read the full text of his report, which was absolutely brilliant and as comprehensive an explanation of a scientific project as I've ever seen. I have no doubt whatsoever that, once he has perfected his equipment, he will achieve the success he has claimed."

"All right then. I'll send him the money he needs. Thank you so much, António. Were you able to obtain the personal information we wanted?"

"Yes. In terms of his education and work experience, I learned enough to be able to write a résumé for him, but I also found out the more pertinent information you require. He lives in Moorestown, New Jersey, and he deposits his checks at Armada National Bank, which I understand has branches in his home town and in Princeton." He handed Jonathan a note showing David's home address. "I was unable to get his account number."

"No matter, António. My bank can handle that. You've done us a great service coming up with all this information. And there's no way I can thank you for what you are doing for Monica, for seeing her so promptly, offering her hope of a cure and freedom from the fear of eventual blindness, and lifting her spirits with the promise of making her eyes beautiful again in just a few days."

Oliveira beamed. "You are welcome, my friend," he said, ignoring Jonathan's proffered handshake of gratitude and enfolding him with demonstrative Iberian gusto in the crush of his strong arms.

They joined the women no longer than fifteen minutes after having left them. Oliveira called his lab and arranged Monica's tests. While the doctor escorted Monica to the lab in another wing of the building, Kimberly completed her daughter's paperwork with receptionist Lucia. Jonathan excused himself, promising to meet his daughter and granddaughter later at the hotel. "I must conduct a bit of banking business while I'm here in Lisbon," he explained. Oliveira accepted Jonathan's invitation to join them for dinner.

At six o'clock with Monica's tests completed, Jonathan's bank business accomplished, Kimberly rested from her sleepless night by an afternoon nap, and his rewarding day behind him, Oliveira joined the family for dinner before catching the 8:20 p.m. train home to Cascais. At one time the doctor had made his daily commute by car, but metropolitan Lisbon's vehicle traffic had exploded in recent years. Despite the building of greatly improved roads between Portugal's capital city and suburban towns, rush hour traffic had become a twice daily nightmare. He much preferred the comfort, convenience and dependable schedule of his train ride. He also savored the walk it allowed him at either end: his brisk, fortifying morning constitutional; his leisurely, calming stroll each evening.

Kimberly left Lisbon for home the next morning. Jonathan and Monica flew to Funchal that afternoon, Tuesday, October 15th, one day before Lynn O'Brien and David Kubasik discovered fortunes at their ATM's.

Chapter 17

Monica enjoyed a late dinner with Jonathan and Natalie on Tuesday, close up against a star-filled sky, high atop Jonathan's seaside cliff. A waxing, almost half moon and a soft rainbow glow from underwater lights were the only illumination at their poolside table. The spotlights that normally splashed color up the white villa walls were doused, as were the garden decoratives and the tiki bar lanterns. No tabletop candles flickered disturbingly. Monica realized that Jonathan had arranged the minimum luminosity they needed to see their food and each other, while preventing any glare from troubling her vulnerable eyes.

When they had arrived at the villa from the airport that afternoon, Monica kept her sunglasses on while she and Jonathan told a delighted Natalie the promising prognosis they had heard from Dr. Oliveira in Lisbon. Monica continued to wear the sunglasses as she lolled about the villa's bright rooms throughout the late afternoon and evening. Removing them before dinner, though, she found her eyes already looked much improved after just three of her twice daily treatments. Cheered by the discovery, optimistic about her eventual recovery, thrilled that her plans to move to Boston and begin neurosurgery training were back on track, ecstatic that no trace of her illness, visual or verbal, would ever reach the eyes or ears of her colleagues and mentors, and happily dining in the dark with no need for sunglasses, Monica was in high spirits.

Natalie too was feeling prime. After months of work on her new movie in Hollywood and on location in New York City and Switzerland, many weeks of which involved six or seven work-filled days, the flick was finally finished. No *paparazzi* had appeared to torment her since she arrived at the villa on Saturday.

She had enjoyed that day and today with Jonathan and tonight with both him and Monica. Her Sunday and Monday alone at the villa garnered her the peace, rest and silence for which she had yearned throughout the demanding months of filming *Alpine Playground*.

Nor did the feminine felicity flowing from either side of him fail to further fuel Jonathan's joy. Monica saw him favor Natalie with a radiant smile before turning to bestow one upon her as well, eager to share the pleasant occasion equally with lover and familial loved one. She watched him refill Natalie's wine glass and found herself focusing on her grandfather's companion. Natalie was good to, good for, Jonathan. She indulged him like a king and treated his daughter and granddaughter with respect and affection born out of her love for him. Monica regretted that she and her mother had not always earned it, let alone reciprocated.

Monica understood that appreciating Natalie's qualities was more difficult for her mother than for herself. Kimberly had been extremely close to her own mother. Jonathan had always been a loving husband and father, and he provided munificently for his family, but Kimberly got to spend little time with him when she was a child. He was always busy, constantly working to build his company from its modest start to the hugely successful international corporation it eventually became. It was Roberta who nurtured and raised their daughter. Her death had greatly affected Kimberly. Even now, she resented Natalie's relationship with her father, despite its having begun a seemly number of years later.

Monica's attitude toward Natalie had been ambivalent at first. Out of loyalty to her mother, whose position on the young actress's intrusion into their life was manifestly clear, Monica had exercised a fair degree of restraint in her early dealings with Natalie. Not that she actually felt any resentment. She was a teenager when they first met, an avid movie-going teenager who could not help being awed by the celebrated Hollywood star. To think that her mother's father, her own wonderful, but certainly elderly, grandfather was Natalie Forthright's object of affection was almost beyond imagination. But from day one Natalie could not have been friendlier to her, and before long Monica responded in kind.

In the intervening years she had grown genuinely fond of Natalie. She hoped her mother might one day also accept and appreciate the beautiful woman who so fulfilled her father's life. Monica knew nothing would please Jonathan more.

The morning after Jonathan's lovely starlight dinner, a horde of *paparazzi* showed up outside the villa. Monica was having breakfast with Natalie and Jonathan when the bell at the gate rang. Jonathan had already swum his morning laps, but it was still early, only 8:30 a.m.

"*Paparazzi*," Natalie said when the ringing persisted.

"I think you're right," Jonathan said, walking to the window. "Good," he muttered, "Carlos and Joán are both in the garden. They'll get rid of them."

Joán's father Carlos leaned into the kitchen a few minutes later and knocked softly to gain Jonathan's attention.

"*Paparazzi*, Carlos?" Jonathan asked.

"*Sim, Senhor*. They are gone for now."

"Did they ask for Miss Forthright?"

"*Sim*. I told them she is not here. They kept demanding to see her. Joán told them they were on private property and that he had called the police."

"That did it?"

"First they insisted on seeing you. I told them you were not here either, and they should call for an appointment. They disbanded soon after," Carlos reported.

Jonathan thanked him. "They'll probably be back," he said.

"*Sim*," Carlos agreed.

But when halfway through the day no one had seen any more photographers in the vicinity, Natalie wanted to enjoy the pool as she had for the past few days. "Care to join me?" she asked Jonathan.

"Sure."

"Monica?" Natalie asked. Monica had taken her drops and pills again early this morning. Her eyes looked even more normal than they had last night, but because she did not dare get chlorine in them, the pool was out of the question. Sitting outside in the sun did not seem prudent either.

"I shouldn't go in the pool," Monica answered, "but I think I could safely sit under an umbrella and watch you. Come to think of it, I brought a book with me. I don't think I'll have a problem reading for a little while Why don't you both go ahead? I'll be out in a few minutes."

Seated on the ocean side of the pool with her back to the sun, Monica settled into an umbrella-shaded lounge chair. She had read no more than a few paragraphs when she happened to glance up and saw two men, *paparazzi*, climbing the palm trees outside the villa wall. They were near the west end of the property, the only place where it is possible to see inside from a vantage point in the trees. The wall there is ten feet high as it is along the villa proper, but whereas the villa itself blocks any view of the gardens and pool, the trees at issue are not beside the villa. They are outside the garage and storage building. There the palms overlook both the wall and that single level structure.

The intruders were some distance from the pool area, but Monica saw that they both had telephoto lenses on their cameras which surely were powerful enough to get close-up photos from where they were. She called out to Jonathan, alerting him to the men's presence. Jonathan climbed from the pool and walked across the garden to the garage area while she and Natalie hurried to the villa and stood where they could observe the action without being seen themselves.

Monica heard Jonathan shout to the photographers that they were trespassing on private property. He demanded that they leave. At the sound of her grandfather's voice, she saw Carlos and Joán emerge from the low building. When the *paparazzi* did not immediately heed Jonathan's command, the father and son disappeared back into the building. They reappeared a moment later. Now Carlos was brandishing a shotgun and Joán one of the machetes the men use to harvest bananas.

The interlopers in the palms evidently did not see Jonathan's men and their weapons. They finished positioning themselves and raised their cameras to their eyes, while Jonathan stood back from the wall where he could see them. Carlos and Joán meanwhile leaned a ladder against the garage wall.

Natalie giggled. "This is going to be fun."

"Carlos and Joán are climbing up to confront them." Monica gasped.

"Yes."

"Carlos won't shoot them, will he?"

"We can only hope," Natalie enthused.

"Natalie!"

"It never fails to amaze me, Monica. These men go through all this just to try to get a picture of me topless by the pool, when all anyone has to do to see my boobs is buy a ticket to one of my movies. Or, better yet, rent a video, put it on *pause* and stare at them all night. You want to have some fun? What say we both go outside topless?"

"Natalie!"

"Oh, come on. We can grant them their last wish before Carlos shoots them."

"You wouldn't!"

"Well, I suppose not." Natalie feigned disappointment. "Jonathan doesn't have enough palm trees to handle the crowd that would show up after that. There would be *paparazzi* storming the gate."

Carlos and Joán were on the roof and had walked to within twenty feet of the trespassers. Busy sighting through their cameras, scouring the garden and pool areas for a glimpse of Natalie, neither of the photographers saw Jonathan's men. Until Carlos shouted, "Get down out of those trees!"

Monica was sure the shock of facing Carlos's leveled shotgun would cause her to fall out of the tree if she were they. Instead, one of them shouted boldly, "What do you think you're going to do with that gun, shoot us?"

"You have been warned. You are trespassing on private property. If you do not leave I have the legal right to shoot you."

"Yeah, right," the loudmouthed one yelled defiantly. His partner, though, had lowered his camera and was studying the cactus plants below him, no doubt looking for a safe place to drop if so rapid a descent became necessary.

"I will count to three. If you are not gone, you will be dead men." Carlos certainly sounded to Monica as if he meant it.

"One . . . two . . . three." BLAM! At the blast of Carlos's shotgun Monica jumped back against the closest wall, her hands covering her eyes. When the explosion stopped reverberating around the villa grounds she heard Natalie laughing and looked up. The men were gone from the trees.

"Did Carlos shoot them?" Monica cried, not at all certain what the answer would be.

"No, he just fired into the air, but they took off like rabbits."

Carlos and Joán scurried down the ladder. They ran to the gate waving their weapons as Monica heard two cars speeding away from the villa.

Jonathan walked calmly back to where the women stood. "Want to go back to the pool?" he asked.

"Yes, we should be all right for awhile before they come back," Natalie said.

"You think they'll return after what just happened?" Monica was incredulous.

"Probably," Jonathan opined.

"I think they saw me leaving the pool, so they know I'm here. And they've got a good story already: climbing palm trees, being shot at," Natalie said, "but they won't be able to sell it without corroborating photos. Yes, I think they'll be back, they or some other macho maniacs, but maybe we'll get enough time for a nice swim. Come with us and read your book," she invited Monica.

"I will."

"What are you reading?" Natalie asked.

"A thriller. Kind of seems redundant now, doesn't it?"

Sure enough, as Natalie and Jonathan expected, *paparazzi* showed up again the next day, this time in a helicopter that circled in from the Atlantic and hovered above the pool. "Unbelievable!" Monica shouted against the noise of its rotor blades. Natalie sighed. Jonathan just looked resigned. "Carlos won't shoot it down, will he?" Monica cried.

"There's an idea," Natalie yelled.

They watched the aircraft for a good ten minutes before its occupants gave up and the chopper angled back over the cliff, edging eastward along the shoreline.

"I think we're going to have to go to the *pousada*," Jonathan announced.

"What about Monica?" Natalie asked.

"All three of us," Jonathan replied.

"I don't think so, Granddad. You two should go. You're not getting any peace here, unfortunately, but I think I should stay until I hear from Dr. Oliveira with the results of my tests. Maybe he'll also have more information on Gunsenhouser's research."

Jonathan had to agree. "I don't like leaving you, though," he said.

"I'll be all right. You don't think the *paparazzi* will stage an amphibious assault and climb the sea cliff to carry me off?" Monica quipped.

"If they do, just get Carlos to shoot them for real," Natalie proposed.

Jonathan asked Monica what she would do all alone at the villa while they were gone.

"It's not as if I'll really be alone. Maria is here, and Carlos and Joán."

Jonathan nodded. "You might be tortured by these crazy photographers."

"I imagine they'll give up if I stay inside the villa, and they don't see any sign of Natalie being here. I can keep you informed about them, though, let you know when it's safe for you to come back. Meanwhile I don't really care to be outside anyway."

"I hope I get a chance to spend more time with you before I

have to fly back to Hollywood, Monica," Natalie said.

"When do you go?"

"The twenty-eighth."

"Eleven days? Surely I'll see you before that. If we decide you can't come back earlier I'll join you at the *pousada*," Monica said, "after I hear from António"

"That's good," Natalie affirmed.

" I'll tell Carlos that you may be asking him or Joán to drive you there," Jonathan said. "One thing, though," he added, fretting, "your mother is not going to like the idea that we took off and left you behind."

"Mom probably will call, but I'll explain what's happening. She'll understand," Monica assured him. "That's another advantage of my staying here, though. I can keep you posted on who calls and pass along any messages I get for either of you."

Jonathan called *Pousada dos Vinháticos*. Not knowing exactly how long they would be staying, he reserved all the available rooms through October 28th, the day Natalie planned to leave for California. Other than three *chambres* already reserved for the forthcoming weekend and two for the following Friday and Saturday nights, the whole *pousada* would be theirs.

The next afternoon, Dr. Oliveira called to tell Monica her tests turned out as he expected. He asked if he could see her again in about ten days to check her improvement from the medication he gave her. She told him how much better her eyes already looked. He said he had initiated contacts with Gunsenhouser's research labs in Europe and the U.S. and would report his findings when she visited him. They tentatively agreed that she, and probably Jonathan, would see him at the institute a week from Tuesday. That would enable Jonathan to accompany her to Lisbon, since Natalie was returning to the States a day earlier.

"Is your grandfather there, Monica?"

"No, he's not, António. He and Natalie are staying at *Pousada dos Vinháticos* for a few days. We've had several incidents involving *paparazzi*. They're determined to get photos of Natalie. She and my granddad went to the mountains to escape their harassment. We think they'll give up when they realize Natalie is not here."

"One would hope so. I'll call your grandfather at the pousada. I have the number there. You be cautious of those crazed intruders, Monica, and take care of your eyes."

"I will," Monica assured him.

Jonathan Kingsley and Natalie Forthright had left for the *pousada* early that morning.

They are still there the following week when Monica arrives with Lynn O'Brien and David Kubasik.

Chapter 18

David parks the Passat, and he and Lynn follow Monica up a set of stone steps to the *pousada's* entrance, where Jonathan Kingsley and Natalie Forthright are smiling brightly, waiting to greet them. Lynn recognizes Jonathan from photos she has seen but thinks he looks younger in person. Close up, life-size, dressed casually in shorts and blouse, Natalie Forthright is every bit as gorgeous as she appears on the big screen and national magazine covers. And being the beneficiary of Natalie's live and in person smile, Lynn feels its warmth and friendliness put her immediately at ease, which she had been apprehensive might not be the case in the movie star's presence.

"Lynn, David," Monica says, "this is my grandfather, Jonathan Kingsley. And of course you recognize Natalie Forthright. Natalie, Granddad, as you apparently already know, this is Mrs. Lynn O'Brien and Dr. David Kubasik."

Jonathan does not take advantage of the opportunity Monica has given him to explain how he knows his visitors. He and David simply shake hands with typical masculine robustness. Natalie likewise, but more delicately, greets David, who says, "It's a pleasure to meet you, Miss Forthright. An honor."

"Thank you, David. Please call us Natalie and Jonathan and let us call you Lynn and David," Natalie requests affably.

"All right, Natalie, Jonathan," David intones.

Natalie meanwhile moves closer to Lynn, who expects the gracious, if pallid, handshake that seems appropriate to the situation and which she would be delighted to receive from the celebrated actress. Instead, Natalie clasps her hand firmly while Lynn expresses pleasure in meeting her, and she continues clinging to it throughout her own response, "I'm *extremely* happy to meet *you*, Lynn."

Then Jonathan, whose eyes Lynn has felt fixed on her throughout the introductory exchanges, steps up very close and whispers, "Welcome, my dear." Lynn returns his smile and lets her hand linger in his as she had in Natalie's. She hopes she does not look as surprised as she feels by the prolonged hand holdings and the endearment appended to Jonathan's welcome. David's expression, though, tells her he finds nothing unusual happening.

Monica accepts kisses from her grandfather and Natalie. "How are you, sweetheart?" Jonathan asks.

"Fine, Granddad. Hi, Natalie."

"Monica, hi, I'm glad you're here."

"I was hoping you would both come home, but this is second best anyway," Monica says with a smile.

"No more trouble with *paparazzi*, right?" Natalie asks.

"Not for a few days. They seem to have given up. I guess they're convinced you aren't there."

"Have we had any calls, Monica?" Jonathan inquires.

"Just António and the man from the bank that I told you about."

"Yes. I called António back, and *Senhor* da Silva telephoned me here at the *pousada*." Lynn and David exchange glances. So da Silva did alert his prize customer after all

Jonathan invites everyone to come inside and leads them to a room that features a small but well-stocked bar. Lynn supposes it is a service bar for the restaurant advertised on the sign out front, but if so there can't be many diners. The bar is unmanned. Natural light from an adjacent lounge filters into the otherwise unlighted space. The lounge is lined by windows overlooking the valley, those Lynn observed from the road.

"I think we can all use a drink," Natalie says, stepping behind the bar. Lynn knows *she* can, and everyone else accepts as well. Natalie pours the same potion into each glass and proposes a toast. "To revelations," she says. Lynn sees that David is as hopeful as she about what that might mean, but they all clink glasses and sample their drinks.

"Mmm, delicious," David comments. "What is this?"

"It's a *poncha*," Natalie replies, "a Madeiran drink. I pre-mixed a batch."

"*Poncha?*" David asks.

"Yes, it's rum, which is called sugar cane rum locally and rather superfluously, mixed with lemon and honey."

"People here like to say a poncho warms you from the outside and a *poncha* from the inside," Jonathan adds. His island aphorism elicits a chuckle from David but no more than a wan smile from Lynn, who hopes that the potent potion she sips will soon serve to quell her unease.

Natalie uses the remainder of her concoction to top off everyone's drinks. "Revelations," she says again. "You first, sweetheart, I should think," she tells Jonathan.

"Right." He suggests they move into the lounge where they can be seated in comfort.

"I think I'll mix another batch of *ponchas* before we start," Natalie suggests as the others settle into chairs. Lynn is about to declare that she, for one, could not possibly drink another sip of the powerful brew, but she restrains herself amid enthusiastic nods from everyone else.

Jonathan addresses the group but looks at Lynn. "We have a great deal to talk about this afternoon," he begins. "Some of it might more appropriately be discussed in private between those of us directly affected, but I have decided" – he gestures toward Natalie, who is pouring rum into a shaker behind the bar – "I should say *Natalie and* I have decided that speaking openly is justified and will be more expedient. All of us here are intimately interlinked. So much so that I, we, believe what ties us together can be shared among us, despite promises being broken and secrets revealed."

Having uttered this intriguing preface, Jonathan falls silent. The others wait in awkward silence for Natalie, whose spirited shaking as she blends her drink ingredients would send any *paparazzo* into ecstasy.

Monica lessens the tension by pointing out the wonderful valley view outside the lounge windows, which they all stand and admire until Natalie enters with her pitcher of *poncha*s. Lynn checks her watch and hopes the expediency of which Jonathan spoke will be expediently demonstrated. What can Patrick be doing all this time? she worries.

★ ★ ★ ★ ★ ★ ★ ★ ★ ★

Patrick is seated in the back of Ben Saber's rented Fiat traveling west on *Rua da Torre* along Madeira's southern coast. Hearing him moving about, Mohamad looks to see what he is up to and is satisfied that he is merely trying to assume a more comfortable position, no easy task when one is handcuffed. Mohamad turns forward to help Saber watch for the landmark that Bhatia and Concierge Alves have told them stands opposite Jonathan Kingsley's villa.

"Here comes a road sign now," Saber says.

"Yes, I see it," Mohamad says, reading it aloud as Saber slows: "Cabo Girão, 5 kilometers."

"That's it!" Saber barks. "So that must be Kingsley's villa on top of the cliff. What a place! Did you ever see anything like that?"

"Yes." Mohamad answers. "Yesterday."

"Yesterday?"

"In Garajau. We saw such homes there, but their locations did not equal this one."

"Kubasik and O'Brien were checking out villas like this?"

"Yes, with a real estate agent."

"Whoa! Your tax dollars at work, Nordin."

"What?"

"The taxes you pay in Telám. From your pocket to Aláz to Kubasik and O'Brien to buy them a nice little villa in Madeira. Sweet!" Patrick erupts into laughter behind them. Saber turns and scowls. "What's so funny, O'Brien?"

"Lynn was in Garajau with Kubasik trying to find the man who sent them money, not to buy a villa."

"Yeah? I don't think so. I believe they already had Aláz's money, and they were looking to buy a cozy little love nest like their compatriot Kingsley's up there on the cliff." Saber hands Mohamad his cell phone, saying, "I'll keep going west while you call your buddy for directions to wherever it is they're all hanging out. I don't like to use these things while I'm driving."

Mohamad dials the number Saber gives him. He hears Bhatia's phone ringing, then a series of clicks, and finally his fellow agent's voice, which sounds muffled and distant.

"Rhali?" Mohamad shouts. He hears nothing. "Rhali?" he shouts a second time.

Finally, Bhatia's voice comes through clearly. "Hello," he says. "Is someone there?"

"Rhali, it is Nordin. Is something wrong with your phone?"

"Ah, there you are, Nordin. I couldn't hear you," Bhatia says, "but now your voice is quite clear. I believe I was talking into the wrong end of the phone. Yes, that is why I could not hear you. I was speaking into the listening end and listening to the speaking end. There are many unexplained buttons on this instrument as well."

"All right, Rhali, never mind that. We have just passed the Kingsley villa. Where are you?"

"I am near a building called *Pousada dos Vinháticos*. I believe it is an inn. The Americans have gone inside it. You will not believe who is there, Nordin."

"Who?"

"Natalie Forthright, the beautiful Hollywood movie actress. I saw her and an older man greet the Americans and the young woman who is with them. Natalie Forthright, Nordin! Can you believe it?"

"I believe it, Rhali. We learned that she is here after you left us at the hotel," Mohamad says.

"Hail, hail the gang's all here," Saber mutters. "Get the directions," he grouses impatiently.

"How do we find you, Rhali?" Mohamad nods at his partner's reply. "Yes, yes, all right. Let me repeat it. We turn right at an intersection where a road sign indicates the distance to *Serra de Agua* and *Pousada dos Vinháticos*. Then as we approach a mountain tunnel we turn left at a similar sign." Mohamad again listens. "Yes, a small sign. I see. All right."

"Tell him to call us right away if any of them leave that building," Saber says. Mohamad repeats Saber's instructions and hangs up the phone. "Rhali said that our second turn, the turn before the tunnel, is an angled left up a mountain road. The sign is easy to miss."

"Okay," Saber says. "Make sure we don't miss it. Before that, though, we make the right turn off this road. Keep your eyes peeled for that."

"What? Peel my eyes?"

"Watch closely," Saber explains with a sigh.

Shaking his head in frustration, Patrick echoes the CIA man's sigh.

★ ★ ★ ★ ★ ★ ★ ★ ★ ★

At the *pousada* Natalie refills everyone's glasses and takes a seat beside Jonathan. Lynn, Monica and David are opposite them across the narrow lounge, a distance of no more than six feet from knees to knees. Jonathan sips his drink, sets it down, looks in turn at his granddaughter, then David, and finally at Lynn, who thinks he is wondering where to start. He decides.

"Lynn and David, I suppose I should commend you for your resourcefulness in finding me. I didn't want you to, but having since considered the matter from your perspective I can understand why you couldn't settle for my remaining anonymous. I should have anticipated you would act as you have. So, now that you are here, I'll explain why *I've* acted as *I* have."

Natalie places her hand on Jonathan's. "Before you decide to beat a hasty retreat," she tells Lynn and David, "let me say that Jonathan is not trying to scare you off, are you, sweetheart?"

"Not at all. Really, I couldn't be happier to meet either of you. Nor could Natalie. We just thought my anonymity would make matters easier for all of us, especially for Monica and Lynn." The two women exchange bewildered glances, neither knowing what Jonathan could possibly mean by that. "But," Jonathan continues, "under present circumstances, we believe I had best tell all of you the whole truth.

"I'll start with you, David. First off, I regret causing you to take time away from your crucial work. Yes, I sent you the ten million dollars you discovered in your bank account. Of course my intent was to help you complete your project, which you no doubt realized. I suspect you just needed to make certain of that fact and learn who your benefactor was, isn't that so?"

"Yes," David answers, "and I was curious about your motivation, why you would contribute such a vast amount of money to fund my work. But I believe I've since figured that out."

"I see. And what is it you have concluded?"

"Well, Mr. Kings . . ., um, Jonathan, maybe I should keep that information to myself for now," David stammers. His reddened cheeks and sheepish tone tell Lynn immediately that this uncharacteristic reserve somehow has something to do with Monica. She sees Natalie look from David to Monica and realizes the savvy movie star has picked up the same vibes as she. Their eyes meet, and they share knowing smiles.

Jonathan is a half step behind the two women, but he catches up with their intuitive leap after a quick look at Natalie. "So then, David," he says, "welcome to my dilemma." He smiles. "Why don't you ask Monica if she objects to your speaking openly."

David stares at Jonathan. He studies the floor. Long seconds go by. "Monica?" he asks hesitantly, finally raising his eyes to her face.

"It's all right, David. Except maybe for Lynn, everyone here knows anyway," she answers.

"Monica has Gunsenhouser's," David says, his voice barely above a whisper.

"How did you know?" Monica asks.

"Your mentions of Dr. Oliveira. That and the sunglasses you're always wearing."

The revelation catches Lynn by surprise. She thinks she must be slipping. Of course! The sunglasses, the references to Dr. Oliveira. Now she also realizes why Monica consistently shifted their conversations away from any focus on herself and why, in Monica's presence, David avoided any detailed explanation of the nature of his research. Monica did not want Lynn or David to know she had Gunsenhouser's. And David, already having grasped that fact, didn't want to say anything about his work until Jonathan or Monica herself first disclosed she was a victim of the disease. There is still one more thing about Monica that Lynn needs cleared up, but she keeps it to herself for now.

"How do you come to know Dr. Oliveira?" Monica asks David.

"Just by reputation," David replies.

"And, Granddad, you sent ten million dollars to David on my behalf because he can somehow help me?" she asks. "I don't fully understand."

"David," Jonathan says, "I promised Monica I would keep her illness a secret. You've just helped me keep that confidence by puzzling it out and filling in Lynn yourself, so let me allow you the pleasure of telling Monica the rest of the story." He sits down and takes Natalie's hand in one of his while hoisting his *poncha* with the other.

David explains the work he has been doing, tells Monica the conclusions he has reached, details his background in Gunsenhouser's and other mitochondrial disease study and research, and outlines the recently published report of his project's status. Monica and everyone else in the room listen in rapt silence until he finishes.

"And you believe you can cure Gunsenhouser's? You can actually cure me?" Monica asks.

"I'm certain of it," David answers.

"Surely António is aware of David's work, Granddad."

"Of course."

"And does he know you sent David the money he needs to complete it?"

"Yes, António and I worked it out hand in hand."

Monica runs into her grandfather's arms. "You're wonderful," she coos.

"You see, David," Jonathan explains, still hugging his granddaughter, "my reason for wishing to act anonymously was because Monica could not allow anyone in the U.S. medical community to learn of her illness. She has been accepted into Harvard's neurosurgery program at Massachusetts General."

"That's phenomenal," David applauds.

"We couldn't let her illness become known and interfere with her opportunity there."

"I understand. Gunsenhouser's and neurosurgery would hardly be viewed as compatible," David says. "So you consulted

Dr. Oliveira, a highly regarded ophthalmologist, safely removed from the American medical community, as well as a family friend."

Lynn's remaining question about Monica has not been addressed, so she broaches the subject. "Forgive me, Monica, but one thing about this still puzzles me. David and I met with two local ophthalmologists in Funchal, and, although they had never met him, both men knew David's name immediately. Yet you didn't recognize his name or know of his work. It just strikes me as odd that a recent medical school honors graduate like you would not have that information."

Monica is about to reply, but David beats her to it. "Let me take a shot at answering that. I can give you two good reasons, Lynn. One: Monica's focus is on surgery, and, even more tightly, on neurosurgery. Ophthalmologists know of my work. Not a lot of other physicians do. Scientific knowledge, medical especially, keeps expanding. The more we learn as a community, the more specialized our particular fields become. I would bet that nine out of ten doctors outside ophthalmology have never even heard of Gunsenhouser's Optic Atrophy, let alone the work of David Kubasik. And number two: reports of my research have only surfaced in recent months. Monica was engrossed in studying for her state licensing examination, a full time job in itself."

"That about sums it up, David," Monica agrees, "except I must confess that in the two months since I passed my state boards, I haven't looked at a medical book or report of any kind. Until the past couple of weeks, I even turned off television news when they got around to their evening health updates. I just took a vacation from everything medical."

Lynn nods. With that loose end tied up she finds Jonathan Kingsley's reasons for sending David ten million dollars completely comprehensible, praiseworthy, and eminently deserving of Monica's eternal gratitude. However, after all this time away from her husband and children, all her travel, all the people she has met and questioned in Madeira, and everything she has listened to this afternoon at the *pousada* while growing tipsy on two powerful *ponchas*, Lynn still has no idea whatsoever why Jonathan Kingsley bestowed upon her the five million dollar gift residing in her bank account back home.

Chapter 19

Natalie asks if anyone would like another drink or maybe a snack. No one is hungry, all of them having eaten lunch not long before, nor does anyone want to risk another *poncha* in the middle of the afternoon. "Could we switch places, Monica?" she asks. "I'd like to sit beside Lynn if you don't mind moving."

"Sure," Monica agrees. Lynn has been seated between her and David with Natalie and Jonathan opposite them. Now Monica transfers to the chair beside her grandfather, while Natalie moves beside Lynn, who is momentarily startled when she feels the actress unexpectedly take her hand. She sees that Jonathan holds Monica's hand. Natalie is smiling at Lynn; Monica at Jonathan. Lynn decides to simply surrender to her confusion, not even attempting to fathom what might be coming next. She thinks she must look as anxious as Jonathan does when he begins to speak.

"It's a shame Kimberly isn't here," he says, drawing a quizzical look from Monica, but she does not comment. "And Patrick," Jonathan adds.

"Patrick?" Lynn blurts, immediately regrets the boisterousness of her outburst, and asks more sedately, "You know my Patrick?"

"Not as well as I hope to," Jonathan answers. "We've met, but it was in a formal business setting. Patrick probably remembers the occasion as one where he was stuck with listening to the boss make a speech. Our meeting meant much more to me, but, of course, he couldn't have known that." Meant more to Jonathan Kingsley than to Patrick? Lynn marvels, but he gives her no chance to consider why that might be. "I'm surprised he didn't travel here with you, Lynn," he says.

"He couldn't get away from work at Atlantic. Too busy. You have, or I guess I should say you *had*, a conscientious employee in Patrick."

"Ah yes, I know that much about your husband, Lynn."

"As a matter of fact, though, he may be here in Madeira now," she announces. "He flew into Lisbon this morning. I'm not sure of his arrival time in Funchal. He had to settle for standby status for a connecting flight over to the island."

Jonathan looks delighted by that information. "We'll get to talk to Patrick too, Natalie," he enthuses. "Isn't that good news?"

"Yes it is, sweetheart," Natalie agrees, "but you'd better get to the point before we drive Lynn batty." She gives Lynn's hand a supportive squeeze.

Jonathan nods and absently reaches for his drink but finds no fortifying *poncha* remaining in the empty glass. He takes a deep breath and begins. "Lynn, I'm sure you and Patrick had to be completely mystified when five million dollars inexplicably showed up in your bank account. It was I who sent it to you. I expected that you would first think that your bank must have made a drastic mistake. But I hoped, once you determined the money was actually yours, you would be satisfied to enjoy it without being overly concerned about its source. With 20-20 hindsight I see the folly of that expectation in your case as in David's. I do regret the confusion and disruption of your lives that I caused you and Patrick by trying to remain nameless. On the other hand, it has had the happy result of bringing you here."

"And Patrick," Natalie interjects.

"And Patrick," Jonathan echoes. "As in David's case, I acted as I did to keep from breaking a promise. With David I tried to honor my pledge to Monica to conceal the fact of her illness. With you, Lynn, I was trying to honor another vow of secrecy, an oath I made to your mother some thirty-seven years ago."

Lynn is not certain she heard correctly. "My mother?"

"Yes."

"Donna Gallagher?"

Jonathan nods. "Yes. She was still Donna Ryan then. She and Michael married a short time later," he says. Lynn stares at him, befuddled. The expression on his face, like the tone of his words, is solemn. She turns to Natalie, whose perfect features now reflect concern, an almost sisterly sympathy. David's expression is expectant. Monica's confusion approaches Lynn's own.

"Michael?" Lynn manages to ask. "Michael Gallagher? My father?"

Jonathan rises from his chair and drops to his knees before Lynn. Natalie puts an arm around Lynn's shoulder. Jonathan reaches for Lynn's hands. "Michael Gallagher is a good man," he says. "He loves your mother, and he loves you. He raised you as his daughter and has done everything in his power for you and your mother, but he is not your biological father, Lynn. I am your father."

Lynn shrinks back from Jonathan, shaking her head, rejecting his words but dazed by them. The room begins to dissolve into an otherworldly blending of bright sunlight, dark secrets, strange faces with printed words floating from them like balloons, shifting, twisting, distorted words forming outrageous sentences. She feels faint and fears falling to the floor. But she doesn't faint. Her inner voice stops her. "He is lying," it says. "Michael Gallagher is your father. Not Jonathan Kingsley." Nor does the room dissolve. The faces in it drift back into focus. The disembodied words disappear into the mouths of their speakers and re-emerge as sounds.

"Lynn, are you all right?" she hears. David's voice.

"Lynn is your daughter, Granddad? She's mom's sister? My aunt?" Monica's voice, disturbed and disbelieving.

"On second thought he must not be lying. He must believe it. He sent you all that money. He is just mistaken. Jonathan Kingsley, your father! Don't make me laugh." Her own inner voice again.

Natalie is holding a glass of water to Lynn's lips. She drinks some of it. "Thank you," she breathes.

David kneels where Jonathan had been. Jonathan is back in his chair, watching Lynn, his face etched in concern, his voice responding to his granddaughter. "Yes, Monica, Lynn is my daughter, your mother's half-sister, your half-aunt, I suppose, if there is such a label for your relationship."

"I'm all right now, David," Lynn says. He returns to his seat. Natalie also sits, again beside Lynn, the water glass in her hand. She offers it to Lynn, who drinks the rest of the water and straightens up, sits erect, nearly herself again.

"You must be mis . . ." Lynn stops; starts over. "Can you be mistaken?" she asks Jonathan, adding no form of direct address, instinctively deciding she can't call him Mr. Kingsley, which he does not want, or Jonathan, as Natalie invited, which now feels even more uncomfortable than it did earlier, and she would surely choke on *father* or *dad*.

"No, dear," Jonathan answers. I'm not mistaken."

"I think you can explain it all now, sweetheart," Natalie says.

"May I?" he asks Lynn.

"Please," she answers, an automatic childlike please and thank you response, while her overwrought brain vaguely ponders what more there could possibly be and is not at all sure she should hear whatever it is.

"Angel?" Jonathan asks Monica, who is staring at Lynn, studying her features, searching for family resemblances but

-215-

finding nothing definitive. Lynn's eyes are hazel, not blue like Kimberly's or Jonathan's; not dark brown like her own. Lynn's hair matches nobody's in the family. Her features suggest no shared genes. She is not tall like Jonathan or Monica, although close in height to Kimberly.

"Yes, Granddad, I wish you would tell us everything," Monica replies. "Please," she adds.

Jonathan stands and walks to a window. He gazes across the valley and back through time and speaks without turning. "Donna Ryan worked for me at Atlantic Glass in the early years of my business. She did our office work, kept our books, wrote my letters. There were no other clerical or administrative employees yet, just Donna and me in the office. She was very intelligent and efficient, but, more than that, she understood what I was trying to accomplish. She saw how hard I struggled to build the company, and she worked right along with me. When everyone in the plant went home at the end of the day, Donna stayed. We put in many, many long hours together, and we grew close, fond of each other."

He turns to Lynn. "You look a lot like your mother did then, Lynn. She was young and very pretty." He sighs. "Anyway, one night we made love. Just that once, but Donna became pregnant. I was already married. Kimberly was a baby." Jonathan looks at his granddaughter. "I truly loved your grandmother, Monica. I had no intention of leaving her." He turns back to Lynn. "Nor did Donna expect or wish me to do that. The last thing in the world she wanted to do was break up my happy marriage and ruin all our lives. I think just about every state in the union outlawed abortion by the 1970's, but even had that option been as available as it is today, Donna would not for a minute have considered aborting her baby, our baby. Neither would she scandalize her religious parents by bearing a child out of wedlock. Nor could she face enduring the burdens of single motherhood.

"I told her I would not abandon her. The dilemma was ours, not hers alone. I offered to provide financial support for your upbringing, Lynn, give Donna money regularly for expenses, or, if she preferred, I would tell my wife what I had done. I knew that would hurt Roberta, of course, but I was sure our marriage could withstand my single infidelity, and perhaps Roberta would even have agreed to our adopting the baby. But your mother would have none of that.

"Michael Gallagher was already Donna's steady boyfriend. I knew he was a fine man and would be good for her. Of course he was unaware of her indiscretion with me. She told him she was pregnant. Michael was in love with her, and, assuming that you were *his* baby, Lynn, he proposed marriage. Donna was sure he soon would propose and she accept in any case. They married within weeks. And in all the years since, she never told her husband or you that you were another man's child.

"Before she left work at Atlantic, which was almost right away, Donna pleaded with me to keep her secret. She insisted I promise never to tell anyone I was your father. She said I owed her that much. I believed I owed her much more, but all she asked was that I allow her and Michael to make their own way, raising you as they saw fit without my interfering in your lives. I promised to do as she wished. And for thirty-seven years, I honored that commitment. I held my silence. It wasn't easy, Lynn. More and more often through the years I've regretted ever making that promise.

"I knew, however, that Michael was always devoted to you as well as to your mother. When you married, I made it my business to be certain your husband was also deserving of you and good to your children, and I know he always has been. You see, with both Michael and Patrick working at Atlantic Glass, it was easy for me to keep tabs on your family. I know you've been happy. But it never seemed fair or right to me that you couldn't benefit from my financial success. I've become very wealthy since I made that long ago promise to your mother to keep our secret. My money has enabled me to do a lot of things for my daughter Kimberly through the years, and for Monica as well. Nothing has been more gratifying to me. I've always been happy that I had the means to help my family. But you're just as surely my daughter as

Kimberly is, and I've never reached out to you at all. That has troubled me for a long time.

"When Monica's illness struck and I learned that David can make her well, I hurried to provide the money he needs to complete his work. Yet I found that my fervor to help Monica, as honorable an emotion as it was, further intensified my guilt at forsaking you all these years.

"Also, I continued to keep my unacknowledged daughter a secret from Natalie, which added to my distress. Natalie and I have always been open and trusting with each other. I was living a lie by keeping this from her. So when I told her about sending David ten million dollars on Monica's behalf, I broke my promise to your mother and told Natalie about you. To my mind, being worthy of Natalie's trust outweighs my aged promise. In addition, and I don't think this is mere rationalization on my part, I can't believe that your mother, that good woman who loves you and wants the best for you, would still hold me to it at the cost of denying you what is nothing more than your birthright." He pauses, affording everyone a chance to absorb his impassioned rationale.

"Jonathan," Natalie says, lifting a momentary silence, "I would like to tell Lynn about our conversation that night."

"Good," Jonathan replies. "I think I've said quite enough."

"Lynn," Natalie begins, "I was aware for a long time that something was tormenting Jonathan, something very important to him. I didn't want to ask him what was wrong. I thought that eventually he would confide in me. So when he finally told me about you and his pledge to your mother, I was not nearly as shocked as you are today. In truth what I felt was relief. I was afraid he had been hiding a medical condition, something seriously wrong with his health, to keep from burdening me with knowledge of it. So to learn of your birth, rather than perhaps of Jonathan's impending death or disability, was nothing short of joyous for me.

"He and I dined alone at the villa the night he told me. It was the Saturday I arrived in Madeira and learned of Monica's illness. That news upset me terribly, but Jonathan explained what he knew of David's work and its promise of a cure for her. I had a relaxing afternoon at the pool. I had weeks of leisure ahead. I believed Monica would be well again, and I looked forward to a quiet dinner with Jonathan. He cooked. Osso buco, my favorite. We shared a delicious Barbera. It was a lovely evening. I was feeling mellow, but Jonathan was troubled. Then after dinner he told me his secret.

"And as I've said, I was relieved to learn about you, Lynn. But only momentarily. When I realized Jonathan was telling me he had never done anything material for you throughout your whole life, I was appalled. 'Jonathan,' I said, 'you're talking about your biological daughter. Blood of your blood! Flesh of your flesh! You've neglected her since she was a baby? How could you? No wonder you were distraught. You must make amends right now.' Of course he was eager to do it, so we concocted our plot to send you money anonymously, just as he was about to do for David. Jonathan's money, but our joint plot, really." Natalie stops talking, smiles at Lynn, and shrugs.

Lynn realizes she has been given a cue to say something. But what? She had been amazed to see Jonathan and Natalie waiting to greet David and her at the *pousada's* front door. She had been surprised when Jonathan said he knew Patrick; astonished that he kept informed about her and her family without any of them ever suspecting he even knew they existed. That he and her mother had once . . . had once . . . She cannot imagine it. Her mother! And that Jonathan is her biological father is beyond belief. And yet . . . and yet . . .

"Are you all right, Lynn?" Natalie asks.

Lynn remains mute, lost in her thoughts. Emerging from . . . from whatever she has just experienced: shock, emotional overload, she is no longer completely disbelieving. The gradually subsiding numbness in her brain is gone, and her thoughts are now sorting through the implications of what she has been told. She nods in response to Natalie's question. Yes, she is all right, she supposes, except for the fact that the foundations of her world have been shaken; except that her life has been a fiction; except that her mother . . . Oh, her poor mother! And her innocent, unknowing father! How terribly this will hurt him when she tells him. And she must tell her mother and father. Her father . . . but Jonathan Kingsley is her father. She shakes her head. "Michael Gallagher will always be my father," she says aloud.

"Of course he will," Jonathan gently assures her.

"Let me ask you, Lynn," Natalie says after a moment, "has your dad ever said or done anything that would indicate he is not actually your father?"

"No, never."

"I just wondered if your mother really kept it secret from him all these years. Apparently she did. When you received the money, whom did you tell about it?"

Lynn reflects. "My boss first, but at that point I was sure I got the money by mistake. Then I told Patrick. His sister Theresa . . ."

"Your parents?"

"Oh yes, I had to tell my parents."

"How did they react?"

"My dad was sure it was a mistake, but when I told my mom and him that all the banking officials I had talked with said the deposit was genuine, he was excited despite his caution. He hoped they would prove to be correct. He wanted it to be mine, I'm certain."

"No indication he knew the source of the money?" Natalie asks.

"No. None at all."

"And your mother?"

Lynn licks her lips. She slides the lower one to the left and grips the right half of it in her teeth. She looks upward and inward, recalling the scene. Unconsciously, her head begins to nod. Yes, she realizes, it was the memory of her mother's reaction that first gave possible credence to Jonathan's claim just moments ago; her mother's odd behavior on learning of Lynn's financial windfall that allowed her to begin considering the possibility that Jonathan might actually be her father.

Donna had not been pleased to hear of Lynn's good fortune. She had been peculiarly cool about her daughter's news, had seemed frightened by it, had appeared to be on the verge of fainting at one point. She did not want Lynn to pursue the matter. That much had been clear. Lynn had not understood her mother's peculiar attitude and puzzled over it afterward.

"Your mother didn't want to hear about it?" Natalie prompts now.

"That was how it seemed."

"Or think you should investigate its source?"

"No."

"Or come to Madeira?"

"Especially that," Lynn concedes.

"She knows Jonathan lives here," Natalie posits.

"I don't know. Maybe."

"She was afraid you would find him, and her secret would be exposed after all this time."

"How she must have worried through the years, trying to keep it from my father, from me, never knowing if Jonathan might contact us or that someone else would learn of it because of Jonathan's prestige, or yours, Natalie," Lynn muses aloud, surprised by her own words.

"It must have upset her all over again to learn Patrick was following you to Madeira," Natalie adds.

"Patrick!" Lynn exclaims. "Oh God, I wish he were here!"

Suddenly the *pousada's* front door flies open and crashes against the wall behind it. Four men thump through the hall. Lynn recognizes Mohamad and Bhatia before she spots Patrick. The fourth man, a stranger, waves a handgun and shouts, "Nobody move!" He shoves Patrick into the sitting room. In handcuffs!

Chapter 20

Patrick stumbles into Lynn's arms. Jonathan and David leap up to help her steady him. Monica screams. Natalie jumps into a martial arts defensive stance.

"Patrick, Patrick," Lynn gasps, "I'm so glad to see you. Why are you handcuffed?" She smothers him with kisses. Mohamad looks quickly at David to see his reaction to the kisses his lover is bestowing upon her husband. Kubasik merely smiles. He is a cool one, Mohamad thinks.

"Hello, Miss, uh, Mrs. O'Brien, Dr. Kubasik," Bhatia says.

"I seem to be under arrest," Patrick answers Lynn.

"For what?"

"Oh, just suspicion of treason, conspiracy, stuff like that. It has something to do with you."

"Nordin, look," Bhatia whispers, "It is Natalie Forthright."

"I see, Rhali."

"Me?" Lynn asks Patrick.

Patrick shrugs.

"We are pleased to meet you, Miss Forthright," the Telámian agents say together.

"Your husband is in my custody," Saber tells Lynn. "So are

the rest of you," he announces. "Everybody stay calm. Mohamad, Bhatia, frisk 'em!"

"What is the meaning of this?" Jonathan demands. "Who are you?"

"Benjamin Saber, United States Central Intelligence Agency," the CIA man replies. "Agents Mohamad and Bhatia are assisting me."

Natalie abandons her karate position. She sits and crosses her legs. Mohamad pats down David. Bhatia swiftly checks Jonathan and moves toward Natalie. She stands, raises her arms above her head and does a little shimmy. Bhatia beams expectantly. Mohamad blushes.

"Never mind the women," Saber growls. Natalie giggles as she sits back down and recrosses her legs.

"Assisting you with what?" Jonathan asks Saber.

"With my investigation of a conspiracy to commit treason against the United States of America," Saber replies. "Are they clean?" he asks Mohamad and Bhatia.

"Clean?" Bhatia asks.

"Weapons, Rhali. Clean, as they say in movies," Mohamad explains. "They have no weapons," he tells Saber.

"No weapons," Bhatia seconds. Saber holsters his handgun and displays his CIA shield. Jonathan examines it closely.

"Mohamad, you and Bhatia are agents of the CIA?" David asks.
"Temporary agents," Saber clarifies.

"We thought you returned to Ractá," Lynn says.

"We deceived you in that regard," Mohamad confesses apologetically.

"But you do work for General Aláz?" David inquires.

"Yes," Mohamad replies.

"Did." Saber corrects him.

"We worked for the general, and we will again," Mohamad explains. "Right now we work for Mr., uh, Agent Saber."

"What exactly is Patrick O'Brien accused of in this alleged conspiracy of yours?" Jonathan asks.

"I'll ask the questions here," Saber says, but then he answers, "O'Brien and his wife received money from General Aláz. So did David Kubasik. You want to tell me why, Kubasik?"

"I didn't get money from General Aláz," David objects.

Lynn supposes that is still true. Maybe the general didn't send David's second ten million yet. Even if he did, David can't know that for certain. "Patrick and I didn't either," she says.

"You didn't meet with Aláz at his presidential palace in Ractá?" Saber sneers. Lynn wishes no one would discuss the general's palace. She can't look at Patrick.

"Well yes, we met with the general," David admits.

"You and Mrs. O'Brien?"

Lynn prays that nobody will introduce the subject of sleeping arrangements at the palace. Fortunately no one does, but she fears she has not heard the last of the subject from Patrick.

"Yes, but . . ." David answers.

Saber interrupts. "You didn't get five million dollars?" he asks Lynn.

"Well yes, Patrick and I got five million dollars, but not . . ."

"And you got ten million, Kubasik?"

"Yes, but we didn't get the money from General Aláz."

"Right. You and the lady just stopped by to give the general your regards before skipping back over to Madeira to buy yourselves a little love nest."

"What?" Lynn, David, Jonathan, Natalie and Monica all ask. Patrick has heard Saber's love nest notion before.

"The villa you were looking for in Garajau with the real estate lady," Saber clarifies.

"Agent Saber," Bhatia interjects, "you may recall that Miss, uh, Mrs. O'Brien and Dr. Kubasik did not exactly stop by to visit the general as you characterize it. Nordin and I took them there after abducting them."

"I know that," Saber snaps. "Why did the general order you abducted?" he asks David.

"He wanted to talk with us," David tries.

"Why didn't he just call you on the telephone?"

Lynn answers. "He doesn't trust the security of his telephones."

Saber laughs. "Well, he's got that right." Mohamad and Bhatia exchange worried glances, each wondering what he might have been overheard saying on those telephones. "So why did he want to talk with you, Kubasik?"

"I can't tell you that."

"Uh-huh. How about you, Mrs. O'Brien. Why did the general want to see you?"

"Actually, he didn't want to see me at all. I was along because Mohamad and Bhatia couldn't leave me standing screaming in the street."

"What?"

"When they abducted David."

"That is an accurate portrayal of events," Mohamad volunteers. Saber glares at him and shakes his head, looking pained.

"I explained that, Saber," Patrick says. "And, as to Garajau, Lynn and Kubasik were there trying to find Mr. Kingsley."

Saber ignores him. "So Aláz only wanted to see Kubasik?" he asks Lynn.

"Yes," she affirms.

"But he talked to you together?"

"Yes."

"About what?"

"I can't say," Lynn answers.

"Why not?"

"He swore us to secrecy."

"I'll bet he did."

"You were actually abducted, Lynn?" Natalie asks. Lynn nods. "How exciting! Why didn't you tell us?"

"We promised not to talk about it."

"This is ludicrous," Jonathan interrupts. "Lynn and David did not get their money from General Aláz. They got it from me."

"Aha. And you got it from the general."

"I did not."

"Do you deny you are the Madeira connection in Aláz's plot?"

"Madeira connection, indeed! What is this plot you keep alluding to?"

"I'll ask the questions here," Saber says again. "*You* tell *me*, Kingsley. Is it nuclear weapons? Missile delivery systems? Oil price manipulation? What *are* you and Aláz cooking up?"

"You must be mad. I know you're wrong about Lynn and Patrick and David. And I would bet you're mistaken about General Aláz as well," Jonathan objects.

"So you do know Aláz."

"I know he is trying to improve his country's economy and the welfare of the Telámian people."

"Or his own," Saber retorts. "And maybe yours."

"Jonathan doesn't need this general's money," Natalie declares.

"What are you, some kind of misguided tinsel town do-gooder siding with these third world zealots at the expense of the U.S. of A., missy?"

Natalie gives him the finger. "Let me see if I've got this straight, Saber," she says. "You've got Patrick in handcuffs because Lynn found five million dollars in their bank account. You think this General Aláz is the source of that money and of David's ten million. To earn it we all deal in military weapons or conspire to destabilize the world's oil supply. Is that about the sum of your delusion?"

"You got it," Saber growls.

"Would you like to know the real reason why Lynn got her money?"

"You talk. I'll listen."

"Do you want to tell him, Lynn?" Natalie asks.

Lynn turns to Patrick, whose eyes widen in anticipation of learning the truth himself about their money. She looks at Jonathan, whose shrug tells her it's all right with him. "Sure. Why not?" Lynn answers. "My father sent me the money."

"Your father? Didn't Kingsley just say he sent it to you?"

"What are you saying, Lynn?" Patrick yells. "You're only going to get us in deeper here. Tell him the truth."

"That is the truth, Patrick."

"You mean Mr. Kingsley is your father? But . . ."

Saber laughs. "You people should get your stories straight. Your own husband doesn't know your father? Come on! You might want to take his advice and be straight with me."

"I *am* Lynn's father," Jonathan says. "She didn't know it until today."

"Phhhh," Saber scoffs, "and I suppose David Kubasik is your

long lost son."

"No, David is a research scientist."

"Oho, the technical advisor. What's your field, Kubasik?"

"Mitochondrial diseases. Specifically Gunsenhouser's Optic Atrophy."

"What?"

"It's a serious eye disease."

"Monica, Jonathan, should David explain why he's here?" Natalie asks.

"I don't like it," Monica says.

"Who are you anyway, miss?" Saber asks.

"Monica Mancini. I'm Mr. Kingsley's granddaughter."

"Oh, and did you just find that out?"

"That's uncalled for, Saber," Jonathan protests. "Monica is my granddaughter. She's staying with Natalie and me at my villa."

"All right," Monica says, "if it will help clear all this up, I'll explain it myself, provided you agree not to tell anyone else."

Saber shakes his head in disbelief at this good looking young chick's cheeky caveat. "Yeah, like the judge, for example. You kidding me? I'm not promising anything."

"It won't matter, Monica," Jonathan says. "Once we clear up this confusion, he'll have no reason to take it further." Monica considers briefly. She meets David's eye. They exchange smiles. He nods.

"I'm a victim of Gunsenhouser's," Monica reveals. "David's research promises a cure for my disease. He needed ten million dollars to complete his work. My wonderful grandfather sent him the money so David can perfect his cure and save my vision."

Saber considers momentarily what Monica has said, but he rejects it with a slight shake of his head and an obstinate scowl. "So Kingsley, you gave Kubasik ten million to save your granddaughter. What about your daughter, Mrs. O'Brien here? Why did you send *her* money, and how come she didn't know you're her father?"

Patrick is even more eager than Saber to hear the answers to those questions.

"Before Lynn was born I promised her mother I wouldn't tell Lynn or anyone else that I'm her father," Jonathan explains. "Until today she thought her mother's husband is her father. And I sent the money because I've ignored Lynn for too long, and I wanted to make up for it."

Patrick jumps in as Jonathan finishes. "Look, Saber, you're getting into a lot of personal information that's none of your business." Saber glares at him, but in looking his way sees that Mohamad and Bhatia agree with Patrick. The CIA man begins to feel alone out on his limb. "A check with Mr. Kingsley's bank will prove he sent the money," Patrick continues. "You can verify David Kubasik's work."

"Yeah, I can do that, and I will. What I haven't heard any skinny on is the visit to General Aláz. I know Mohamad and Bhatia took you and Mrs. O'Brien there, Kubasik. I think the money you got came from the general. Mohamad and Bhatia also believe that's so. I want to know why Aláz thought it was so urgent to meet with you that he sent two of his men to grab you, paid for their flights to and from the States, covered their expenses for the past couple of weeks, and even ate the cost of sending his personal jet back and forth between Madeira and Ractá."

"Also to Lisbon," Bhatia adds.

"What?" Saber asks.

"He also sent his plane to Lisbon. We were first supposed to capture. . ."

Mohamad, looking as if he would like to choke his associate, interrupts. "When we were unable to capture Dr. Kubasik in Lisbon, we flew to Funchal in the general's plane."

Natalie speaks up. "Saber, I think you've heard enough to be able to figure out why your general had to see David."

"Is that right? Well, maybe I missed something, or then again maybe you have information I don't have."

"You've heard everything I've heard. I just see more mystery movies than you do. The plot here doesn't seem all that complicated. Think about it! Monica has this disease she wants kept secret. So her grandfather sends David the money he needs to cure her, but he sends it anonymously.

"Your General Aláz also needs to see David. He doesn't want anybody to know about it either. So he has David abducted and swears him to secrecy about their conversation. The elements are essentially the same in both instances. Except we know Monica's secret, and we don't know the general's. Now, you tell me, Saber, what do you think he's trying to hide?"

Mohamad and Bhatia quickly turn to each other. "Nordin," Bhatia whispers, is it possible the general has . . .?

Mohamad's warning grimace stops him dead. "Don't say it! Don't even think it! We know nothing," Mohamad cautions.

At the same time, Saber checks Lynn's reaction and then David's. Lynn is sure he reads the truth in her eyes as well as in David's. Saber says nothing to acknowledge that Natalie has deduced the fact of the matter, but everyone can see his screws are dead in the water.

"Are we finished here?" Jonathan asks.

"Not quite," Saber answers. "I got the gist of your theory, Miss Forthright," he says, somewhat more respectful of the movie star than he formerly was, "but I've heard a lot of tall tales here. Without some kind of proof, it's all just talk. First off, Mrs. O'Brien, do you want to tell us now why these two men abducted you and Kubasik?"

"I told you why they took me," Lynn says.

"Yeah, right, standing screaming in the street. What about you, Kubasik?"

"I can't say, but I think you know," David answers.

Jonathan takes control. "You're perfectly welcome to check whatever you want, Agent Saber," he says. "I'll give you my banker's name and number. You can verify my wire transfers to both Lynn and David. And you can look into anything else you care to. But I'm afraid we're finished here."

"Is that so? I think I'll decide when we're finished."

Jonathan sighs. "I can call Langley if you like. Maybe we should see what the director has to say about all this."

Saber can't resist laughing at that, considering what he himself has to go through to talk to the guy one rank above his own. Get through to the director? What a joke! The president himself waits on hold to do that. "You're talking about the Director of Central Intelligence?"

"Yes. Why don't *you* dial, so you can be sure I'm not calling somebody else?"

"My pleasure." Saber follows Jonathan into the bar room. The others trail behind them. Jonathan picks up the phone; hands it to the CIA agent.

"Just tell them Jonathan Kingsley is calling."

Saber grins and dials. "The director, please," he says. "Jonathan Kingsley calling."

His grin vanishes. "She's ringing somebody," he says. He waits. His smug expression reappears. "He's not in," he tells Jonathan. But the smirk flees his lips as quickly as it formed. "She wants to know if you'll talk with the deputy director."

"That will be fine," Jonathan says.

"That will be fine," Saber repeats, and almost immediately his face collapses in panic. "No, sir, this is Agent Benjamin Saber," he says. "Yes, sir, yes, Mr. Kingsley is right here." He hands Jonathan the phone.

"John, how are you?" Jonathan asks. "Yes, I asked for George. Mm-hmm, he's out of town. Certainly you can. Here's the situation." Jonathan describes the afternoon's encounter in some detail; listens briefly to his listener's response. "Yes, it's just been a huge misunderstanding. Certainly. All right," he says. "Nice talking with you, John. How's the family?" He listens again before adding, "Good, good, glad to hear it. Give George my regards too, will you? And thanks for your help." He holds out the phone to Saber. "He wants to talk to you."

"Yes, sir. Saber, Benjamin. Yes, sir. Uh, Rácta, sir. R-A-C-T-A. Yes, sir, the capital of Telám. Five years, sir. Twenty in the region." He listens, his body turned away from the group to muffle his conversation as best he can. "Yes, sir. No, sir. All right. I understand. Yes, I'll return to my regular post right away. Thank you, sir."

Saber returns the phone to Jonathan, happy to get away from it himself. "Yes, John?" Jonathan asks. "Of course," he replies. "We're still living at the villa. Can you stop by again this year?" Jonathan listens; smiles and nods his head at what he has been told. "That's absolutely true: Christmas week and New Year's Eve are great fun here. But don't even bother looking for hotel rooms in Funchal this late in the year. The town will be full. Stay with us at the villa. You're always welcome, John. George, A.B. and the wives as well. Wonderful! Yes, talk to them. I hope you all can make it. What's that? No, right now we're up in the mountains at a *pousada*. Natalie is with me. Right. My daughter and granddaughter, too. Also a friend of the family. Okay, John. Call me when you firm up your vacation plans. And thanks again for your help here. Goodbye."

Chapter 21

Lynn awakes on Monday morning and reaches for Patrick, but she finds only pillows on his side of the bed. A soft breeze off the Atlantic Ocean wafts into their guest room on the top floor of Jonathan's villa. It is cool and carries a light scent lifted from the gardens below. Lynn sniffs and purrs. Sweet. Exotic. Jasmine, she thinks.

The clock tells her reluctantly opening eyes that the time is 7:45 a.m. She doesn't care. The morning is glorious. She can linger in bed if she wants to. No work today. No kids to get off to school. Patrick is already up and out. She stretches and yawns luxuriantly but soon slips into a bathrobe Natalie has given her and pads barefoot across the silk-carpeted floor to a window. There is Patrick in the pool, swimming laps with Jonathan as he has done each of the past three mornings.

Everyone had left the *pousada* on Thursday shortly after Jonathan and Ben Saber finished their phone conversation with the CIA's deputy director. Saber had hastened to remove Patrick's handcuffs, expressed regret for the way he had been treated, and, finally, apologized to everyone for his unfounded suspicions about them. He asked to speak with Mohamad and Bhatia alone for a moment before he returned to Funchal. The Telámian agents followed him outside to his car, hoping they would not be asked to return the $25,000 each that Saber had already paid them. They fully expected that he would want his money back.

To their surprise the first thing the CIA man said was, "You can keep the money." Bhatia did a little dance in the *pousada's* parking lot, chanting, "Thank you, thank you, thank you."

Mohamad could not help laughing at Bhatia's antics, but in his experience money was not so easily earned. "You said we could keep the money regardless of the outcome of our investigation," he said. "You are a man of your word, Agent Saber. I add my thanks to Rhali's more demonstrative expression of his."

"You realize I want something more from you," Saber said.

"Well, we have actually done very little to earn the money, and the whole affair proved to be a colossal misunderstanding, so . . ."

"I want your pledge of silence about all this. No mention of CIA interest in General Aláz. You keep what we think we've learned about the general to yourselves. You make no attempt to expose my informer at the palace. If we ever meet, you act as if you don't know who I am. In total, you conduct yourselves just as you would have if we had never met."

"Rhali?" Mohamad asks.

"Who is this stranger talking with us?" Bhatia questions in reply.

"Our lips are sealed," Mohamad says. "We will go back to Ractá and simply report that Kubasik has returned to the United States. That fulfills our mission, after all."

"Good. Just make sure he leaves before you do."

"I don't suppose you would like to ride home with us in the general's jet?" Mohamad asks with a grin.

"That would be about all I need after this fiasco. No, thanks. I'll manage."

"Nordin," Bhatia says as Saber drives off, "maybe Dr. Kubasik won't leave the island right away, and we can get a few more days here."

"I hope so, but I thought you were in a hurry to go home."

"Why is that?"

"Women," you said.

Bhatia shrugs. "Ah yes, poor creatures. They surely pine for me, but they will just have to wait a little longer. And what of the pretty little serving girl at General Aláz's palace who has eyes for you?" He blinks in a hilarious parody of a moonstruck lover.

"She too must wait," Mohamad says when he stops laughing long enough to speak. He puts his massive arm over Bhatia's shoulders. "Come, my friend," he says. "Let's find out what the Americans plan to do."

The group had reconvened in the *pousada's* sitting room. Jonathan was speaking, but he stopped when Mohamad and Bhatia entered.

"Pardon our interruption," Mohamad said. "We wish to add our apologies to those of Agent Saber. We are most happy that you are not guilty of any wrongdoing. Truthfully, neither of us believed you were, did we, Rhali?"

"No. We have come to know you, Mrs. O'Brien, and you, Dr. Kubasik. You are not criminals. No doubt all of you here are upright, respectable persons," Bhatia granted.

"Thank you," Lynn said. David stood and shook their former abductors' hands. "No hard feelings," he added. "You had your orders, and you carried them out with as little inconvenience to us as possible under the circumstances."

"You are most gracious, Dr. Kubasik," Mohamad said. "In fact, though, our mission is not completed. We are required to continue following you until you return to the United States."

"Of course. I should have realized the general would want

your assurance that I've returned to work. Yes, and I must do so right away."

"Hold on a minute, David," Jonathan said. "I was just getting to that." He went on to invite David, Lynn and Patrick to spend a few days with Natalie, Monica, and himself at his villa. David thought he should leave for the States immediately, but he agreed with Jonathan that remaining in Madeira for the weekend would cause his research little additional delay.

Lynn watched Monica and David exchange smiles at his decision to stay. Wondering if Natalie observed it also, she turned to the actress and was rewarded by a conspiratorial wink. Natalie knew what was going on.

Lynn and Patrick welcomed Jonathan's invitation. Both wanted an opportunity to talk further with him, and a holiday on Madeira at his fabulous home sounded idyllic. They knew Theresa would not object to housing Kerry and Sean for a few more days.

When a conversation about the logistics of hotel checkouts and return flights to the U.S. threatened to bog down in tedious detail, Natalie stepped in to solve everything. "I'm flying to L.A. on Monday in a chartered jet with plenty of room for all of us," she announced. "Forget about taking scheduled airlines. We'll all enjoy the weekend together and leave from *Aeroporta da Madeira* at four o'clock Monday afternoon. I'll drop David in Newark and Lynn and Patrick at, um, I guess Atlantic City is closest to home for you?"

"It is," Patrick said, "but my car is in Newark."

"Easier yet," Natalie said. "Just one stop." She suggested that everyone go together to the Hotel Savoy, check out, and drive to the villa.

Natalie promised the Telámians she would give each of them autographed photos on Monday at the airport, where they would be on hand to witness David's departure.

Jonathan called ahead to his chef Maria, arranging dinner for six at his villa. He also asked her to have Carlos or Joán pick them up at the Hotel Savoy. Finally, he and Natalie packed their bags, stashed them in the trunk of David's rented Passat, and rode with him and Monica. Lynn and Patrick made the trip down from the mountains with Mohamad and Bhatia in their rental Mercedes.

Late Thursday night Lynn called Theresa from Jonathan's villa. As usual at the Conlin home, Molly answered the phone. "Hi, Aunt Lynn," she said. "I've got one for you. Oh, wait, you're still in Madeira, aren't you?"

"I am, Molly, but I've got one for you this time."

"Oh, good! Danny is here too. Can we both try to guess?"

"Sure. I had dinner a few nights ago at a restaurant here in Madeira, the Cliff Villa. What movie stars' photographs are on the wall there?"

"Whose photos are on the wall of a restaurant way over in Madeira? Come on, Aunt Lynn! That's not a fair question. How are we supposed to know that?"

"Now wait, Molly. Just think about it. What movie actress do you know is in Madeira?"

"Natalie Forthright! You didn't get to meet her, though, did you?"

"I did. She's here with me now. Would you like to speak with her?"

Lynn jerked the phone away from her ear as her niece shrieked. "Danny, Aunt Lynn is with Natalie Forthright! She's putting her on the phone!"

"No way!" Lynn heard her nephew's changing voice shout, cracking as it slipped from his developing baritone to his childlike tenor.

Natalie took the phone. "Hi, Molly," she said.

"Omigod, you're really Natalie Forthright! In person! Talking to me! I don't believe it!"

"Your aunt tells me you and your brother are into movie trivia."

"Uh-huh."

"I've got one for you," Natalie said.

"Danny, Natalie Forthright has a movie trivia question for me!"

"I've got one for Danny, too, but you first. I'll give you a clue about who was in one of the other photographs."

"At that restaurant?"

"Yes."

"Okay."

"It's a man. He co-starred in *Erin Brockovich*."

"Albert Finney?"

"That's right, Molly. Good work."

"That was awful easy, Miss Forthright. You're just being nice, but thanks. I'll bet you could stump us if you wanted. Shall I put my brother on?"

"All right. I enjoyed talking to you," Natalie said.

"Thanks, Miss Forthright. I loved it! Good luck with *Alpine*

Playground. Here's Danny."

Lynn's nephew got Roger Moore on his second attempt at identifying the last of the Cliff Villa photos. He first named Sean Connery. His clue from Natalie was that the actor in question was one of the men who had starred in James Bond movies.

Lynn spoke with Theresa. "We're at Jonathan Kingsley's villa for the weekend. Uh-huh, with Natalie. I'll explain it all when I see you. Is it all right if the kids stay with you for a few more days? Thanks, Theresa. We'll be home late Monday night. If you'll get them out on Monday and Tuesday, we'll pick them up Tuesday afternoon after school. We're going to stop to see my mom and dad Tuesday morning. How about meeting us for lunch at the Anchorage? Our Treat. Um, about noon? Fine. See you then. Yes, and tell you everything. Thanks again, Theresa." Lynn and Patrick each spoke briefly with Kerry and Sean, both of whom had to say hello to Natalie to verify their cousins' claim that they had spoken with her.

Jonathan was present throughout the entire call, and, although he had chuckled as Natalie conversed with Molly and Danny, Lynn saw him hang his head and sigh when Patrick talked with Kerry and Sean. She realized he wanted to hear his grandchildren's voices.

"Jonathan," Lynn said, becoming accustomed to addressing him in that manner, "we'll call you from home Tuesday evening. Kerry and Sean will want to talk with their grandfather, but Patrick and I must tell Mom about you first."

Jonathan nodded and smiled. "Of course. That will be wonderful. Tuesday then. By the way, Lynn," he added, "you seem to have enjoyed dinner at the Cliff Villa?"

"Yes, it's in such a beautiful setting, don't you think?"

"It is, but at night you can't really appreciate the view of the harbor."

Lynn beamed. "When David and I were there, I thought the very thing and wished we could be there for lunch instead."

"How about we do that: all have lunch there on Monday before you fly home with Natalie?"

"That would be perfect," Lynn said. Natalie, David, and Monica all endorsed the idea. Patrick smiled politely. His glance told Lynn he would go along with the group without objection, while it also managed to convey his preference not to visit the sites of her dining escapades with David.

The weekend at Jonathan's villa was delightful. Lynn was especially glad that Patrick and Jonathan hit it off really well. Openly eager to learn everything he could about Lynn and her family, Jonathan was by her side or Patrick's constantly, doing his utmost to absorb a lifetime of inside family history in just a few days. He and Natalie were genial hosts. David and Monica were also good company when they joined the others, but that was not often. The pair preferred to be alone together as much as possible. Lynn got to work out on Jonathan's treadmill and Stairmaster on Friday, Saturday and Sunday mornings, pushing herself hard after having gone so many days without training.

Lynn skips exercising on this, their final day in Madeira. It will be busy enough without it, she thinks. Jonathan wants to make a stop at his bank. Then there's the luncheon, and they are expected at the airport by three-thirty.

"Monica is flying back with us this afternoon," Patrick tells Lynn when he returns to their room after his swim.

"You're kidding!"

"I'm not. She and David came out to the pool to tell Jonathan right before I came up here."

"What did Jonathan say?"

Patrick shrugs. "It seemed all right with him. I think he was surprised, though. And he was concerned about her missing their appointment with António. That's her ophthalmologist, right?"

"Uh-huh. Dr. Oliveira. Jonathan's friend."

Patrick nodded. "Jonathan said he would cancel the appointment. Your buddy David asked if Jonathan and António would want to come to Princeton when his equipment is ready for use."

"Oh, how nice! So Dr. Oliveira can treat Monica as soon as possible."

"I guess. Monica said she's going to work with David until she has to go to Boston. She wants to help him finish his work. She's going to stay at her mother's until her move. How come she's moving to Boston?"

Lynn explains about Monica's neurosurgery training at Massachusetts General. "That's very impressive," Patrick marvels. "She must be really sharp. This is quite a bunch you've gotten us involved with, Lynnie: a multi-millionaire, a movie star, a scientist, a brain surgeon; not to mention foreign agents and the CIA. Will you be able to settle back in to life as usual at home after your adventure here?"

"Maybe we'll add a few upgrades that we couldn't afford before, but absolutely, I can't wait to get home."

Patrick looks pensive. He takes Lynn in his arms and kisses her. "We'll be all right, won't we?"

"We'll be spectacular, Mr. O'Brien."

He sighs. "I'm going to shave and shower. Jonathan wants to talk to us before we all leave."

"He does? Just the two of us? Patrick nods. "What about?"

"He didn't say. Just that he would like to see us before he meets with his bank manager today."

"Hmm. Any particular time?"

"We agreed on nine o'clock. He has to be at the bank at ten-thirty."

Jonathan is waiting in his library when they arrive. He kisses Lynn's cheek, shakes Patrick's hand, gestures toward a silver tray on which coffee, juice and pastries await their pleasure. After some light conversation about sleeping well and the weekend weather, Jonathan says, "I wanted to see you both, together, this morning before we make our stop at the bank. There are a few more things I haven't told you."

Lynn and Patrick nod encouragingly but have no idea what they are about to hear. "When I said at the *pousada* that I had completely ignored you all your life, Lynn, what I actually meant was I never contacted you, never acknowledged you as my daughter to anyone but myself. However, I was not so remiss as to overlook your welfare altogether. I always hoped that someday I would be able to reveal that I'm your father, and I took some steps to prepare for that time.

"I started a trust fund for you when you were a baby, just as I did earlier for Kimberly. It has long since matured. Its proceeds were invested and are managed by *Banco Espirito Santo*. At maturity on your twenty-first birthday, it amounted to a million dollars, and, I'm happy to say, in the fifteen years since then it has more than tripled in value." Jonathan sits back and sips his coffee.

"And that three million or so dollars accounts for the bulk of the five you sent me," Lynn states. She does not mean it to be a question, presuming that Jonathan is just explaining his gift to her in greater detail.

"No, no, Lynn. Your trust and its later earnings are completely separate from my gift."

"You mean we have an additional three million dollars?"

"Actually closer to four million. About a third of it is presently available as cash, I believe. The balance is in securities."

"Jonathan, nine million dollars. I . . . I don't know what to say. This is just overwhelming. I feel like jumping up and down the way sweepstakes winners do on TV. Nine million dollars, Patrick!"

"I'll jump up and down with you," Patrick volunteers.

Jonathan laughs, clearly feeling good about himself, reveling in his long-denied freedom to tell his daughter of his forethought and prudent financial planning on her behalf throughout her entire life. Instead of jumping, Lynn extends open arms, which Jonathan stands and fills, hugging her while she lavishes kisses on his cheek. Then she hugs Patrick, who lifts her off the floor and swings her in a circle.

"*Senhor* da Silva can tell us the exact amount of your cash and securities this morning," Jonathan says when they're all seated again.

"*Senhor* da Silva? That fox! So he knew all about us when David and I met with him?"

"About the trust and investments. I asked him not to tell you about them until we could meet with him together. He doesn't know you're my daughter, though."

"I'll bet he's never even asked why you established a trust for me. He would die of curiosity first, wouldn't he?"

Jonathan chuckles. "I think you're right. I confess I've sometimes had a little fun at his expense trying to get a rise out of him. The man never takes the bait. He has done a splendid job for us, though, wouldn't you say?"

"I surely would. A splendid job indeed."

"There is one thing more," Jonathan says.

"More?" Lynn asks.

"I started trusts for each of your children, my grandchildren, when they were born, the same as I did for Monica."

"Kerry and Sean have their own trust funds too? Oh, Jonathan, thank you. How wonderful for them. And for us. You are so generous. How can we ever thank you?"

"Just stay in my life. Come visit as often as you can. Let Natalie and me get to know my grandchildren. We can talk by phone, send e-mails. I'd like you both to meet Kimberly. As a matter of fact, I expect to be coming to New Jersey with António when David is ready for him to treat Monica. Princeton is close to both you and Kimberly. I'd like us all to get together when I'm there. You can meet your half-sister. I'll get to know your children." Jonathan pauses. "I would really like that. All contingent on your mother and Michael sanctioning it, of course. I don't want to cause you trouble."

"Patrick and I plan to visit my parents on Tuesday morning. Honestly, Jonathan, I don't know what their reaction will be, but whatever it is, I'll tell you when we call you Tuesday evening."

"And in any case, once we've told everyone that you're Lynn's father," Patrick adds, "there will be no reason Lynn, Kerry, Sean and I can't do everything you've mentioned. We'll look forward to all of it, won't we, Lynnie?"

"Positively."

"As will I," Jonathan says. "Once you've talked with your family, Lynn, Patrick," he adds after a moment's thought, "consulting a financial counselor should be the next thing on your agenda. Also a tax advisor; perhaps an attorney. "

"Yes. Our bank manager back home said that too."

"Good. I suggest you do it as soon as possible. You'll want knowledgeable and trustworthy guidance as you learn to manage your money. You don't want to tackle it alone, at least not early on."

"Are there people you would recommend?" Patrick asks.

"You want to find experts with good reputations in your local area. The bank manager you mentioned can help you find them. Also Monica can tell you about Philadelphia firms that she and Kimberly use. They've had good success with these individuals. I'm sure you'll do fine. Besides, anytime you have a question or want to discuss anything, you can just call me. I should be able to help. I've been at the game for a long while."

Senhor da Silva is his courtly Iberian gentleman self at their meeting, affable to Jonathan and Patrick. To Lynn as well, but only she gets to see the glint in his eye reserved for the fairer sex. He is charmed by the feigned hands on hips, upturned nose scolding Lynn gives him in response to his insincere apology for concealing the truth from her at their first meeting. Lynn and Jonathan sign dozens of papers arranging for the banker to wire accrued cash on hand to her bank and authorizing him to sell or otherwise dispose of her securities, except for her stock in U.S. firms. Those certificates she takes with her.

Their luncheon at the Cliff Villa proves to be great fun. The view of Funchal's harbor, framed as it is by the cliffs that give the restaurant its name, justifies Jonathan's praise and fulfills Lynn's imaginings. Patrick is so impressed that he seems to have forgotten his notion of returning to the scene of the crime, as he termed it. The food is delicious. They all drink some *Vinho Verde*, and everyone except Natalie and Jonathan, who nevertheless are good sports about it, relishes the attention the beautiful Hollywood superstar's presence commands as dozens of diners visit their table for autographs and a few words with her.

The day flies by and soon they are at the airport. Natalie carries two autographed photos of herself. She slips them to Bhatia, who is standing near the exit and accepts them smilingly but wordlessly. Lynn sees Mohamad watching from across the way, ensuring that none of his countrymen observe any contact between the agents and the Americans. Catching Lynn's eye, he gives her a furtive wave as she and the others exit the terminal.

The pilot, co-pilot, and even a pretty flight attendant are waiting to welcome Natalie and her guests aboard. While the crew readies the plane, David and Patrick shake hands with Jonathan and thank him for his hospitality. David promises to keep him informed of his progress with Gunsenhouser's. Patrick restates that he and Lynn will call tomorrow night.

"Goodbye, Granddad," Monica says. "Thank you for my sight, you wonderful man," Lynn hears her say, but misses her whispered, "and thank you for David." Monica promises that she and Kimberly will call him and see him soon.

Lynn kisses her birth father, puts her lips close to his ear and says, "There is no way I can thank you enough for everything, Father. She kisses him a second time before turning to board the plane. Through a window she watches Jonathan and Natalie's passionate farewell kiss.

Natalie is crying as she enters the plane. Lynn stands to console her with a hug. Natalie manages a bittersweet smile. "What can I say, Lynn? I love the man."

"And he loves you," Lynn replies. "I understand why in both cases."

Jonathan stands on the tarmac watching their plane taxi away, a solitary figure so important to all of their lives. To Lynn a kind of guardian angel who has enfolded her in his protective wings since she was a baby and only now materialized for her to see. He waves one final time before turning to leave.

Chapter 22

Patrick turns onto Atlantic City Airport's entrance road. Lynn rides beside him. She always prefers that he drive, whether in her new BMW SUV, as now, or his Lexus, which they left back home in their garage. She turns to smile at their children and sees Sean salute the guard at the FAA Technical Center as they pass. Kerry clucks and rolls her eyes at her younger brother. "What?" he asks.

"Oh, nothing," Kerry sighs in older sister exasperation.

Lynn is glad they don't have to waste half an hour searching for a parking place, as was the case until recently. The airport's long-needed parking garage is finally built. They drive in, and the Conlins: Bill, Theresa, Molly and Danny enter right behind them.

It is the Monday before Easter. Five months have passed since Lynn and Patrick flew home from Madeira in Natalie Forthright's chartered jet. Kerry and Sean have been excused from school a few days early to allow them to visit their grandfather for the holiday. Lynn is satisfied that the gym can operate without her while she's gone. Patrick is temporarily unemployed, having left his job at Atlantic Glass just the previous Friday.

Once again the O'Briens will be flying with Natalie Forthright in a chartered aircraft, but this time all four family members are going, traveling in style, round trip to Madeira. Natalie's plane is due to arrive from Los Angeles shortly. Theresa and her family are on hand to bid Lynn and hers *bon voyage*, and because there is no way Molly and Danny are going to miss out on meeting their favorite movie star when she will be as close by as the local airport.

While she lay awake the night before, too keyed up by travel preparations to fall asleep right away, Lynn reflected on all that had happened since she and Patrick returned home a few days before last Halloween. As planned, they had visited her parents the morning after they arrived.

"What are you going to say?" Patrick had asked her at breakfast.

Lynn shook her head and hunched her shoulders. "Whatever comes out of my mouth, Patrick. I've tried not to mentally orchestrate it. I just want to do it and get it over with." He reached across the table and patted her hand. This promised to be difficult for Lynn.

Her mother answered the door. She did not faint or draw back at the sight of them as Lynn had feared she might. Neither was there the feigned hearty welcome home scene that, despite herself, Lynn had pictured her mother attempting. Instead, Donna maintained her composure long enough to ask, "You found Jonathan?"

"Yes," Lynn answered. Patrick avoided his mother-in-law's eyes.

"So you know."

"Yes, Mom."

"I'm sorry, Lynnie," Donna cried. She threw herself into her daughter's arms, reaching with one hand to pull Patrick into their embrace as well.

"It's fine, Mom. Don't be sorry. I understand," Lynn whispered.

"I have to tell your father now," Donna said after a moment.

"We'll come with you," Lynn said.

Donna nodded, resigned. "All right."

Michael Gallagher was in the kitchen, finishing his second cup of coffee and reading the Atlantic City Press obituaries. Satisfied that he didn't recognize any of the names listed, he looked up to see his wife, daughter, and son-in-law come into the room. He saw Donna's tears, Lynn's pain, Patrick's wish that he were somewhere else, and spoke before any of them could. "You don't have to tell me. I already know."

"You know?" Lynn asked before Donna was able to assimilate her husband's words. Now her mother looked as if she *would* faint after all. Patrick pushed a chair under her.

"I've known all along," Michael said softly.

"Oh, Michael," Donna sobbed, "if you knew for all these years, why didn't you say something?"

"You didn't want me to know. I just tried to respect your wishes. None of it mattered to me, Donna. I never felt anything but love for you. And I never loved Lynn one little bit less because I wasn't really her father. As far as I'm concerned, I'm way ahead of Jonathan Kingsley on this. I'm the guy got to keep you both."

Lynn sat down, shaking her head in wonderment, and watched Donna struggle to recover her equanimity. Patrick exhaled forcefully, his tension defused. He started to say something, thought better of it, and asked instead, "You got any more coffee, Mike?"

"Sure. Help yourself."

Patrick offered it around, but no one wanted coffee. Michael moved closer to his wife and held her hand.

"How did you find out, Dad?" Lynn asked.

He paused, but so briefly that only Lynn noticed it. What he filtered from his reply in that silent instant was that there had been talk at Atlantic Glass about the pretty secretary who worked late at night with the boss. Crude, smart-ass remarks that Michael did not like and quickly put an end to by announcing that Donna was his girl. What he answered Lynn was, "When your mom didn't become pregnant again after a few years of marriage, I wondered if, uh, if I . . ."

"If you were infertile?" Lynn suggested.

"Uh-huh. I went for some tests and learned that I have Immobile, or maybe it's Immotile something-or-other Syndrome. It's a condition where a man's sperm count is normal, but the critters don't move the way they should. In my case they're also abnormally shaped. I don't recall the medical terms, but there was no way I could be your father, Lynnie."

"And you knew about Jonathan and me?" Donna mumbled.

"You spent a lot of time together. I knew you admired him." Michael shrugged. "He was the only man who seemed a possibility. I could see how it might have happened."

Donna was relieved to be freed from the awful effort of hiding the truth from her husband and daughter and the unrelenting self-recrimination that chaperoned living her lie. Now she worried aloud that others would learn of it. Michael told her nobody would hear it from him. Lynn knew there was no use telling her mother that she shouldn't care what anyone knew or thought they knew. Such rugged individualism was not in Donna's makeup.

"Patrick and I will tell the children," Lynn said. "And we owe the truth to Theresa and Bill and to Patrick's mom and dad. As far as I'm concerned, that's it. All I'll say to anyone else, if anything, is that the money came from some long-lost relative. People can think whatever they want." Lynn told her parents about the trust fund Jonathan had set up for her when she was an infant and the additional money that had accrued from investments since it matured.

Michael was stunned. "Nearly four million dollars, Lynnie. So in all, what, close to nine million?"

"Yes, plus he has arranged similar trusts for Kerry and Sean."

"He's a good man," Michael said simply.

"He is," Lynn agreed. "He's a wonderful man. So are you, Dad. You would have done the same if you had Jonathan's money."

"That's true. I would have."

"And you'll always be my dad. Don't ever forget that or doubt it for one minute."

Michael nodded, becoming too filled up to trust his voice further. Donna wept openly. Patrick couldn't watch.

Later that day Patrick and Lynn met Theresa for lunch as pre-arranged. By then Patrick's sister had figured out that Jonathan Kingsley must have sent Lynn the money. There were only so many reasons she could dream up to explain why he did it. The actual one was among those she considered. Nonetheless, she could hardly believe her ears when Lynn told her.

That night, as promised, Lynn called Jonathan at his villa. Jonathan was overjoyed by her report that, all-in-all, Donna took the news well.

"She wasn't angry? She doesn't hate me for telling you?"

"She cried, Jonathan, but she was relieved not to have to conceal the truth any longer."

"That is such a burden off my mind, Lynn. I was afraid she would be furious that I told you. And Michael? Was he hurt when you told them? What did he say?"

"My dad said you're a good man."

"Really?"

"Yes, and, Jonathan, he already knew."

"He knew? Donna had told him?"

"No, Mom never told him. Until today, she had no idea that he knew about your affair or that he's not my biological father."

"He knew but never let on to Donna?"

"That's right. He respected what he thought was her wish."

"The same way I did."

"Yes. He kept her secret, even from her."

"Did he say how he came to know?"

Lynn explained about her father's suspicions and their confirmation by the results of the fertility tests he took.

"Oh, Lynn, how foolish we've been, wasting so many years because of. . .of . . ."

"Secrets, promises, appearances, omissions, cover-ups, pretense, what people might think, unwillingness to face consequences, lack of forthrightness," Lynn offered. She laughed along with Jonathan at that last of her characterizations.

"Forthright. Yes, I think in our places Natalie would have been, don't you?"

"Absolutely," Lynn agreed.

When Lynn finished talking, Patrick said hello, thanked Jonathan for his hospitality when they were at the villa, expressed once again his gratitude for all he had done financially for Lynn and their family, and put each of the kids on the phone with their grandfather. Lynn listened to their open, straightforward conversations. They talked about their ages, their schools, their interests, their friends. Sean said, "Granddad? Not grandpa or grandfather? That's what who calls you? Monica? Who's Monica? Oh, a cousin? Cool! Granddad, huh? Yes, I do. I like it. Now we have a pop-pop, a grandpop, and a granddad."

As they come running toward her now, yelling that Natalie Forthright's plane is taxiing toward the terminal, Lynn remembers how proud she had been of Kerry and Sean that night. Jonathan had been enthralled by them.

Natalie stays on the plane. The O'Briens and Conlins watch for its passenger door to open, their pre-arranged signal to come aboard. It does, and a flight attendant steps down to meet them as Lynn and Patrick lead the scurrying pack to the aircraft.

"Are you sure this is okay, Lynn?" Theresa asks. "I feel funny about it."

"It'll be fine," Lynn reassures her. "Wait till you see."

Natalie welcomes Lynn and Patrick with kisses and hugs and, "It's so good to see you both again." Then to everyone's amazement she greets each of the others by name. "Hello, Theresa, it's nice to meet you, and you, Bill," is surprise enough, but the teens and 'tweens are wowed that the famous actress actually remembers their names. "So, Molly and Danny, I guess you didn't get to see *Alpine Playground* because of its R rating?" Natalie ventures.

"No, we didn't," Molly replies. "You're still our favorite actress, though. Mom and dad said it was great – for adults. They might let us watch it at home when it comes out on video."

-256-

"Well, we certainly will now that we've met Miss Forthright in person," Theresa says, adding, "As long as you close your eyes whenever I tell you."

"And we'll definitely get to see *Chanteuse* when it comes out this summer," Danny says. "It will be PG 13 like we've read, won't it, Miss Forthright?"

"Yes. My first PG 13 in four years. Also the first time I get to sing in a movie."

Molly and Danny have come armed with trivia questions they're hoping will stump Natalie, obscure facts about forgettable, mostly forgotten films. She answers them without difficulty. Molly tells her that she and Kerry are taking voice and dance lessons and have joined the dramatics club at school. Danny says he plans to be involved in dramatics, too, when he gets to high school. Right now he and Sean are eager for baseball season to start. Both of them play for community league teams. Natalie encourages them all.

When the Conlins leave the plane, Patrick sits with Kerry and Sean who are excited by every aspect of the flight, the first ever for both of them. Natalie invites Lynn to sit beside her so they can talk. They have not seen each other since they flew together in the opposite direction last fall, although each is fairly well up to date on what has transpired in the interim.

"Will Monica and Kimberly be at the villa?" Lynn asks.

"Yes, and David, too."

"David? Well-well."

"Mmm-hmm. With Jonathan, my poor baby. He's wearing an eye patch. Only for about a week, though, I think."

"I'm sure he'll be fine," Lynn assures her.

"Oh, I know. António told me. I called him shortly after he removed the cataract, and I can believe *him*. Jonathan, on the other hand, probably wouldn't have told me if there had been complications. Anyway, I'll get a chance to baby him while he wears the patch. The real news from António is that Monica's follow-up examination and tests showed no signs of Gunsenhouser's. Everyone expected they wouldn't, but now we all know for certain that the disease is gone for good."

Lynn nods, already having learned about Monica's test results. Jonathan had flown from Madeira, and Monica, Kimberly and David from the States three days earlier to meet in Lisbon at the Oliveira Ophthalmic Institute. António had pronounced Monica cured and replaced Jonathan's occluded natural lens with an artificial one the same day. That was Monday. On Tuesday they all flew back to Madeira, António and Mrs. Oliveira included.

"Everyone will be at the villa," Lynn says.

"Yes, the whole gang."

"Oh, this will be fun. It was a shame you had to miss our get-together back in February, Natalie. That turned out to be quite a party too."

"I hated that I couldn't be there," Natalie says, "but after the cast of *Chanteuse* took a two-week break from filming at Christmas, I couldn't get away again so soon."

Jonathan and António had gone to Princeton in February when David's project was completed. Monica, who had worked side by side with David until she had to go to Boston after the holidays, returned to Princeton for the single treatment she needed from António. Kimberly was also there. That night Jonathan stayed overnight at Kimberly's home. The next day, after António and David finished treating a second Gunsenhouser's patient, Jonathan got to meet his grandchildren as he had hoped he would. Lynn and Patrick invited him to bring everyone along, so Kimberly, Monica, David and António all joined him for the visit to Somers Point.

"Did Jonathan tell you that my mom and dad were there?" Lynn asks.

"Oh, yes. He said they both thanked him for all he had done for you and your family. He was touched by that, Lynn, and even more so by their acceptance of him in your world."

"I'm glad. I felt the same way. We couldn't accommodate everyone at our old house, so I arranged with my old boss to use the aerobics studio at the club," Lynn says.

"Old house. Old boss," Natalie says. "Things are changing for you."

"Actually, we're still in the old house, but not for long. We bought a beautiful home in Linwood, the next town north of us. We'll be right on the Patcong River. Six bedrooms, a family room, a huge kitchen, dining room, living room; even a pool. We make settlement next month. You must come visit us and see it."

"I will. With Jonathan, after you get situated. And I understand you bought the health club where you used to work?"

"We did. The Patcong Fitness Center. Charlie Jacobs, the owner, had been after me to manage the place for him so he could retire. When Patrick and I told him we wanted to buy it, he was downright thrilled. We settled the deal in a matter of weeks."

"How is business?"

"It's pretty good. Charlie always managed to make money. We plan to upgrade equipment and programs, which will eventually improve profits, but we want to hold off until we're confident we know what we're doing."

"Get your feet wet first?"

"Yes. Patrick just left his job at Atlantic Glass. We'll be working together. I know fitness. Patrick can supervise people.

Also, he was a business major in college, and he's taking graduate courses in accounting and finance now to help us manage the money Jonathan gave me as well as our health club finances."

Jonathan has a huge van waiting for them when they land at *Aeroporto da Madeira*. Carlos honks its horn as Natalie and the O'Briens exit the airport terminal. He climbs out to store their bags and help the group board the van.

"Wow, Granddad," Sean says after kisses and handshakes and welcomes are exchanged, "this is a humongous van! It looks like a little bus, doesn't it, Mom?"

"It does," Lynn agrees.

"I rented it for the week so we'd have a vehicle we can all ride in together, Sean."

"Cool!"

Natalie admonishes Jonathan for coming out in the sunshine, but her scolding is such burlesque, accompanied as it is by endearments and baby talk about his poor eye that Lynn and Patrick both have to laugh. Jonathan's repentance is no less insincere, but he does promise to follow doctor's orders and behave himself at the villa.

"I wonder how our old buddies Mohamad and Bhatia are doing," Lynn muses aloud at Jonathan's enormous dining room table one evening during a sumptuous duck and passion fruit timbale dinner at the villa.

"Mmm," David intones before swallowing a bite of the delicious dish. "I saw them in Princeton when António treated General Aláz."

"You did? When was that?" Lynn asks.

"The day after we treated Monica," David replies.

"The day of our party in February?"

"Uh-huh."

"You saw the general and Mohamad and Bhatia that day. Why didn't you tell us?"

"Same reason as after you and I saw him in Ractá. He swore us to secrecy."

"Us?"

"António, Jonathan and I. Until this week General Aláz was still afraid that one of his enemies or underlings would learn that he had Gunsenhouser's."

"This week?" Lynn asks in mock exasperation. Already having gotten the picture of what must have taken place, she makes David explain anyway.

"The general came to Lisbon with Mohamad and Bhatia Tuesday morning. António tested him as he had Monica the day before. He's completely cured, too, and I feel that releases us from any further obligation of secrecy. Don't you?"

"I'm sick of secrets," Lynn responds.

"I gave him back half his money," David adds.

"And David returned half of mine as well," Jonathan interjects.

"I received enough grant money to cover the cost of finishing my project," David explains, "but I couldn't in good faith accept it when I had already gotten private funds from Jonathan and the general. So I declined the grant money, spent half of Jonathan's and half the general's and refunded five million to each of them."

"I wondered," Lynn admits.

"I knew you would. That's why I asked Jonathan if he objected to my telling you."

"Of course I didn't mind," Jonathan says.

"Mohamad and Bhatia told me they are now the general's private bodyguards. It's a promotion for them," David tells Lynn. "And Ben Saber? They told me he returned to the States and has a better job at CIA headquarters in Langley."

"No! How could that have happened after his blunder with us?" Lynn marvels.

"I can answer that," Jonathan says. "At Christmas when my CIA friends and their wives were here at the villa, they told me what was going on with Saber. Actually, we were largely responsible for his promotion and transfer. After the mistakes he made with us, they didn't want to risk his continuing as a field operative for fear he might foul up something that really matters."

"So they promoted him?" Lynn is incredulous.

"Right. Pushed him upstairs where he can't do any real harm."

"Unbelievable!" Natalie agrees with Lynn.

"It's really not that unusual. Happens all the time in the business world," Jonathan says. "And in fairness to Saber, I was told he had done excellent work throughout his career and should have been returned to the States years ago. The man Saber reported to was also promoted. Both of them were ordered to make no further mention of General Aláz's medical condition or Saber's debacle with us."

The group's Easter vacation is enjoyable for all of them. Kerry and Sean love the pool and their van rides around the island. They take scores of photographs. Lynn and Patrick are glad they were able to bring them along. Jonathan is enchanted by his grandchildren and cherishes being with Natalie and all his family. Natalie is always happiest when she can be with him, and she is pleased to be included in this primarily familial vacation. Kimberly, relieved to know that Monica's cure is complete, is so relaxed she is even friendly with Natalie. Monica and David appear lost in each other from time to time, as usual, but, clearly a pair now, are more accessible to and involved with the rest of the gang.

"This has been so grand," Lynn says the night before they all must return to reality. She raises her glass of *Vinho Verde* with the toast, "To our next time together."

"Together," Jonathan repeats.

"Together," everyone echoes.

"I wonder when that next time will be," Lynn ponders aloud.

"Monica?" David asks. Everyone's eyes turn to her. She nods. They all turn back to David. He puts his arm around Monica. "In June," he says. "At our wedding."

ABOUT THE AUTHOR

Joseph Keough and his wife Margaret (artist and cover creator) live at the Southern New Jersey seashore. Their grown and loving children, Lonnie, Karen, Brian, Susan, Martin and Dan, to whom this book is dedicated, live nearby. In addition to *ATM*, the author has published reader-acclaimed *Shattered Peace*, which also is currently available in paperback and as an e-book from Amazon/Kindle. Three additional novels are in the works.

Made in the USA
Columbia, SC
29 October 2020